Keeping a Christmas Promise

Jo Thomas

PENGUIN BOOKS

TRANSWORLD PUBLISHERS
Penguin Random House, One Embassy Gardens,
8 Viaduct Gardens, London SW11 7BW
www.penguin.co.uk

Transworld is part of the Penguin Random House group of companies
whose addresses can be found at global.penguinrandomhouse.com

First published in Great Britain in 2022 by Penguin Books
an imprint of Transworld Publishers

Copyright © Jo Thomas 2022

Jo Thomas has asserted her right under the Copyright,
Designs and Patents Act 1988 to be identified as the author of this work.

This book is a work of fiction, and, except in the case of historical fact, any
resemblance to actual persons, living or dead, is purely coincidental.

Every effort has been made to obtain the necessary permissions with
reference to copyright material, both illustrative and quoted. We apologize
for any omissions in this respect and will be pleased to make the
appropriate acknowledgements in any future edition.

A CIP catalogue record for this book
is available from the British Library.

ISBN 9780552178679

Typeset in 11/14pt ITC Giovanni by Jouve (UK), Milton Keynes.
Printed and bound in Great Britain by Clays Ltd, Elcograf S.p.A.

The authorized representative in the EEA is Penguin Random House Ireland,
Morrison Chambers, 32 Nassau Street, Dublin D02 YH68.

Penguin Random House is committed to a sustainable
future for our business, our readers and our planet. This book
is made from Forest Stewardship Council® certified paper.

For those who were taken from us too early and the friends and family they left behind. They never really leave us. Their words, advice, love and laughter are still always there, all around us, in who we are and become.

For Liz Weedon, Polly Beavon and Jane Wenham-Jones

PROLOGUE

Then

'This is the best hen party ever!' says Laura, as she opens the sun screen, squirts a dollop into her hand, then rubs it over her arms and long legs.

'I can't believe we're here,' says Meg, getting comfy on her sun-lounger. Joanna had been out earlier and put towels on four, right by the pool. She had our day planned.

'A whole week in the sunny Costa del Sol just chilling!' says Laura.

'It's going to be brilliant. I've loved organizing it. I've got it all planned!' says Joanna, who clearly didn't plan on us just chilling.

'It had better be, because I'm only ever doing it

once,' says Meg, picking up the sun screen and slathering it on, squinting against the already hot sun.

'I wonder where you'll be celebrating your twenty-fifth wedding anniversary,' I say, sitting on my lounger, planning a swim and wondering what's on the lunch menu.

'Where we'll all be!' says Laura.

'Happy!' says Joanna, applying lip gloss with one eye on the lifeguard.

'Here's to one more down, and one left to go,' Meg says to me. 'You're the only one left, Freya.'

'I'm happy as things are,' I say. 'I have my career to think about. There's not a lot of time for romance in a busy kitchen.'

'I'm worried things will change once I'm married,' says Meg. 'I don't want you guys to think I'm not here for you.'

'You worry too much, Meg,' I tell her kindly. 'You have to put yourself first sometimes. We'll always be there for each other.' I produce the bottle of cava I bought in duty free on the way over, and the plastic glasses from our apartment bathroom. 'Too early?' I ask.

'No!' they chorus. I pop the cork and pour.

'Here's to us!' I say, raising a glass and taking a sip. Then I pull a pad and pen from my bag. 'I've had this recipe idea knocking around in my head ever since dinner last night.' I open the pad and jot down the ingredients and flavours I'd come up with.

'You work too hard,' says Joanna.

'It's not hard, it's just what I do.' I smile.

'Well, don't work so hard you forget to live!' Laura says. 'Now . . . time for a game of Truth or Dare?'

'No!' we cry.

'To friendship!' Meg lifts her glass.

'Do you think we'll still be doing this when we're in our forties and fifties?' says Joanna. 'Going away together as friends? We should!'

'We should agree to do it every year,' says Meg, lying back with her face to the sun.

'What would you like to do before you're forty?' says Laura.

'Have a family,' Meg says quickly, opening her eyes.

'Get thin!' says the ever-thin Joanna, sliding her hands over her slim hips and once again glancing in the direction of the lifeguard to see if he's noticed. He has, of course. Everyone notices Joanna.

'Eat at a Michelin-starred restaurant?' Laura asks me, with a knowing grin.

'Get a Michelin star!' I laugh.

'Live in Paris,' Joanna says dreamily.

'Work in Paris,' I join in, the idea gathering pace.

'See the Northern Lights!' says Laura, wrapping her arms around herself. 'At Christmas time. On my birthday!' She warms to the idea. 'Sipping a glass of something lovely with you guys and seeing them for real. I've always wanted to see them. They just seem . . . magical. The Northern Lights, in Iceland. That's what I'd like to do by the time I'm forty.'

1

Now

'Oh, good grief! What's that pong?' says Meg, screwing up her face and holding her nose as I follow her through the heavy door into the light, bright modern hotel room.

I drop my case by the door and head straight to the window to take it all in. It's mid-morning and only just getting light. But we're here. I'm so excited. I just want to get on and see it all.

I look around the bedroom, which has the same inviting, chilled, laid-back feel of the hotel lobby. Clean lines, functional and modern, with crisp white linen, blue blankets, and towels in a roll. It's smart, neat and could be anywhere in the world. The wonder clearly happens outside the window. I stare at the mist rising over a milky blue natural pool, like a blue topaz nestled in a bed of jewellers' cotton wadding, as the snow continues to fall and settle on the rocks around it. There's a small wooden bridge and on the other side I can see women in bikinis and men, shoulders showing above the water. They're sitting and chatting with mud packs on their faces as the snow falls around them, the mist rises and the golden flames of the candles flicker. We've made it to Iceland. I look up slightly to stop any tears that might threaten. We're here for Laura. She can't do it so we're doing it for her.

'We're going to find the Lights, Laura,' I whisper and hug myself. I breathe in deeply, feeling my shoulders relaxing. Meg's not wrong. I wrinkle my nose. There is a strange smell. 'Could be the plumbing. It smells like . . .'

'Farts!' Meg finishes seriously, her hands on her hips. She looks at me as if I'm one of her children, and I'm trying not to laugh. But then she cracks up and I join in. It feels good to laugh, reminding me of the fun times we used to have. When we stop, I finally reply, 'I was going to say rotten eggs.'

'Why would a bathroom smell of rotten eggs?'

'It's not a smell you want in your kitchen either. That's for sure!' I say.

It's a beautiful bathroom. Clean, functional, with everything you could want from oversized white bathrobes to stacks of fluffy towels, cleansing products and shampoos. If only I could read which was which . . . I pat the top of my head to find my reading glasses, which I need all the time, these days, to follow recipes and bookings for the restaurant.

'Moisturizer, cleanser, scrub . . .' I read off the labels. Everything I could think of. I let out another sigh, trying to dispel the guilt I feel at being here and not at work.

'Just what we need,' I say, as we take stock and remember why we're here.

'Apart from the smell,' says Meg, and laughter bubbles inside me once more. It's like we're in our twenties again, when it fuelled our friendship group of four.

By the time we reached our forties, it was more about supporting each other through tough times as life left its scars on us. But it looks like the laughter is still there and it feels good to find it.

'Don't unpack. We need to change rooms,' Joanna instructs, as she bursts in from next door, her mouth downturned and disapproving. We stop laughing. She's as tall and slim as she was when she was working at the Grand Hotel, before she married the owner's son.

'I'll get this sorted now. Follow me!' she says. We do as we're told without question.

A lot has changed since those days at the Grand Hotel, I think, as Joanna ushers us back the way we came in, weekend cases on wheels bumping along the corridor, letting her take charge, like schoolchildren on a day trip.

'It's the sulphur in the hot water,' explains the smart receptionist in perfect English. 'It's geothermal. It comes from underground. It's a natural smell. It's perfect for bathing in, but not drinking, just like our natural warm pools. All our hot water is free here in Iceland,' she explains politely. 'We run our heating off it too. It's an excellent use of our resources and working with nature.'

'Right, yes, of course,' says Joanna, running a hand over her smart, sleek bob.

'Wow!' says Meg. 'I didn't know that!' We nod in approval.

'Truth or Dare!' A young hen party arrives in Reception behind us and we turn to look at the boisterous group in black T-shirts with their job titles in white: Mother of the Bride, Maid of Dishonour, Bride. The wording is stretched over the latter's large bosom and takes a moment or two to read. They have sashes and cowboy hats, and are clutching bags of duty-free they've picked up in the airport.

'Oh, no,' says Joanna. 'Hardly a good start to a relaxing weekend. Sorry.' She turns on her heels – white lace-up fake-fur-trimmed boots – and ushers us back down the corridor to our rooms. 'Sorry about the smell,' she says to us.

'It's fine,' Meg says, trying to keep up with Joanna – her legs are shorter.

'Joanna, stop apologizing. The smell is fine. Like the

receptionist said, it's natural. It's amazing they have hot water on tap,' I tell her.

'I thought this place would be quiet and out of the way. Most people head to Reykjavik and the Blue Lagoon,' she says.

'Honestly, it's perfect,' Meg reassures her.

'Well, I'm sending you the weekend's itinerary on the WhatsApp group. I've got it all planned.'

'I just want a quiet weekend in the spa hotel, with lots of treatments and a hot spring to chill out in,' Meg says.

'And see the Northern Lights. That's what we always said we'd do,' Joanna says.

'And that's why we're here,' I confirm. 'We promised. I really hope it happens.'

'That's it,' says Joanna, having pressed send.

Our phones ping into life.

'It's all there, along with our leaving schedule and flights home on Monday,' she says.

'Let's not think about that right now. We've just got here!' I say, wanting to enjoy every moment of our trip before I head back into the busiest time of the year.

'I've got seven missed calls. I'd better answer them,' says Meg, turning away. I watch her, as does Joanna. This is just the break she needed. It was a struggle for all of us to get away, and I'm so glad we've made this weekend happen.

'It'll be more wedding stress,' I say to Joanna,

watching Meg put her phone to her ear, stepping into her bedroom, snow falling beyond the big window there, steam rising from the hot spring. I know she won't be looking at any of it while she's on the phone to one of her many family members.

'That'll be her ex-mother-in-law making demands again,' Joanna tuts. 'Or the grown-up children changing the seating plan and refusing to sit with Tom's family.'

'No!' I say, incredulous.

'Yes. Didn't you hear the latest?'

'I . . .' I feel bad. 'I hadn't realized. I've missed lots of the WhatsApp messages, what with the Christmas menu to prepare, and a new restaurant opening,' I say, cross with myself. 'But Meg's wedding is only . . .' I do a mental count '. . . two weeks away.'

'I've offered to take over the organizing as chief maid of honour,' Joanna says.

'You're chief maid of honour?' I say. I don't know why but suddenly I feel hurt.

'Well, it makes sense. You don't have the time, especially if your boss offers you the new restaurant to run. But Meg seems determined to do it all herself.'

She's right. I don't have time. I shouldn't even be here, but there was no way I was going to miss it. 'You're so good at organizing. Keep me in the loop, though.'

'If you read your messages,' she says, half joking.

I check them now. I find a lot from my boss, sending photographs of new premises, restaurants and shops for lease or sale. I wish I was there to oversee what's going on, to have a hand in choosing the new place, so I can feel really invested in it, but there was no way any of us was going to miss this trip. I double-check my messages. It's all work, nothing from anyone else. I turn off my phone, like we'd promised each other we would, then switch it back on quickly, just to check I haven't missed anything from the restaurant. But there's nothing. It seems they're managing, with my long lists of instructions, and I switch it off firmly.

Joanna is absolutely right. I certainly won't have time to help with the wedding. Especially not if Wilfrid goes ahead with his promise to give me my own restaurant and executive-chef title. Taking time off now has been hard enough. But we've had this trip planned for a very long time, from before Meg announced that she and Tom were finally getting married and before I knew there might be a new job on the cards. But I'd had to make this weekend. There's no way anyone would have missed it. We're here to see the Northern Lights on what would have been Laura's fortieth birthday.

'You okay?' Joanna asks.

'Fine. Just checking I'd done everything I needed to do before leaving the restaurant.' I bring myself back to the here and now. Outside, in this snowy wonderland, we'll relax and celebrate our lovely friend Laura.

'You know you did. You work too hard,' Joanna says again.

I laugh and wave a hand. 'It's not work, it's a way of life. You don't have any other when you run a restaurant.' I wouldn't have it any other way. It's my life. It's who I am.

'Not just any restaurant.' She raises an eyebrow. 'An award-winning Michelin-starred restaurant. You don't blow your trumpet enough! Laura would have you shouting it from the rooftops.'

She's right. But my head is still buzzing, doing a mental check of everything back at work. I need to switch off, I know I do. Everyone tells me I do. It's not that easy, but I'm going to give it a good try. This weekend is for Laura.

'Right,' she says. 'We have forty-five minutes to unpack, then get to the spa before lunch in the restaurant. I have a car booked to go out later and find the Lights. Have you got the bottle of fizz we bought at the airport?'

'I have.' I touch my handbag, which holds the vintage champagne. 'A special bottle to toast a special lady.' It's a far cry from the cava we celebrated with in the Costa del Sol when Laura first told us of her bucket-list wish: to see the Northern Lights. Now, on her fortieth-birthday weekend, we're here. Just like we promised we would be when time was running out for her. It all happened so fast. After her diagnosis we thought there would be time, and there wasn't. We did have time to promise we would celebrate her fortieth for her, though, and find the Lights.

We were twenty when we started the bucket list. Only it wasn't a bucket list then, just a bunch of ideas, things we wanted to do, to see, dreams for the future.

I wanted my own restaurant, never stopped thinking about recipes. I dreamt of going to Michelin-starred restaurants and eventually to work in one. Now I do. I dreamt of working in Paris, which I did for a while, learning my skills from the best chefs. That was after my mum died. Before then, I just focused on working at the hotel, cooking for her, and that was where I met Mark. We worked side by side in the hotel kitchen.

Joanna wanted a certain lifestyle. She dreamt of a big house, holidays, fast cars and skiing holidays. Her first marriage, to the son of the owner of the hotel where we worked, fell apart: he had a cocaine habit and was finally written out of his parents' business until he could sort it out. He didn't. She found her man and matching lifestyle second time around. He was a customer, who used the hotel on business trips, older than her and ready to see the world with his new wife.

Laura wanted to experience life: zip wires, whitewater rafting, running a marathon, and seeing the Northern Lights.

Even then Meg wanted a big white wedding and a family. If only we'd known how things would pan out by the time we hit forty. Meg also divorced, but somehow kept the mother-in-law and gained some stepchildren, as well as working all the hours she can. As for me, well, I nearly had it all. But I'm happy where I'm at. I'm in a good place.

I think about the new restaurant, my kitchen, run to my rules, and smile.

'We're going to have fun this weekend.' Joanna claps her hands. 'Sleeping, relaxing, massages, sitting in the hot springs, watching the Lights,' she says, as I open her WhatsApp message to Meg and me and gaze at the busy schedule.

'It's not too much, is it?' She looks as anxious as a contestant on *The Great British Bake Off*, waiting for her feedback from Paul Hollywood.

'It's fine. Really great, honestly!' I tell her. 'Thank you for arranging it. If it wasn't for you, I'm not sure we'd be here.' She had booked the flights and the hotel, which I would never have got round to. Neither would Meg, who works in a care home, as well as arranging her wedding and dealing with tricky stepchildren and ex-in-laws.

'So let's get on with the unpacking and head for the spa. We'll go out to see the Lights after lunch. I just want it all to be perfect,' Joanna says.

'It will be!' I say, shoving my phone away. This weekend I'm definitely not thinking about the restaurant. I promised myself I wouldn't. And I promised my friends that, just for the weekend, I'd leave work behind. This is a celebration of Laura's life.

2

Cold! So cold! I can feel the hairs up my nose freeze as soon as I step out of the changing room, through the glass door, with trails of condensation running down it where warm meets freezing. I push it open and have half a mind to run back inside, but in front of me is the wooden duckboard path, leading to the warm pool beyond, shrouded in rising mist. It's now or never. I dash, in the bitter cold, towards the steps and climb down them into the water. I can see Meg and swim towards her. The warm water is heaven and I'm getting used to the pong. Although my body is warm, my head and shoulders have yet to be convinced.

I join her and we watch Joanna make her way elegantly across the duckboard, in a powder blue bikini, tall and beautiful as she ever was. She dips into the pool and joins us.

'All okay?' I ask her.

'Yes, I was just checking our bookings for tomorrow's treatments and our early dinner reservation. This place has a very highly recommended restaurant of European and international cuisine.' She gives us a satisfied smile.

'Can't wait.' My stomach lets me know it's excited at the prospect too. 'And thank you again, Joanna.'

'No need. All your treatments are listed on the schedule, mealtimes too.'

'That's brilliant, isn't it, Meg?' I ask, but Meg is lost in thought. 'How were your phone calls?' I ask tentatively.

'Tricky,' she says, frustrated. 'Why can't everyone just get along? Now I've got to change the seating arrangements again because Tom's aunt Marion has fallen out with her sister's second husband and refuses to come if she has to sit anywhere near him. Frankly I have no idea who to put her next to because she falls out with everyone, especially after two glasses of fizz. I've told the kids not to let her have more than two, but I can't be sure she won't help herself and then her filter will be well and truly gone. Who will she upset next?' She slaps a hand into the warm water. 'What about you? All okay back at the restaurant?'

I swish my hands in the water as if I'm running a bath and mixing in the bubbles. 'Well, Wilfrid wasn't happy about me coming away. In fairness, it couldn't be a worse time, but I've made all the arrangements for this weekend to be covered in the kitchen. As long as I'm back on Monday for evening service and the start of our Christmas taster menu in the week before Christmas, everything will be fine.' I let out a long slow breath I didn't know I'd been holding. 'It's all fine,' I repeat, and I'm not sure who for, them or me. 'I've organized it all.'

'How about you, Joanna?'

She waves a hand. 'All the usual stuff in the run-up to Christmas, clearing the calendar . . .'

'Oh, my God! It's flippin' freezing!' The hen party's arrived outside to squeals and screeches of laughter. They have neon nails, bikinis, and are deeply tanned with a hint of orange. The bride is wearing a plastic tiara and the others have plenty of festive glitter.

'Geronimo!' shouts one, and runs towards the water, pulling her friend in with her.

I feel our hearts sink as one.

'That was us, last time around,' Meg says, nodding towards the party as they crack open a bottle of fizz, pour it into plastic glasses and hand them round, while sitting in the hot spring, keeping their made-up faces out of the water. We smile at the memory.

'So, how are the rest of the wedding plans going?' I ask, hoping to get to the bottom of what's going on with her.

'Oh, you know . . . weddings!' Meg sighs.

'But I thought this was going to be simple and straightforward, different from last time. You said, "We're not kids any more."'

'It was! But things just snowballed! And now my ex-mother-in-law is upset because she isn't invited. And the kids think I'm excluding their granny! Phfff! Oh, that reminds me. Wedding favours! I must make a note. I thought of them on the plane.'

'But I thought you weren't going to do all that,' I say.

'I know, but I saw these cute little boxes the other day and I was thinking maybe I could learn to make them.'

I shake my head and smile. Meg was never going to be able to keep things simple. She always has a hundred things on the go, and everything has a list.

'Well, make sure you take time off for the honeymoon.'

'I'm fine. Just busy.'

I swear I can see little sparkles of tears in the rims of her eyes, but it could just be the snow, the light.

'We all have a treatment booked,' Joanna says. 'That should help.'

'Yes!' we agree, as we climb out of the warm water into the cold air and run to the changing rooms.

The giggle bubbles up in me as the young woman runs her exfoliating machine over my feet.

'Sorry, sorry,' I say. I'm trying to relax. I really am. I

breathe in and out, trying to ignore the tickling. This is the best treatment for me. I spend all day on my feet and this will be good for them.

The treatment room smells amazing. And it's so lovely and warm as I sit in the chair, looking out through the tinted glass to the slowly falling snow, and it's only two o'clock in the afternoon.

'So, what are you doing about Christmas?' Meg asks, having a manicure next to me, while Joanna has the full head and face massage with what looks and smells like warm honey. I'd like to taste the honey, and my stomach rumbles again. Breakfast at the airport seems a long time ago. Since then I've arrived in a winter wonderland, bathed in a hot spring, and am having my feet placed in warm water and massaged with lavender exfoliator. My eyelids are feeling heavy.

'Um, Christmas?' I reply, to stop myself dropping off. 'Well, it'll be the usual, really. We've got the Christmas taster menu starting on Monday and we run it right up to Christmas Eve, and separate menus for Christmas Eve, Christmas Day and Boxing Day.' I'm wide awake again as the beauty therapist slips my feet into warm bootees and tells me to relax. I *was* relaxing, I think, just for a moment. But now all the work thoughts have come rushing back in.

'What about you?' I ask Meg.

'Well, with the wedding being just after Christmas, I thought I'd keep it low key. But we've still got twelve for lunch, or maybe more, what with our kids, his parents and, of course, Granny . . .' She trails off.

'Meg, Granny is your ex-husband's mother. You're not supposed to invite your ex's mother to Christmas dinner after you've divorced,' I tell her.

'I know, but she likes to see the children.'

'They're hardly children any more. They're adults!' Meg sighs. 'It's just, well, it's hard to say no.'

'You need to delegate more,' says Joanna, her head tipped back, eyes shut, a therapist working on her nails as another massages her head.

'Have you got Christmas sorted?' I ask her.

'The caterers are confirmed, and decorators are coming next week to put up the tree and do the house. Drinks order is in, and we're giving them all a holiday to Turkey as their main present. I've ordered stockings from a company that specializes in gifts for adults. They'll come wrapped and we'll have those with Bucks Fizz mid-morning, after a breakfast of smoked salmon and scrambled eggs. Then a walk, as usual, with the dogs. After that lunch will arrive. Then we do presents to and from each other. On Boxing Day there'll be drinks before a cold-cuts lunch.'

'And you've got people in to do all of this?' Meg is incredulous.

'Yes,' says Joanna, matter-of-factly.

'But don't you miss getting involved?' she asks. 'Choosing presents, late-night wrapping, searching for the Sellotape, trying to remember where you've hidden things?'

'Getting up early to put the turkey in?' I join in. 'Prepping veg to carols on the radio?' I think back to those early days of working as a kitchen assistant. 'And making a last-minute dash to the petrol station for more mustard or whatever the chef's run out of.'

'Remembering to get the turkey out the freezer!' Meg laughs. 'Or turn the oven on . . . Oh, that was a year!'

At first Joanna says nothing, then, 'It's just tradition. It's how we've always done things. It's important how it all looks.'

'How it tastes!' I say.

'Making sure there are no fights!' Meg laughs again.

I look at the therapist as she takes my feet out of the warm bootees. 'What kind of things do you usually eat at Christmas? Do you go out?' I ask her.

'We bake a lot. At home.' She's dabbing undercoat onto my toenails. Her face lights up as she talks. 'We all get into the kitchen and cook. We have a buffet for Christmas, with all our favourite dishes. And, of course, with all the family off work, we make soup, lots of soup. And there's fish. We eat a lot of fish. My mother loves the wind-dried fish, very salty, with cold butter. It's delicious.' She starts to apply a light pink nail varnish. 'We mostly eat what we can make or have preserved. So we bake, we eat lamb for our

Christmas feast, with potatoes, done in the pan with brown sugar and rhubarb jam. We do lots with rhubarb.' She laughs. 'Imported food is so expensive and eating out is practically impossible if you don't have a fortune.'

'It sounds like a lovely time,' I say, imagining this young woman and her family in the kitchen.

'It's where one generation hands down the recipes to the next.' She smiles. 'And on Christmas Eve, we give books to each other.'

'I love books as Christmas presents,' says Meg. 'They can be so personal.'

Joanna lifts her head and opens her eyes, as if she's listening to somebody reading a Christmas classic to her. 'So, you put on your clean or new pyjamas, eat chocolate and read a book. A peaceful sleep before the big day of cooking and family.'

I nod and smile. 'I like that,' I say.

'I might do it,' says Meg.

'You have enough to do already!' I laugh.

'What kind of books?' Joanna asks.

'It can be anything you think the other person will enjoy.'

'Well, that's a cookery book for you, Freya. And . . . home interiors for Joanna. And a romance for me! Something that takes me to a lovely place and I know will have a happy ending.'

'Escapism.' I feel the same about cookery books.

'I have no idea what kind of book I'd like,' Joanna says, and there seems to be sadness in the way she speaks.

'Maybe a diary, so you can plan a whole new year afresh,' suggests a therapist.

Joanna looks at her and nods slowly. 'Maybe.' She swallows.

'A diary is great for you. You love planning,' says Meg.

'Well, that's you ladies finished,' says my therapist. 'What are you doing for the rest of the day?'

'I'll check the app!' Meg laughs.

'Joanna has it all planned,' I say, with a smile.

'A late lunch in the restaurant and then we're off to see the Northern Lights.' She beams, her little wobble clearly behind her.

'You're looking for the Lights?' My therapist raises her neat eyebrows and looks at the other girl.

'You think we'll see them?' asks Meg eagerly.

She begins to clear up. 'The weather forecast isn't so good. Are you going on your own?'

'Yes,' says Joanna, suddenly looking troubled.

—'It might be hard,' says the therapist, with an apologetic shrug.

We pull out our phones, even though we've agreed not to, then head out of the serenity and warmth of the spa into Reception, heads down, comparing weather apps.

'Now what are we going to do? How on earth are we going to see the Lights now?'

'Come on, it's Laura's birthday!' says Joanna, jollying us along, as she always did. 'Let's remember why we're here!' And she's right. 'Let's get changed, have a drink before lunch and try to figure something out.' Joanna doesn't do plans that fail, but I have a sinking feeling that these will.

'There's nothing we can do about the weather,' I say.

After a hot shower in my lovely bathroom and getting changed, I knock on my friends' doors and we head for Reception.

'Which way's the bar?' Meg says. I point to the gently lit purple seating area and to a board and drinks list. Christmas is in the air all around us. There are lots of beautiful fake trees, decorated in the same purples and blues, blending with the green. Twinkling lights, full of Christmas promise, and gently piped Christmas music remind me of all the work I've left behind, and what is going on at the restaurant right now with me away. But I make a huge effort to push it out of my mind.

'Blimey, look at those prices!' Meg says, her eyeballs nearly popping out.

The hotel foyer is bright and modern. 'Sleek and stylish', I remember seeing in the details that Joanna sent over when she arranged the trip. There are brightly coloured wicker chairs around coffee-tables in the foyer, neat high-backed sofas and deep square arm-chairs in front of a glorious flame-effect fire by the airy, high-ceilinged bar, with its shades of purple and blue. Ferns with trailing fronds festoon the lighting hung across the seating area, creating a sense of the outdoors when you're really inside. Because, believe me, you wouldn't want to be sitting outside in this weather. We find a table in the glass-roofed observatory bar, where lit candles have been placed in all the windows. Snow is falling and settling partway up the panes.

'I'll go to the bar,' says Joanna, looking in her bag. 'Oh, I've left my purse in my room.'

'I'll go,' says Meg, pulling out hers.

'Let's make a kitty,' I suggest.

'Good idea!' says Joanna. 'I'll put mine in as soon as I get my purse. Or I can put it all on my credit card and you just give me the cash.'

'Sounds good to me,' I say, and pull out some notes, peering at the price list that's lying on the table. My eyes smart. It's really expensive even by comparison with upmarket places in the UK. But we're here for Laura. It really doesn't matter.

An air of disappointment hangs heavily around us.

'I think we just have to accept that we won't see the Lights tonight,' says Meg.

'Let's check the weather again for tomorrow. These things can change quickly,' I say, once again doing the thing we said we wouldn't and pulling out my phone. But nothing has changed. 'Still not looking good.'

'But we're only here for three nights!' Joanna practically crumples.

'We've come all this way for the Lights,' says Meg. 'We can't leave without seeing them.'

'We won't!' I say, trying to stay positive, but our spirits are plummeting.

Across the bar area, the hen party is in full swing.

'Do you want to join us?' they call over. 'You look like you're at a wake rather than on holiday! Come and join us. We're playing Truth or Dare.'

I raise my hand politely, turning them down. 'Thank you, but no.' I smile.

Meg hands me a drink as Joanna pays with her credit card. 'About the Northern Lights?' I hear Joanna ask the barman.

'Ah, you're chasing the Lights.' He shakes his head. 'You won't see any tonight. The snow is too heavy.'

'What if we went further inland, to the mountains?'

He nods, as he pours her gin and tonic. 'Sometimes you have to hunt them out. You need a Light-seeker.'

'A what?' says Meg, spinning round.

'A Light-seeker. Someone who knows the area well and can find them for you,' he says, a jazzy version of 'Jingle Bells' playing softly in the background.

'Do you know one?' Joanna asks eagerly, and my spirits start to lift.

'Yes.' He shrugs. 'Me.'

'You're a Light-seeker?' Joanna says eagerly.

'When I'm not here, yes. I take out tours.' He pushes the drink towards her.

'Can you take us out?' She picks up the glass by the stem and grips it firmly.

He looks out of the window and shakes his head. 'I'm working this evening. Besides, the weather is not good. Maybe another day.'

Meg stands up and joins Joanna at the bar. 'But we're only here for three nights. Please, we've always wanted to see them.'

'It's really important.' Joanna puts on the pressure.

I join them at the bar.

'We can pay.' I grimace at how crass that sounded.

'And we'll tip really well,' Meg joins in.

'Okay, okay. I can't take you out but I'm here all weekend. I can tell you where to go, though I can't promise you'll see them. The Lights don't come out to order. But I can tell you where you'll get your best chance to see them. A little off the beaten track.'

'Will it be safe?' Meg is concerned.

'We'd have to be careful,' I say. 'It's a bit risky.' I turn to Joanna.

'It doesn't look that bad out there,' she says. 'It'll be fine. These cars are designed for it.'

'Well, in that case . . .' I say.

And we chink glasses. 'To Laura!' we say.

'Let's have lunch, pick up the hire car and get going!' Joanna smiles.

Maybe we'll see what we came here for after all.

'Could I have salad Niçoise, but hold the anchovies and add extra Parmesan shavings, dressing on the side.'

I listen to Joanna's order, wondering about the air miles that must have brought in all those non-local and unseasonal products.

'And tell Chef please that I want the egg yolk really firm.'

I cringe, as does Meg. Joanna has always been the same. She has lived the lifestyle she always wanted, in her first and second marriages.

'I'll have the soup, followed by pasta,' I say, still baulking at the prices and the strange mix of Mediterranean dishes on the menu. Nothing that would tell us we're in Iceland.

'And me,' says Meg. 'I know what you're thinking,' she adds, as the waiter finishes taking our order and leaves.

'What?' I laugh.

'You're looking at the menu, thinking how you'd change it.'

'I'm not!'

'You are,' they say.

I put the menu down. 'I was thinking about Icelandic food.'

'What is Icelandic food?' Joanna asks.

'Well, apart from what the spa therapist told us this afternoon, it's always been known as . . . putrid shark, and there's puffin,' I tell them.

'Ewwww!'

I roll back my shoulders. Maybe I should have had a massage after all.

My thoughts turn back to the new restaurant, the customers, the high prices paid for perfection. And, very briefly, I think about the recipes, warming and comforting, I used to make, and quickly shut down what I remember from when Laura was still here. We're celebrating her life, not being sad that it's over. I swallow my sadness.

After a lunch of bland soup, pasta and a sad-looking salad, wine like vinegar, and the background noise of Truth or Dare from the neighbouring round table, whose occupants have taken to glaring at us as if we're a bunch of old grumps, I can take it no longer. It's hot inside the hotel. I need some air.

I excuse myself and say I'm going to use the bathroom before we head out to find the Lights. I go to my room, grab my coat and hat, then head downstairs. I go outside and breathe in deeply, the snowflakes tickling my nose. It's really cold. I stamp my feet and think of the bland lunch I've just had. So many things could be done to make it better. But some other part of me wants to stop thinking about food and just focus on seeing the Northern Lights.

I walk around the outside of the hotel. At the front door there are candles, big ones, in storm lanterns, with wax dripping down their sides, warm and welcoming against the snow and reflected in the glass of the entrance. There are a few chalets, with lights over the doors, and I can see the steam rising from the hot spring. I wonder if the hen party will head back in later, ordering more prosecco. Maybe they're right: maybe we are a group of grumpy old women. But we're in our prime! Meg is getting remarried. Joanna is happily married to her millionaire and is enjoying her stepchildren's successes. I'm about to get a new restaurant to run. This is what Laura would have wanted. She wanted us to embrace life and live it, and we have.

For the past two years we've grabbed the opportunities. Meg is in charge of two care homes, which are going from strength to strength. Joanna has travelled the world, eaten in the best restaurants, skied and partied in the best resorts. We went out and seized the day, didn't look back. Laura wanted us to look forward, not back.

I keep walking, gazing up at the sky, hoping for a hint that the snow is stopping and the Lights might peek out.

Suddenly I hear a shout, then a door slam. I've been wandering along, eyes on the sky, and realize now that

I'm at the back of the hotel, away from the beautifully lit front entrance and the hot spring. There's another shout from behind the kitchen door and then I see a young woman, standing in the cold, hugging herself. I should turn and walk away. Give her some privacy. This probably isn't even a public area. I see her take a huge breath and her shoulders shudder. She must be freezing.

Suddenly I'm right back there, a young woman, getting bawled out in the kitchen, working as a pot-washer and then a commis chef. I remember how I felt. I remember the angry tears, the humiliation. I remember thinking I should just walk away, not take the abuse from the foul-mouthed chef or the younger ones, vying for his favour. But all it did was fuel me: I wanted to make it, wanted to be the one taking charge, my ideas on the plates in a kitchen run without shouting, swearing and bullying.

'Are you okay?' I ask the young woman.

She looks up, startled. 'Oh, yes, fine. Sorry.' She turns to go back in.

'Wait!' I say.

And she stops, upset still evident on her face.

'Take a moment. They won't miss you. And if they do, good. They'll see what a great job you're doing.' The words tumble out of me as if I'm talking to one of the younger members of my kitchen brigade.

I put a hand on her shoulder, then pull off my scarf and wrap it around her. 'Chef's in a bad mood, is he?'

She nods and sniffs. 'Someone complained about his salad Niçoise. Said it lacked flavour and seasoning.'

It was Joanna. But all the food here lacks flavour and seasoning.

'And did it, do you think?'

She looks up at me as if no one has ever asked her opinion before. 'Yes,' she says, surprising herself.

'But you can't tell him or her.'

'No. Him. He says he's Italian, but I'm not sure.'

'Can you get another job? Somewhere where the chef doesn't shout and swear at his team?'

She shakes her head. 'Jobs are few and far between. I need this one. I want to cook, but there are very few places around here.'

It infuriates me: dreadful food, appalling people skills in the kitchen, and the customers expected to pay these rip-off prices. 'In that case, take a deep breath. Hold your head up, lift your chin a little and remember why you're here. Promise yourself that, one day, you'll run your kitchen differently.'

She smiles. 'Do I know you? Are you from around here?'

'No. But I do know what it's like to work your way up in a kitchen. Don't give up.'

'Thank you,' she says. She goes to pull off my scarf.

I put my hand up. 'Keep it, for when you need to get some air and remind yourself why you're here.'

She smiles. 'Thank you again. And if you're eating in

tomorrow, don't go for the fish curry. It was supposed to be today's fish of the day but he dropped it!'

'Good tip. Thank you. I won't.'

She takes a deep breath, lifts her chin a little, turns towards the kitchen door and opens it. Indecipherable smells tumble out on a wave of steam and hot air.

'Where have you been? You're needed!' I hear the chef shout.

She glances at me over her shoulder and smiles again.

'You were missed! Good!' I say. Then she goes back into the kitchen and the door shuts behind her. A reminder of the twenty-year-old me, pot-washing and commis-cheffing in the finest restaurant I could find. A twenty-year-old who, when shouted at, dug deep and found the determination to become the best chef I could be. I'd show him. I hope that young woman does too.

I walk slowly back towards the front of the hotel, the candles burning brightly around the entrance, giving the place a golden glow while the snow continues to fall heavily.

Joanna spots me from where she's standing beside a big four-by-four and attempts to run over to me, slipping, sliding, long limbs flailing. She rebalances herself, then slows to a considered walk. 'Where have you been? We were worried! We're ready to leave. I'm meeting the Light-seeker here to get all the details.' She drops her voice as if he's a member of the Magic Circle. It makes me smile.

'Is it safe?' I look out at the dark, snowy night.

'He knows what he's doing. He's a Light-seeker. He knows all the right places. He's giving me details of the best locations. We'll get to see the Lights! Here.' She hands me a hip flask and I take a swig. 'We're doing this for Laura, remember? Finding the Lights! What we always said we'd do. When will we have the chance again?'

She's right. I have no idea when I'll have another break, let alone come back to Iceland. I take another look at the four-by-four and don't need asking again. 'You're right! Let's find those Lights!'

3

I march over to the car. Once I'm in, Joanna locks the doors.

'Let's do this!' I say.

'You're sure it's safe?' Meg asks.

'That's him,' Joanna says, pointing to a man waving at us.

'Who?' says Meg.

'The Light-seeker!' Joanna says, as the young man from the bar comes out of the front doors. He steps forward to speak to us.

She presses the button to lower her window and accidentally lowers all four, freezing us again.

'Give me your number,' he says, 'and I'll send you what you need to know.' He's wearing a padded gilet, a beanie hat, and thick thermal gloves. It's like a drug deal in a car park, but with satnav and card details changing hands for the heavy tip we promised.

'Yes, they're there,' says Joanna, through chattering teeth, looking at her phone as a message pings through. 'I've got all your instructions.'

He nods, then frowns.

'Problem?' I say.

'Oh, er, your payment hasn't gone through,' he says to Joanna.

'Oh!' she says, clearly flustered.

'Here, take mine,' I say, reaching through the open driver's window, shivering and waving my card at him.

'Okay.' He taps a small white machine with it and watches. 'That's worked. Thank you.'

'No! Thank you!' we respond.

'It means a lot to us,' says Joanna.

'Good. And again thank you for the tip,' he says, holding up his white card machine, clearly pleased.

'Drive carefully,' he says.

'Is it always this cold?' Joanna wonders.

He laughs. 'Colder sometimes! You get used to it. Now, enjoy your trip. Stick to the main road,' he says, 'and remember, be back by ten, before it gets really cold. There is more snow on the way.'

Joanna raises the windows and pulls away. 'So we must return before ten. It will get cold then and start to freeze,' Joanna says.

'Cold then? What's this?' I laugh.

'Winter apparently,' she says, and we all laugh, as she pushes the vehicle into gear and rolls up the drive. 'Okay, everyone ready? Let's see if we can find those Lights.' Snow is falling steadily in the darkening afternoon.

'Let's do it!' I say.

'Whoop!'

This is it. We're on our way to find the Northern Lights for Laura. And I feel a thrill of excitement, and satisfaction. We're going to find them!

'So, like he said, the conditions aren't ideal. Snow is forecast all night, getting heavier after ten and for the rest of the weekend.'

'Does that mean no Lights?' Meg asks anxiously.

'He said it means they'll certainly be shy,' Joanna smiles, 'but told us where to try.'

She doesn't seem nervous at all, unlike me. I look out at the darkening afternoon, onto the expanse of white wilderness. Usually as evening comes I'm in the kitchen, preparing for service, checking and double-checking that everything's in place. The better prepared the kitchen is, the smoother the service.

Joanna was on Reception at the restaurant where we worked. Meg and Laura were waitresses. Meg always struggled with silver service. Nerves would get the better of her and cutlery would slide. She once had to fish a knife out of a gentleman's dinner jacket – it had fallen off the plate she was clearing. She never enjoyed working there, but Laura always had her back. She had a way with people – a smile and a laugh, putting them at ease. Laura and Meg worked as a team. We all did. And we partied together after work.

I blink, or try to. My eyelashes might be frozen. Even my eyeballs are freezing.

'Okay, so it's all programmed into the satnav,' says Joanna.

'Let's hope we see them quickly,' says Meg, huddling into the front seat.

It's nice to see her smiling, maybe even relaxing a little. She looks exhausted. All the wedding planning has taken it out of her. I hope that's all it is. She's shivering, her hat pulled down over her ears, her arms wrapped around herself, her teeth chattering. Joanna turns on the engine and the air-con is blowing full blast, but not hot air.

'Quick! Heat!' Meg says.

It's nearly as cold in the car as it is outside, and although it's just early evening, it's so dark – a kind of gloom that makes you want to go inside, light candles and snuggle up until spring. I look back at the hotel with fondness. There's the hot spring, and a list of treatments I'm going to work my way through tomorrow. As soon as we've seen the Lights, we can relax for the rest of the weekend.

Joanna pushes the car into first gear and it seems to

grip the snowy road as we crunch out of the drive, with a wave from a hotel worker, clearing the snow from the front step.

Meg puts on some music and we're soon driving along, staring into the dark, snowy night.

'Anyone else hot in here?' asks Joanna, and we all nod and fan our faces. The heaters are working well and soon we're stripping off hats and gloves.

'A group of perimenopausal women should be known as a flush,' says Meg, making us all smile.

Joanna opens the windows, only for us to be rewarded with a huge dump of snow from the car's roof on our faces. We close the windows again, and strip off our coats as well.

Eventually Joanna pulls up. 'This is it,' she says, looking around at the other cars and coaches in the parking spot. 'This is the best place to see the Lights!'

It's barren. Big areas of nothing more than snowy wilderness. Despite my hot cheeks, I shiver. Imagine being out there in that. I shudder.

We sit and wait. One by one, cars start to leave and head back the way we came. Some far too fast for this weather.

We wait, unsure what to say to each other, all thinking the same thing. We're here for Laura. We're here to see the Lights. We promised.

The sky is dark, snow is falling and there are no stars.

'It's not clear enough,' I say finally.

'Let's move on,' says Joanna, starting the engine and checking the satnav.

I stare out across the blanket of snow, with more snow drifting down, like snaking white ribbons in the wind. I'm in awe at the enormity of it. We're in the middle of nowhere. I find the open space almost terrifying. It makes me feel so small, so . . . inconsequential. For someone who spends all day in a kitchen, surrounded by people, I can't imagine life like this. It feels so isolated. No one for miles. Slowly and steadily, rolling forwards on the car's chunky tyres, we continue further west, each of us alone with our thoughts as the snow whooshes towards the windscreen and flakes dance in the headlights. The wipers do their best to get rid of the snow but, really, it feels like trying to push jelly uphill. The more the wipers swoosh, the more it keeps coming.

Joanna puts on the soundtrack she's made for the trip, all the old songs, and soon we're bobbing along to them, looking out, ever hopeful.

'Okay, let's try here,' says Joanna, checking Google Maps and pulling off the road to what I think might be a parking area. A couple of other cars are there. We put on our coats and hats and tentatively step out into the snow. Already the cold is biting at my feet, fingers and nose, and then I feel it in my bones. The snow is falling heavily. Lots of tiny flakes, tumbling, flying, flipping and falling, as if laughing at the mischief they're creating. After a little while of looking out over the edge of a cliff to a plateau below, the other Lights tourists get back into their vehicles. We look at each other and shake our heads. I motion for us to get back into the car.

'Don't worry, I know of another place,' Joanna says, still smiling. It feels like the middle of the night.

'Is it safe?' Meg asks again, as we pull out onto the snowy road.

'It's fine. We still have another two hours. And the hire company told me we have the best tyres, studded ones. And we'll drive slowly.'

I'm starting to get a little less sure about this and wonder if we should turn back now, try again tomorrow or the day after.

We set off. The road is increasingly snow-covered, and is clearly less used.

'I wouldn't like to try this in my Merc,' says Joanna, still upbeat.

Meg and I look at each other. Joanna likes to remind us every now and then of how well life is going for her, and it grates a bit. Especially for Meg who is working so hard, but will never have a Mercedes on what she earns. I know how much this trip has meant to her, how she's saved for it and with the wedding on top.

It's really dark now and I'm watching the clock. The windscreen wipers are working as hard as they can, swooshing away the snow as it keeps falling. Every now and again they freeze. Joanna stops and I jump out to shake them so they start again, then get back into the car, rubbing my hands up my arms.

Soon, Joanna is pulling up again. This time there's no car park. We're further off the beaten track than before, and the anxiety seems to be increasing, like the snow-fall. This time she's got a map out, with markings on it, made by the Light-seeker, who told her to be prepared. She checks it, and the satnav, but that's not working.

'This is it!' she says, with delight. 'I'm sure of it.' She double-checks the map, then steps out with it. It flaps and flutters, trying to escape her in the bitter, biting wind.

We follow her into the unwelcoming wind and I can hear the rush of water.

'Be careful on the edge,' Joanna tells us. 'There's a waterfall here, coming from the mountain. Cleanest water you can get.'

We stand and listen and look up at the sky.

'Sometimes the Lights come out over the waterfall,' she says.

We can't see a thing, except flurries of snow racing towards us.

'I wish she was here,' says Meg, over the noise of the wind and the waterfall, which we can't see, below us.

'Me too,' I say, hugging myself. My nose is so cold, it feels like it might freeze and drop off.

'She'd have told us to keep going, not to give up,' Joanna says firmly.

'She'd have told us nothing was impossible. If we want it enough, we'll get there,' I agree.

'She'd have told a joke, made sure we didn't get sad,' Meg says, 'told us to keep moving forwards.'

'Is there anywhere else we can try?' I ask, reminding myself how important it is that we do this.

Meg pulls out her phone to check the time. 'It's getting late. We must be back by ten when the weather's going to worsen,' she reminds us, and I know we're all feeling desperate now.

I tap my phone, hold it up and spin around, searching for a signal.

Disappointment is heavy in the air.

'We have to see the Lights. It's why we're here,' Meg says, and no one argues with her.

'There is one more place he told me about.' Joanna bites her bottom lip.

'I'm not sure we should go any further.' The tone of her voice has made me even more nervous.

'But we're only here for two more days and this is really important,' Joanna says.

'We're celebrating,' Meg adds.

'Yes, we're celebrating.' I swallow.

'On her birthday. We can't give up now. We promised to do it for her. On her birthday.' Meg looks at us firmly, like the mum she is.

'We did promise,' I agree quietly. I remember the last few days when she was at home on the sofa, under a huge duvet, and I tried to make things she might like to eat or drink, or just to enjoy the memories they prompted. Paella from our trip to Spain for Meg's first hen party. Fish and chips like we used to have by the beach on days off. Christmas cake, which reminded her of her nan, heavy on the brandy. Sunday roasts and curry, with chips on the side. And pancakes! In the end I made soups, with her favourite flavours: rich oxtail, like beefy broth, a hug in a mug, from the days we'd watch the rugby in the stands. Obviously not the Christmas cake. I made ice cream for her, laced with cinnamon and rum-soaked raisins. Cold, yet with warming flavours. Fish soup, with plenty of garlic. It's not like she was going to be kissing anyone. She laughed and coughed. I tried to find a way to bring out smells and flavours in a way she could enjoy them.

'We promised we'd find the Lights and raise a toast to her with this.' Joanna pulls the bottle from my bag. I even remember making champagne sorbet so she could let it sit on her tongue and savour the flavour.

She looks at us and the bottle as we hold our breath.

'We promised not to cry, only laugh,' Meg says.

'Okay, there's this one last place. Are we all up for giving it a try?' Joanna asks. 'One last go and we'll head back for today. I can't promise I'll find it. But I'll try. It's a bit off road. A village called Villiá – it means Wild

River apparently.' The map is spilling over to cover Meg in the passenger seat. 'Over there.' She points down from our vantage point. My stomach flips with excitement and fear. 'Where the river flows from the mountains, down the waterfall and onwards to the sea. Where the wild salmon swim, the Light-seeker told me.'

'I've never heard of it.' Meg picks up the travel guide that Joanna has also brought in book form. Belt and braces, that's our Joanna. Never just rely on the satnav.

'It's not somewhere tourists flock to, apparently. It's a bit . . . off the beaten track,' she says, more seriously. 'We don't have much time if you want to try it.'

'It's up to you. We've got just an hour before we have to head back. We can give it one last shot?' Joanna looks at us seriously.

We look at each other.

And my stomach tightens with terror. This really is madness.

'But this would have been her fortieth,' says Meg.

'We won't have another chance,' says Joanna.

'We want to!' we all agree. 'For Laura!'

'Just drive carefully. Laura wouldn't want us to die in the process!' I add.

We travel in silence, no tunes this time. Inside the car, the air is heavy with anxious anticipation. Outside, the snow seems to be falling heavier. The car is slipping and sliding, occasionally getting stuck, and the windscreen wipers are freezing. Once again, I get out to release them. Joanna drives much slower and with care.

'We'll need to head back soon,' she says, and we all agree, looking out at the snow swirling around us.

'We can always try again tomorrow,' I say to the others. 'It might not be her birthday, but close to it.'

'Weather's getting worse,' says Meg, chewing her fingernail through her glove.

The tension in the car is growing.

'I've read books like this. Three people go up a snowy mountain and only two come down.'

'Maybe we should turn back now,' I say.

'We've come this far! You can't play it safe all your life,' Joanna says.

I bristle. I don't think you could call running a Michelin-starred restaurant in a male-oriented kitchen playing it safe. But now is not the time.

'Yes, we'll be fine. Just a little further! Joanna's used to driving big cars,' Meg says reassuringly.

'Not in weather like this.' She confirms my worst fears. Meg reaches back from the front seat and I take her hand, squeezing hard as Joanna sets off again, uphill in the direction of Villiá.

'What is this guy doing?' Joanna says, as we spot the red taillights of a car through the snow in front of us. 'He's never going to make it in that. This hill is way too steep. Idiot!' She throws up a hand.

I crane my neck to see the long hill. We'll be heading

over the top, then down to what must be the village of Villiá.

'Look, let's go back,' I say. 'Laura wanted us to see the Lights, but not risk our lives doing it.'

Reluctantly, the others nod.

Joanna stops the car. 'Sure?' she asks.

We nod again.

'Sensible call,' she says. 'I'm sorry. I've let everyone down.'

'You haven't!' we say.

'It's the right thing, Joanna.' I put my hand on her shoulder.

Joanna looks ahead, and for a moment I'm worried she'll keep going, regardless. She has that steely determination on her face. I hold my breath.

'You're right. I know that,' she says. 'We'll turn here.' She starts to manoeuvre the car and I can barely look, but when I open my eyes, the car is facing back the way we came. I breathe a sigh of relief as she steadily drives back down the road. Meg and I let go of each other's hands.

Joanna puts on another soundtrack, mellower this time. We all start to relax a little as we make for the hotel, a hot bath, an expensive gin and fish pie.

The car behind us has had the same thought, I think, as I see the headlights of a car behind us: it must also have turned around. I'm feeling altogether happier – until, suddenly, Joanna swings the steering wheel and the car swerves to the right. Meg and I grab each other's hands again awkwardly. Joanna doesn't brake but swerves expertly as a bank of snow tumbles down the hillside in front of us and brings the car to a stop. 'Everyone okay?' she asks.

'Yes. What happened?'

'Falling snow. It's happened before when I've been skiing.'

'Can you get us out?' Meg asks.

'It'll take some digging,' she says, pulling on her hat. 'There's a shovel in the boot. The guy at the hire place insisted on it.'

She goes to grab the door handle. Checks the rear-view mirror. 'Oh, no!' she says.

'What?' we ask.

'Hang on. It'll be okay,' she says, screwing up her face.

'What wil—'

Bang!

The four-by-four lurches forward, and we hear the hiss of airbags inflating.

We are surrounded by white.

'What happened?' Meg wants to know.

'Everyone okay?' asks Joanna, again.

'Think so,' I hear myself say shakily.

'We hit a rock in front when the car behind skidded and crashed into us. I'll see if the driver's okay,' Joanna says. She clambers out of her seat, then over me, and pushes open the back window.

'I'm a first-aider.' I snap into action, undo my seat-belt and start to climb out of the window after her. 'I'm coming with you!'

'Hello! Hello!' Joanna says, tapping on the driver's window and I join in.

The door opens slowly.

'I'm okay,' says the woman, who's about our age, maybe a little younger.

'Is anyone else in the car with you?' I ask.

'No. Just me,' she says, pale and shaken.

'Now what?' I say. We're in the middle of nowhere. There's just snow as far as the eye can see.

Joanna glances around. 'We're not going anywhere this evening,' she says.

'*What?*'

'It's going to take some time to dig the cars out of here. And we need daylight.'

'We can't stay here!' I pull out my phone. 'No signal.' I feel panic rising.

'Don't worry. I spotted a farm up there.' Joanna points.

'Okay. We'll go and get help. You two stay together,' I say, to Meg and the lone driver. She gets out of her car and into the four-by-four's boot.

'Stay together!' Joanna instructs very firmly, as we start to walk.

I see she's limping. 'You're hurt.'

'It's okay.' She waves me away. 'Just cramp.'

'No, you stay here. I'll go for help.'

'It's just over there. That farmhouse.' She puts her hand on my shoulder.

'I'll be back!' I call to her, squinting.

'Be careful!' says Joanna.

I've never been so scared. My heart is banging against my chest as I set off along the road, squinting into the snowy distance.

And then, I see a light, a farmhouse, and my spirits rise.

4

'Hello!' I shout, and bang the red front door, so cold I could cry, but I suspect the tears would freeze. I'm shaking with cold and fear. Who knows where we are? It's desolate out here and really dark. What if we're stuck for the night? I stamp my feet.

'Come on,' I say impatiently, through chattering teeth, but there's no reply. I bang again, even louder this time, and see a bell, which I ring. Then I go for a combination of all three. 'Hello! Hello!' Knock, knock! Ding, ding!

When there's still no reply, I know I can't wait. I see smoke from a small building just beside the farm-house, rising from a chimney. If there's smoke, there must be someone about. I have no idea who or what might be there. There is an indentation in the snow I can see, as I hold my phone up, that resembles a path-way. I take a deep breath and start to walk along it.

I trip, and fall face first into the deep snow.

'Damn!' I pick myself up. 'What on earth is this place?' I'm angry with myself for agreeing to come out here. The anger has replaced fear. I just want to find someone to help us get out of here and back to the hotel.

Teeth chattering, I'm heading for the little building at the end of the path. I can smell more than I can see. Suddenly my stomach roars with hunger. The smell is familiar yet different.

I reach the little wooden door, with a heart shape cut into it.

I take a deep breath – and, suddenly, a bark makes me leap out of my frozen skin. A black-and-white dog, a collie, partly covered with snow, sits up and barks again outside the door.

'Okay, good boy. Just looking for your owner,' I say. He doesn't seem angry, just alerting someone that I'm here.

'Good boy,' I repeat. 'Good boy.'

'Hello?' I knock on the wooden door of the little hut and, when there's no reply, pull back the door slowly. The warmth in there pulls me in. The smell is amazing. And then I see it, rows and rows of pink, turning orange, smoking salmon. My mouth waters. There is an earthiness about the smell as the smoke winds, twists and curls its way upward and out of the chimney. It's wonderful, comforting, soothing and, frankly,

I could just sit here until morning comes. And if I can't find anyone, I may just suggest that that's what we do.

But if the smokehouse fire is lit, someone must be around. We need help to get away from here. We can't stay out all night. This is serious. I mean, people die out here.

I step out of the smokehouse, the smell staying with me and wrapping itself around me.

'Hello!' I shout, then put my hands around my mouth and give it all I've got over the vicious wind. '*HELLOOOO!*'

A door opens in an outbuilding behind the farm-house, and a shaft of light floods out. I see torchlight moving towards me. Oh, thank God! I could cry with relief.

'Hello! Hello!' I wave at the torchlight. 'Hello!'

I jump up and down, partly to keep my feet from freezing but also so that whoever it is can see me. 'Can you hurry, please? It's really cold out here!'

'No!' comes the answer, which surprises me. I'm not sure I've heard right.

'Hello? Can you help, please?'

'No! Go away! Get off my land!'

I stand and stare, in utter shock, then see the torch turning as its owner goes back towards the shed.

'No! Wait!' I struggle into the snow, toppling, then

right myself, determined to go after the light. 'Please! You have to help!'

The light turns back and someone is walking towards me through the snow. As they get closer I see their face in the torch they're holding up. I see a very much younger man than I was expecting. He's also much better-looking than the grumpy voice led me to suppose.

'I told you! I told your boss! Don't send anyone! We're not interested! It's a no! Now, if you'll excuse me!'

I wonder what to say next. I try to put my words into the right order as he tsks and mutters that they can't even send someone who speaks Icelandic.

He turns back towards the small building, opens the door and the golden, fiery light pours out, then disappears as the door slams shut.

I'm standing in the freezing cold, the vicious wind biting at my skin, and my friends are in a car in the middle of nowhere. We need help. How dare that man just walk away from me?

'Hey!' I march as best I can through the snow to the door and, without waiting to knock, fuelled by fury, fear and the prospect of freezing to death, I wrench it open.

A blast of hot air rushes towards me. There is a work bench, with tools and instruments of all kinds. The man has a mask pulled down over his face and a blow-torch, firing out a blue flame, in the other.

I'm too angry to be scared. 'Hey,' I repeat.

He straightens, holding the blowtorch in one hand.

'I don't know who you think I am, but I need – we need your help!'

Slowly he pulls back his face mask. There's something familiar about him. But I don't have time to ask: he's already putting down the blowtorch, clearly ready to shoo me out.

I take a step back, then put my foot in the door. Large clumps of snow fall from my inferior footwear and make puddles almost immediately on the concrete floor. The warmth in the workshop taunts me as I stand in the cold, snow falling on my head and face. 'Please,' I say politely, less confrontationally. 'I don't know who you think I am, but I've never been here before. No one sent me. But we need help. There's been an accident. Our cars are stuck, just over there.' I point in the direction I think I've come from.

He doesn't need telling twice. He whips off his face mask, whistles and the collie comes bounding through the snow. He pulls on a coat hanging on a hook by the door, adds a big fake-fur hat with ear flaps, slips out of the shoes he's wearing, pulls on big boots and strides into the snowy outdoors.

'Why didn't you say?' he says.

'You didn't give me a chance!' I reply, as he heads in the direction of the gate and the road. Soon I'm puffing, trying to keep up.

'What are you doing up here anyway?' I hear him ask as he looks back at me, slowing for me to catch up.

'Looking for the Lights.'

'On a day like this? You read the weather reports?' he says, and I feel like I'm being told off. In fact, I am being told off.

'I know. We thought we had the timing right. We were heading back to the hotel. But we came off the road.'

He shakes his head. 'You should have come with a guide. Or taken advice.'

'We did!' I reply.

'Well, they should have known better.'

I feel foolish now, as well as cold. 'But we did tell him it was really important that we see them.'

The wind is howling, the snow zipping around, causing chaos.

He looks at me for a moment, but doesn't ask any more. 'Anyone hurt?' he asks over the wind.

'Not too bad. Shaken. But it would be good to get inside and ring for help.'

He pulls down his hat further against the wind, whistles again and the dog is immediately by his side, staring up at him, awaiting instruction.

'Okay,' he says, and sets off along the road, which is covered with fresh snow now. I follow as quickly as my shorter legs will allow, hit a deep patch and fall face first again.

'I'm fine,' I say furiously, righting myself and wondering, not for the first time, what on earth I'm doing here, when there's so much I could be doing in the restaurant kitchen at home. The snow is falling so heavily that I can barely see the figure in front of me. All I can hear is the wind. It's stinging my face. Which way was the car? Which way was the farmhouse? Am I going mad? The wind sounds ridiculously like laughter.

Suddenly someone's right beside me. 'You okay?' the man from the farmhouse says, over the wind.

I nod, squinting against the snow, scooped up on the gusting gale. I've never seen anything like it. This is real snow. Big snow. It's actually terrifying. Then I shake my head. Actually, I'm not okay. Far from it.

'Take my hand. It can be a little scary if you're not used to it.'

'You can say that again!' I'm suddenly reassured by his thick gloved hand taking mine.

'Let's find your friends and get them to the farmhouse.'

Whoever this man is, he's going to help us and I'll be grateful to him for ever. The dog barks to let us know he's found the car, leading us to my friends. Relief floods over me. We're safe. For the time being.

5

Finally, the four of us, we three and the woman who drove into us – she is shivering badly and very pale – make it to the lights of the farmhouse. We stagger through the heavy snowfall, the wind still wailing around us, arms slung around each other, and the stranger we're stranded with, in the freezing cold, dark, scary wasteland.

'Here are some blankets. Come into the living room where it's warm,' directs the man. 'I'll make some hot drinks,' he says, as we stand, silent with shock, beside long sofas. The dog jumps up onto a sofa, looking at me with his blue-flecked eyes, until his owner returns with a tray of mugs, and tells him to get down because he's wet. Then he calls him and rubs him with a towel, thanking him for his help. We strip off our coats, and leave them in the hall over a warm radiator, along with our soggy gloves and hats, our boots beneath. I take a moment to look at him. He's a little younger than us perhaps, with gunmetal grey hair, silver streaks running through it like liquid mercury. He's wearing a thick patterned jumper and a grey scarf around his neck, a shade darker than his beanie hat, and is attractive . . . very attractive indeed.

'Are you okay, Meg?' Joanna says, and I turn to look at her.

'Yes, just a bit of a shock,' she says.

'You'll feel better once we're at the hotel. What's going to happen now?' Joanna asks the man, her directness making me wince. 'How are we going to get back?'

'Drink your coffee and I'll organize beds for the night,' the man says, handing around the mugs.

'The night?' Joanna says. 'Oh, no, we really couldn't put you out. We'll just get back to the hotel.'

'What were you thinking? That you'd try to get back tonight?' He looks at her with a relaxed smile.

Joanna gazes at Meg and me, a nervous laugh in her throat, as if she's talking to a madman. 'Well, yes. If you could ring for a taxi that would be great, or help us tow the car from the snow,' she says, her usual forthrightness wavering.

'Joanna, he's right. We're not going anywhere in that weather.' We all know it's true.

'Especially not with the four-by-four stuck in the

snow,' he says. 'We'll need to get help to shift it.' He shrugs. 'It all depends on the weather. Out here, you have to work with the weather, not the other way around.'

'But we don't even know you! You could be anyone!' says Joanna, and I cringe at her crude summing up of the situation. Although, to be fair, she's right. She's saying what we must all be thinking. We have no idea who he is.

He turns back to us, with a tray of shot glasses. 'I'm Pétur Snorrison. This is my home. My family's farm. Now you know who I am. Oh, I have a brother too. Hilmar Snorrison.' My eyebrows shoot up. I know the name. The famous Icelandic opera singer. 'He and his wife are about to move back here, with their family, and look after the farm.' His blue-grey eyes match the silver flecks running through his hair and his close-shaven beard. His eyes seem to twinkle in the candles he's lighting around the room as he speaks. 'Now . . . who are you?'

'We're . . . umm . . .' I look around at us and the stranger in our group, who is staring into her mug, clearly in shock.

'Drink your coffee. It will help to warm you. I will heat some soup. It's important to get dry and warm after being in the snow.' He hands around the little shot glasses, which contain a clear liquid. 'The weather shifts rapidly here. You can experience all types, sometimes at the same time!' he explains.

I take a glass and bend to sniff it. Wow! It's power-ful. I wonder if drinking it is a good idea, but then I see Joanna throw hers back. Maybe it'll help me make sense of all this. We're in the middle of nowhere in Iceland, stuck in a snowstorm with a famous opera singer's brother. I follow Joanna's lead and knock back the shot. It burns as it goes down and for a moment I can't speak or even really think.

'What *is* that?' I croak.

'Firewater,' he says matter-of-factly. 'We brew it our-selves. It helps in the winter months.' He laughs, as if this is all perfectly normal. Then he tilts his head back, and I see his Adam's apple bob up and down as he swallows a shot. 'A top-up?'

'Perhaps later,' I say, putting my hand over my glass.

For a moment no one says anything. All that can be heard is the wind, and I'm thinking that, actually, another firewater might help.

'So, tell me, who are you all?' he says, as he moves back to the kitchen and pulls a large pan onto the hob, clearly the soup he's about to warm up. 'Oh,' he turns back to me, 'I'm sorry about earlier, when you first knocked at the door. I thought you were someone else.'

'Clearly.' I find myself smiling at him. 'It was really good of you to help us,' I say, and feel my cheeks pink-ing, which must be the firewater.

'Out here, we look after each other,' he says, adjust-ing his hat. 'Otherwise, well, we'd all die.'

Meg splutters on her firewater, and the young woman pats her on the back.

'Anyway, you're welcome and, as I say, I apologize for my earlier abruptness.'

'Who did you think I was?' I say, emboldened by the firewater.

He waves a hand. 'It's fine. Nothing to worry about. Let's just say someone who would not be welcome in my home. Now, tell me who you are and then I'll serve the soup.'

'I'm Joanna, this is Meg and that's Freya,' Joanna says, pointing to me. 'We're just here for three nights, staying at the hotel down by the hot springs and hoping to see the Lights. And . . .' We all look at the woman from the other car. She looks pale.

'Frankie,' she says, in a British accent. 'Short for Francesca.'

'And you're all here looking for the Lights?' he asks.

'Yes,' we say, as does Frankie, nodding.

'Well, it's clearly not the night for it,' he says.

'Does this happen often? People getting stranded out here?'

'We get a lot of tourists who don't take things seriously enough around here. They think it's a playground, a fun place to explore and see the Lights.'

'Like us, you mean.' My cheeks burn.

'It's not safe. People die if they don't know what they're doing in these conditions.'

For a moment none of us says anything. We're thinking about what might have happened out there this evening. Finally, Pétur, our rescuer, breaks the silence.

'Now, I've put the soup on, there's bread too. I need to check the sheds, the sheep and the smokehouse. Go ahead and help yourselves. I'll be back,' he says, as he walks towards the door where his boots, coat and dog are waiting.

'Oh, and this is Jón!' he says, rubbing the collie's ruff. He looks up at his master with complete contentment.

And I can't help but notice the difference in the man who first turned me away and this one. I find myself with pink cheeks again and feeling warm. But then, that's a regular state for all of us: warmth and pink cheeks are common in perimenopausal women.

'Come on, let's sit,' says Meg, pointing to the table in the open-plan room.

As we head into the kitchen area and sit on the chairs around the long pine table, I head straight to the cooker and stir the soup, leaning over it, breathing in its flavours. There are mushrooms, different types – I can smell them, earthy – and lots of pepper. Some alcohol, and plenty of cream, making it rich and smooth. Delicious. I find some bowls in the cupboard and the lights flicker off, then on. I turn back to stirring the soup feeling my toes warm, itch and ache as they thaw on the warmth coming up from under the floorboards. Then the lights go out and we all look around at each other.

'I should go,' says Frankie, tossing aside the blanket that's over her legs and getting to her feet.

'I'm not sure that's a good idea,' I say, putting down the soup spoon. 'It's probably best if we all stick together.'

'No, really,' she says. 'It's best if I try to pull the car out and get on my way.'

'Really. It's not worth it. Come and have some soup. We'll get you out as soon as we can,' I insist.

'No, thank you. You've been more than helpful.' She pulls on her coat, her woollen hat, and heads for the door.

'You can't go out in that!' exclaims Meg, and then to us, 'She'll die! We've got to do something.'

We look at each other. Meg's right. We should do something. But what? We can't let her go out in this weather. The atmosphere has become as chilly as the wind outside sounds. What if . . .

'Captain Oates!' says Meg.

'Who?' asks Joanna.

I stand up. I can't just let someone walk out to their death.

Suddenly the door opens and a cold blast blows in. It's Frankie again. Her teeth are chattering so much she can barely speak. 'You're right. No point. Frozen,' she manages.

'Look, let's just stick it out and we'll sort it in the morning.'

'I can't stay here,' she says.

'It doesn't look as if you have a choice. We'll just say we're all together if you're worried about whose fault it was. I'm sure the insurance is used to things like this,' I say. 'We were just as stupid, persisting in looking for the Lights when the weather was turning. It's our fault as much as yours, and we should look out for each other. Now, sit and eat. You'll feel better.'

'Maybe the hotel will send out another vehicle to find us when we're not back. Someone will notice we're missing and come looking for us,' Meg says optimistically.

I check my phone for signal. There is none. 'I'm sure you're right,' I say, realizing this must happen a lot. 'They'll send help. Don't worry.'

And with that, Frankie does as she's told, barely able to hold the spoon for shaking hands and chattering teeth.

As we eat the soup, I cut into the loaf of bread on the table. I pick up a slice and breathe in. It smells amazing. I start to work out the flavours, but there's something I can't put my finger on. I bite into it. It's delicious. Nutty, with a thick crust and soft centre. I take some of the light, nearly white butter from the table and spread it on thickly.

'This is really good!' I say, thinking of nothing but the fresh bread, malty and nutty, with the creamy butter slowly melting into it in my mouth.

At that moment the door opens and Pétur comes in with Jón at his heels.

'How is it?' I ask, making polite conversation.

'The storm's bad. The sheep and barn seem safe, though. But no one's going anywhere tonight . . . or coming in for that matter.'

We all look at each other. This can't be happening, can it?

6

'So, this is your accommodation.' He leads us up the steep white wooden stairs from the hallway with a battery-operated lamp. He reaches the top and indicates two rooms opposite each other with their doors open. Two long rooms, in the eaves, wooden-cladded and each with two sets of bunk beds nestled under the sloping ceilings.

'I hope you'll be comfortable. You'll be safe here,' he says, taking in our clearly tired and worried faces.

'Thank you,' we say as one, exhausted and a little shell-shocked.

'There is a shower room,' he points to a door off the hall, 'and if you need anything, my room is downstairs, at the far end of the hallway.' He holds out a hand and we step into one of the long bunk rooms.

'It should warm up pretty quickly.' He puts a hand

on the radiator. 'Even when we have no electricity here, the hot water that comes from underground has a back-up system and keeps pumping, so we still have heat at least.'

I'm hearing what he's saying but not really taking it in. I walk over to look out of a window at the far end of the room. The snow is throwing itself at the glass and, despite the wind whipping through the wide-open expanse around us, in here I feel safe.

'There are sleeping-bags. All you have to do is pick a bunk,' he says, as if this was the most natural thing in the world.

It seems so surreal. 'What is this place? How come it's here?'

'These were my brother's and my rooms when we were young. But in the summer we used them for fishermen to stay. Still do. But now also school parties.'

'School parties?' Meg asks.

'Small groups who come here to learn about life outside the city, how we live with nature.'

'At this time of year?' Joanna is horrified.

He laughs. 'No, not at this time of year. Which is why you're lucky.'

'I'm not sure "lucky" is the word I'd use,' says Joanna, looking around in obvious dismay.

'And for tourists who are looking for the Lights and get caught out by the weather.' He raises an eyebrow, gently reminding us of our recklessness.

'We would have been fine if it hadn't been for . . .' Joanna looks at Frankie, who shakes her head ever so slightly. And Joanna, not known for her diplomacy as a rule, says no more.

'It's empty now, but in the spring and autumn, the schoolchildren come out here to learn about the rivers, the sea life and see where the wild salmon come home to.'

The simple room may be basic, and far away from our luxury rooms at the hotel, but it's only for one night and we're safe and warm. I shudder, thinking of what could have happened if we hadn't found this place.

'Thank you for everything,' I say, and there's an unusual shake in my voice. I'm usually the one giving instructions. It feels strange to be out of my comfort zone, like being a new young chef all over again, wondering if I'll ever understand what's going on around me.

'You're welcome. I'm downstairs if you need anything.' He smiles.

'Does this happen often?' I ask.

'The snow or tourists searching for the Lights?'

'Um, both.'

'Yes,' he says, and smiles, then tuts. 'The Lights will show themselves when they're ready to. Hunting them down won't make them appear. Some things can't be rushed.' He smiles again, and I can't help but hold his stare for just a second longer than necessary. His eyes are the colour of clear water.

'Goodnight, ladies. Sleep well. Oh, and a little firewater for a nightcap,' he says, producing a bottle from his pocket and four shot glasses. 'And I'll leave the lamp. There's candles on the tables if you prefer.'

'Thank you. Let's hope we're out of your hair in the morning,' I say.

'Let's hope,' he says. 'We'll be able to see the condition of the road and the cars better then and can work out a way back for you.'

'At least we'll be in the hotel for our afternoon spa treatments,' says Joanna, with a sigh of relief. But I can see from Pétur's face that it may not be straightforward.

We hear him head down the staircase to where his dog is waiting at the bottom and reach into our pockets for our phones. We pull them out, hold them up, and walk around the room.

'No signal still.'

'Nothing,' Frankie confirms.

'Oh, God! Tom won't be able to get hold of me. What if he thinks something's happened to me?' Meg worries.

'Meg, something has happened! We were involved in a crash in a snowstorm and we're stuck in the middle of nowhere.' Joanna has reverted to type.

'Look, let's get some sleep. We'll be out of here in

the morning and we can just put it down as a great adventure. Now, who wants which bunk?' I say, feeling calmer. We'll be away in the morning and this will just be a good story to tell when we get back.

'I can . . . sleep in the other room if you like,' says Frankie shakily.

'Let's stick together,' I say. 'We'll feel safer that way.'

'If you're sure?' She looks at Joanna.

'Yes, of course,' says Joanna, who's not half as cold-hearted as she may seem.

'Besides, we have just the one lamp.' I try to lighten the mood.

'Okay, thank you. I appreciate it. It was, after all, my . . .' The words catch in her throat. 'Who's first for the bathroom?' she says, and clears her throat.

'You go ahead,' I say.

'Maybe if we dialled nine-nine-nine or tried texting,' says Meg.

'Meg,' I say, more firmly than I intended, 'this is just one thing you can't fix for everybody. We have to wait until the morning.'

Her face falls and she sits down heavily on a bunk.

'I'm not sure I can do this,' says Joanna, holding up her phone. The torch is throwing out a stark white light over the room and she looks as if she's been asked to spend the night in a bath of rats and snakes, like a contestant on *I'm a Celebrity*.

'Oh, for goodness' sake, Joanna!' snaps Meg, to our

surprise. 'It may not be the Ritz but, like Freya says, we're lucky to be alive and to have found this place. It may not be up to your usual standard, but it's really very clean, safe and warm.'

Joanna closes her mouth.

'Let's get ready for bed,' I say, trying to calm the tension.

'I wonder how Frankie is,' says Meg, looking towards the bathroom.

We turn to the door just as she reappears, pale, shaken and puffy around the eyes.

'Don't worry. It could have happened to any of us,' I say.

'We were all taking a risk. We'll sort it in the morning,' Meg says, comforting her.

She nods gratefully.

We take it in turns to use the bathroom by phone light. The water is lovely and hot.

Pink, warm and fresher, we all grab a sleeping-bag and head for the bunks.

Meg takes a bottom bunk and so does Joanna . . . because of her vertigo, which is a new one on me. But I'm happy to try a top bunk. I throw my day rucksack on the bed. It doesn't have anything particularly useful in it for a night in the wilderness. Frankie takes a top bunk too. I look at the bottle and four glasses. Well, it might help us all to sleep. I pour the clear liquid into the small, heavy-bottomed glasses and hand round shots of the firewater. Then I grab my sleeping-bag from the bunk, shake it out, step into it, and sit at the little round table by the triangular window at the gable end of the house. I open the door on the little lantern there and light it with the matches left beside it. For a moment we soak up the silence and listen to the crackle as the candle sparks into life.

'Well, I know who would've found this funny.' Meg breaks the silence, checking her phone again, then sliding it under her pillow, presumably in the hope of getting signal when the storm passes.

In the light from the candle we smile, and raise our glasses.

'She always did get us into trouble,' says Joanna.

'I wish she was here,' says Meg, rolling her glass between her palms.

We all sip at the firewater as we remember our friend.

'A friend who's not with you any more?' Frankie asks tentatively.

We nod.

'Sorry, we should have explained. We lost her two years ago, to cancer. It's her birthday. She always wanted to see the Northern Lights and we promised we'd do it for her. So it feels like she's right here, with us.'

'That's a good idea,' she says, her voice quiet and thoughtful. 'To absent friends.' She sips the ferocious firewater and falls into her own thoughts.

The wind is whipping up outside, but other than that, there is no sound, just the flicker of the candle in the square, glass-sided lantern, lighting up the white wooden walls, and the warm glow from the lamp. No cars, sirens or late-night drinkers on the streets.

'Guys.' It's Meg who breaks the thoughtful silence. 'You do think I'm doing the right thing, don't you? Getting married again?'

There's a beat while Joanna and I take in what she's just said. Then, 'Of course!' we say together.

'This is Tom we're talking about!' I say.

'He's gorgeous,' Joanna says.

'He adores you!' I add. 'And you adore him!'

'I'm just . . .' Her voice cracks. 'I don't know. The wedding is just two weeks away, but . . .' she takes a deep breath '. . . I'm not sure I'm doing the right thing.'

Joanna and I are stunned. We'd no idea she was having any second thoughts.

'It'll all look better in the morning,' I say. 'We should get some sleep.' I'm worried about where our weary minds are taking us. I blow out the candle and scramble into my top bunk, with a shove from Meg. What happens if and when I need the loo in the night? I'll cross that bridge when I come to it, I think.

They fall into exhausted sleep, Joanna snoring, as she always has and has always denied. I'm worrying about Meg and Tom. But I'm also thinking about the flavour of the firewater and about Pétur. And I think of

Laura, her final words to me. 'Don't look back. Go and live life.' Then I'm working out how to pair the flavour of the firewater with something to make a new dish. It's my go-to place when I need to escape and eventually I, too, fall asleep.

7

It's morning. A clock on the wall is telling me it is. It's early, but still morning. I slept right through the night without having to get up. But now I do, much as I'd like to stay in the warmth of my sleeping-bag.

I test my phone for the torch. It's dead.

I make it down from the bunk in the dark but decide not to wake any of the others by trying to get back into it. I get dressed in the bathroom, by lantern light, and tiptoe downstairs to the kitchen, which is warm. I look around, finding solace, comfort and familiarity in the ingredients on the shelves, the flour in jars, the preserves and pickles. I light the candle in the middle of the table – clearly Icelanders are used to power cuts – then turn back to the shelves. The dried mushrooms in jars, clearly used in the soup yesterday. The preserved berries, dried and pickled. The dried fish that the woman doing my nails told me about. The nuts, the rhubarb jam.

There's just a couple of recipe books on the shelf. I reach up to pull one down and flick through the pages, enjoying the comfort it brings from being in my hands. The ideas, the suggestions, recipes that can be mixed up and made into something new. Something I haven't felt in a long time.

Suddenly I'm back in the kitchen, in my last job, where Mark and I worked side by side in the busy, noisy, well-known restaurant. The closer we worked together, the closer we grew, staying after work and creating our own ideas, sharing our sample plates, with a glass of wine, all of which led us to bed. At the time it suited us both.

With one hand I hold the lantern to the shelves. The glow lights up the glass jars. With my other hand, I run a finger along the jars and stop at rice, which reminds me of our girls' trip to Venice one January and the dish I created when we got home: a take on creamy risotto, with flavours of Aperol spritz to remind us of Happy Hour, a hit of prosecco and a little floral flavouring. It wasn't Michelin-starred cooking then. It was comfort food for my friends. Food has brought me comfort and comforted those close to me, kept the memories alive – and then I'm thinking of Laura. I slam the book shut and toss it to one side.

'Sorry! I didn't mean to disturb you.'

I swing round to see Pétur walking into the room

wearing his grey beanie and a high-necked grey jumper. I'm flustered. 'Oh, no, you didn't . . . I'm – I'm sorry.' I don't explain any more. I can't. 'Sorry,' I repeat.

Pétur's face is set, his laughing eyes far more serious than they were last night. There's no smile this morning. I'm worried I've offended him, but we'll be leaving soon, and as kind as he's been, I want to get back to the hotel.

'I'm going to check the sheds, the weather,' he's pulling on another pair of thick socks, 'and the road, see if it's clear for you to get back.'

'Can I come? I'd . . . I'd like to check the road, too.'

He hesitates, then says, 'Sure. Help yourself to warmer clothing.' He gestures to the rows of coats and waterproofs, the baskets of hats, gloves and socks under the stairs by the front door. 'We always have spares,' he says.

'For lost tourists who are stupid enough to be hunting for the Lights,' I reprimand myself.

He laughs. 'Come on, let's check the animals and sheds, and find out if the road is clear.'

He opens the door and the wind lashes us, throwing swirls of snow our way. Even Pétur's dog, Jón, looks out of the door dubiously into the darkness. Pétur hands me a large torch and a small one to wear on my head.

He pulls his hood over his hat. I do the same, then fall into step behind him, suddenly remembering the disorientation I felt last night when we went to find the car. He seems to understand. 'Stay close. It's okay. I know my way around. It's my farm,' he says, as if this is all totally normal, and maybe to him it is.

The hairs freeze in my nose as the cold wind bites at it, making it itch and sting.

'Jón,' he calls to his dog, who turns to his master and falls into step with him.

In front of us is the long straight drive I trudged up last night through the snow. I squint into the darkness, getting my bearings.

'Let's start with the sheep,' he says, and points to his right. I follow closely, every now and then stumbling in the thick snow, putting my hand out in front of me to stop myself tripping and finding myself falling against his back.

'You okay?'

'Fine,' I say, walking where he walks, unable to see anything but darkness and snow. Finally he comes to a stop. I'm out of breath. I've walked just a few hundred yards but it seems so much further. My lungs are cold and raw, and my legs ache with effort.

I watch as he kicks the thick snow away from a door in a big metal-sided barn, then pushes it with his shoulder to open it. 'It's the cold. It sometimes sticks,' he says.

'You mean this isn't unusual?' I look around, stamping my feet.

'It happens,' he says, and smiles that warm, friendly, lazy smile again. 'Come in.' He leads the way into the barn.

Inside, the torches light up the faces of the sheep, sleeping or chewing the sweet-smelling hay in their pens.

'We keep sheep, about thirty, and they're all in the barn for the winter,' he says, walking forward, touching a head, moving the torch to inspect them carefully. Their eyes glitter in the light. 'In the summer they live out on the land, and in autumn, we round them up from the hills around here. It's a big annual event. Everyone joins in with the round-up. On horseback mostly.'

At the far end of the barn, bigger eyes flash in the torchlight. I hear a whicker, and I can make out the outlines of horses. Pétur swings a leg over the fencing around them, pats and checks them, talking gently to them. 'Looks like they're all okay, and the shed has held up well.' He runs the light over the high ceiling. In here with the wind outside, the baa of the sheep and the shuffling of horses in straw, it feels calm.

'I'll feed them, then show you the rest of the farm . . . what we can see,' he says, 'if you'd like to.'

'I would,' I say, then remember the important thing. 'How will we know about the road?'

'Soon as it's light, I'll walk down there. See if it's clear.'

'Okay.' I wonder how long we'll have to wait for daylight. But, in the meantime, it feels good to keep busy.

'As long as we're back for our flight home,' I say, half joking, half serious. I don't mind missing my treatments in the spa but I have to be home on Monday.

'Let's feed the horses first. They get grouchy if we leave them too long,' he says, and I follow him into a tack room, with tack along one wall and buckets on the other.

'We have a smokehouse too, if you'd like to see it,' says Pétur, as we leave the safety of the barn and head out into the wind and snow, his dog circling us. My mind flips back to the smokehouse I stepped into last night, when I felt a rush of comfort from the spiced scent that greeted me.

I nod. 'I'd love to.' I'm trying to see if it's getting lighter or if I'm imagining it.

'Do you like smoked salmon?'

I nod again. 'Very much!' I follow him towards the front of the farmhouse, then to the little hut I went to last night. I'm sure it's getting lighter. I wonder what time it is and how long it will be before we're back at the hotel.

'Come in,' he says, kicking snow from the wooden door. I can smell the smoke before we're even inside. 'This is where we smoke salmon, lamb and cheese.' He indicates the warm, dark but inviting shed.

My shoulders drop as I gaze at the racks of smoking salmon. 'Is this part of your business?'

'We do a lot of things to get by here. In the summer, we welcome fishermen, for the salmon fishing in the river. While we still have some.' His smile slips for a moment, but then, fixing it back on his face, he says, 'We smoke the salmon for them. And for locals. This is fish I caught in the summer and has been in the freezer. But with the power out, it's best I smoke it now. I can always sell it online if I have too much. Would you like to try some?'

My stomach rumbles, reminding me I haven't eaten yet today. 'Yes, please.'

He puts down his torch and turns away from me. I breathe in the smell of the smoking straw, twisting its way out of the chimney.

'Here.' He holds out a knife with a sliver of smoked salmon.

I pull off my gloves and take the salmon. First I hold it to my nose, then put it into my mouth and let it sit on my tongue. It's divine. Smoky, soft and melting. 'It's gorgeous!'

'Thank you,' he says. 'It's the waters we have here that make the salmon so good and keep them coming back.'

'Are we far from the river?'

'No.' He laughs, then seems to realize I have no idea where we are. 'We're not far from the river and the waterfall, which the salmon return to, or the sea for that matter. Come the summer, wild salmon always return to where they were born to spawn. They always come home. But, sadly, for many rivers there are fewer each year. We are lucky. The numbers are still good. We just have to keep it that way because if the salmon are in trouble, we all are. If the water isn't good enough for them to come back to, how will anything else survive?

'Here, water is all around us. And it's good, clean water. The fish thrive in it. Our community relies on it. Good fishing is why people come here and what we rely on for business and to feed ourselves. The waters don't get much better than they are here. And we mean to keep it that way,' he says seriously.

I can hear his passion for his home. I almost envy it, the passion for something you believe in so whole-heartedly.

I take another piece of the freshly smoked salmon from the knife he's holding out to me. It's as glorious as the first, but this time I know what to expect and I'm smiling before it's even reached my mouth, and his smile returns as he watches me.

'This is fantastic,' I tell him. 'I can see why it matters so much to you.' And for a moment we hold each other's stare, in the half-light of the torches.

'Let's get these inside,' he gestures at the salmon he's put into a basket, 'then see if we can find out about the road for you guys,' he says, bursting the warm little bubble in the smokehouse. 'You must be keen to get back.'

As we step outside, I note that it's definitely getting lighter. 'What's that over there?' I ask, pointing to the big shed I found him in when I first arrived last night.

He smiles. 'You want to see?'

'Yes.' I'm more and more intrigued by this place. The snow is swirling, the wind is whipping around us, and here is a farmer, making a living from and loving the place he calls home.

He pulls back the door and I can see inside the building quite clearly now in the half-light. 'What is this place?' I ask, walking around, taking in the tools and machinery there.

He smiles mischievously. 'It's the other way I make my living. Can you guess?' He points to a glass cabinet.

I step forward, and gasp. 'They're beautiful! You made them?'

He nods. 'I'm a jeweller. It's what I do when I'm not smoking fish or looking after horses and sheep.'

'It's amazing.' The glass cabinet contains silver jewellery: a necklace of clear crystal sitting in a fan of silver flames, earrings in the shape of flames, a bracelet of crystals and silver triangles, delicate yet bold, a statement piece. All, in fact, are big and bold.

'It's about this place, right?'

'Where I live, my home. It's what inspires me, yes.'

Tears prickle in my eyes and I have no idea why. But I think they're about the pride and passion this man clearly has for his life and work. I wonder why, all of a sudden, I feel empty inside.

'We may be remote here, but we live with nature. We look out for our neighbours and Mother Nature. She's our closest neighbour. We work with her and she provides for us. It's a mutual agreement . . . Now let's find out about the road. You and your friends will be ready to leave,' he says.

Slowly I turn away from the jewellery, not wanting to take my eyes off it. 'What do you do with it? I mean, how do people know to come and buy your work?'

'Mostly commissions. I'm . . . known,' he says. 'But, also, I have a big exhibition coming up, next year, in London. It will get my name known wider,' he says.

I have to admit I admire this man very much. He's certainly living his best life. Everything that Laura wanted for us. 'Live your best life,' she told me at the end.

'Good luck,' I say, with a crack in my voice. 'And thank you for taking us in last night. I can see we should never have tried to come out this far.'

'No problem. It happens. And good luck to you with whatever you do, back home. What do you do?'

'I cook,' I say.

'I can tell,' he says. 'You know good products when you taste them. You must take some smoked salmon with you when you go.'

'I'd like that, thank you.' I'm drawn to this man who loves his food and where it comes from.

It's bizarre to think that I don't know him, he doesn't know me, yet I'll be looking out for his name. I'll know where his jewellery comes from and what inspires him.

'Here, you take the salmon and go back to the farmhouse, see your friends. They may be worried about you. I'll check on the road and the car.'

'Cars,' I correct.

'Cars?'

'Uh-huh.'

'We didn't all come in one car. Frankie was in a car behind us and ran into us.'

'Oh, yes,' he says. 'I forgot. So Frankie isn't the friend with the birthday?'

'No, she died. Two years ago. Yesterday would have been her fortieth.'

For a moment he says nothing, then, 'I'm sorry.'

I shake my head and tears spring to my eyes, surprising me. 'It's the one thing we promised we wouldn't do. We wouldn't be sad. We'd celebrate her life. That's why we're here.'

It's probably the tiredness and the cold, but the day is turning darker again, and colder. I'm staring straight ahead, letting the snow settle on my eyelashes. 'It was just before her thirty-eighth birthday.' I try not to let myself go all the way back in my head. 'She made us all write out a bucket list of things we dreamt of doing.'

'So what did you put?'

I think for a moment. I've only just met this man: why am I telling him my innermost thoughts? But I'm not likely to see him again and it's taking my mind off the fact that we're out in the dark, in the middle of nowhere. 'I wanted to create a menu worthy of a Michelin star.'

'And did you?'

'No.' It's true. I may work in and run a Michelin-starred kitchen, but the recipes we use and the menus I devise are not mine.

'And seeing the Lights?' He jerks a thumb towards the snowy sky. 'This is what your friend wanted?'

I nod. 'This was Laura's. She always dreamt of seeing the Northern Lights. That's why it's so important we do it for her.'

We fall into silence.

I get the feeling he's going to ask another question and hope he doesn't. I'm not sure I have all the answers right now.

'You take the salmon. I'll check the road,' he says, Jón at his feet.

I watch him go, wondering how people can live like this from day to day.

I pick up the salmon in the basket and, as daylight puts in an appearance, I head back into the farmhouse, feeling that I've tasted a tiny slice of the real Iceland and would have liked to taste more. But it's time to leave.

I go into the kitchen where the others are gathering.

'What's happening?' they ask as one.

'We wondered where you'd gone. Thought you'd left without us,' Joanna says, in her hat and coat, clearly ready to depart. 'We've treatments booked this afternoon,' she says, looking at the Fitbit on her wrist, which isn't working, and tapping it.

'Pétur's gone to look at the road, see if it's passable and if we can get the cars out,' I report. 'I've been checking the farm animals and barn with him. It all looks in one piece.'

There's anxiety in the kitchen as we wait. I look at the shelves again, and the book.

I'm thinking about the taste of the smoked salmon and of the firewater, still with me from last night, and my mind is making mental notes of the flavours and pairings that would work.

Finally Pétur comes in.

'Someone's not happy this morning,' says Meg, quietly, to me. 'Something someone said?' She raises an eyebrow.

'What is it?' I ask. 'What's up?'

'There's been an avalanche. Overnight,' he says, straight to the point.

For a moment, no one says anything.

'It happens. Sometimes. The road is blocked, both ways, for now. We just have to wait. Help will come. The phone reception is down, like the electricity, but we are used to this,' he confirms. 'We need to check that everyone else in the village is okay and accounted for, and the sheep on the other farms are all safe in their sheds.'

Still none of us says anything. Until Joanna breaks the silence. 'So . . . the repair truck, for the cars?' We all look at her in horror. 'Well, someone has to ask. How are we getting out of here?'

He shakes his head. 'I'm sorry. No one's going any-where until the road is cleared. Your car is deep under snow.' I know now why his usual cheer is missing. 'You're lucky – it could have been you,' he says, to all of us.

None of us says anything. Then Joanna speaks again, saying this time what we're all thinking. 'You're saying we're stuck here?'

'For now.' He shrugs. 'Yes.'

We look at each other, eyes wide. This wasn't part of the plan.

'I can't believe this is happening!' Meg puts her head into her hands.

'There must be a way out,' Joanna persists. 'We only have two more nights.'

'There is one road in and the same road out. Right now, it's buried under metres of snow. I can't tell you any more, I'm sorry. It's how things are here. Now, I have to check on the other villagers.'

Meg checks her phone again, tears brimming. 'I knew this was a bad idea,' she mutters.

'You said it was a great idea!' Joanna responds.

'No, you did, Joanna! You and your Light-seeker, with your maps and satnav. I have to get back to the family. And I have a wedding to go to!'

Suddenly I'm panicking. The restaurant. What if I'm not there for the Christmas-week taster menu? I'm due there Monday evening. We have to get out of here soon. Then I take a deep breath. The one thing we don't do in the kitchen when things go wrong is panic.

'Look, we'll be out soon,' I tell everyone. 'Let's stay calm. This happens all the time, right?' I look at Pétur for support.

'Not quite like this,' says Pétur, apologetically. 'This one took everyone by surprise.'

'I wouldn't have driven you out here if I'd known the weather was going to turn like this,' says Joanna, looking upset.

'I wouldn't have either,' says Frankie, who has been very quiet until now.

'You weren't together? What were you doing out here?' Pétur asks Frankie.

'Like these guys,' she swallows, 'I wanted to see the Lights. Always have. I have to be getting back. Just here on a bit of business and thought I'd get the lie of the land and see the Lights.'

'Well, next time go with a guide,' says Pétur, firmly.

'I will,' she says quickly.

'So, can I just get this straight?' Meg says. 'Our cars are under an avalanche and –'

'– we're stuck here!' Joanna finishes.

Pétur nods. 'That's about it! For today anyway.' He turns back towards the door, changes his beanie hat for the thicker fake-fur one with ear flaps, and puts his gloves back on. 'I have to meet others at the school-house. We have a small wind turbine there for electricity for cooking. It's just enough in an emergency for the village. Then we'll check on the other local people. A lot of them are quite elderly. We need to make sure no one was trapped in the avalanche or caught out by the lack of power.'

We all look at each other and I can feel panic rising again, like in the kitchen when orders are coming in thick and fast and the only thing you can do is keep going.

'Wait! What? You're leaving us here?' Meg suddenly asks.

'Like I say, we need to check on the rest of the villagers. Check everyone is safe, the sheep too.'

'Can't you stay?' Joanna asks.

'I need to help. It's what we do here. I'll meet my cousin there. He's good with sheep. He checks the ewes when they're pregnant. He'll check the farms and I'll deliver food. It's what happens when we have an emergency. We have our routines. We'll meet at the schoolhouse, split up, deliver food and check on the villagers . . . If we don't help each other in a place like this, we die.'

This is real. This isn't some cute image of Iceland. This is life and death. Despite the warmth in the kitchen, from the geothermal hot water and the candle lit on the table, I feel cold, really cold, and scared.

'The best thing we can do is keep busy,' I say to the others. 'What can we do to help?' I ask Pétur.

'What can you do?' Pétur raises an eyebrow.

'I cook!' I remind him.

'Ah, yes! Excellent! Well, we can always do with extra hands. We will make soup, stew, and take warm drinks to the older ones.'

'We're your women!' I say, and the other three look at me in horror.

'I had a hot-stones treatment booked for three. I'm guessing I won't make that,' says Joanna.

'Not today,' says Pétur. 'All we can do is wait and hope the road is cleared soon. The rescue services will come when the weather eases up . . . You came to see Iceland, right?' he says, clapping his gloved hands together. 'Well, you're about to see the real Iceland, not the spas and fancy restaurants bringing their food into the country at vast expense. Looks like the elves are clearly not happy.'

'Elves?'

He smiles. 'And trolls. Trolls can be tricky! Mind you, so can elves,' he says, almost as if he's talking to himself.

'He's joking,' I say, to the others. At least I think he is. No one believes in elves, do they?

'If you ask me,' he says, 'the elves are very unhappy. And no one around here jokes about them.'

I open my mouth to joke back and I'm stopped in my tracks. He's not joking.

'The Yule Lads have definitely arrived in town.'

'The Yule Lads?' I ask warily.

'Their mother is a troll. They arrive from the mountains in the days before Christmas. Tonight is the night for Hurðaskellir. Door-slammer. When you hear the doors bang, you know he's around!' His lazy smile returns as he looks at our incredulous faces. 'You're welcome to stay here,' he says.

'On our own?' Joanna sounds horrified.

'Yes.'

'Was he serious about the elves?' Meg whispers to me.

'It's your choice,' he says. 'But I have to leave. We have only a few hours of light.' He turns to step outside, Jón at his heels. I'm pulling on my gloves and hat and follow him.

'Well, you can stay,' I say, 'but I'm going to help.'

'You always need to be doing something,' says Joanna. 'It's okay to stop, you know.'

'Right now, I'd rather keep busy. Besides, we might actually get to do what we came for and see the Lights.'

'She's right. That is why we came here.'

'And to relax and have massages,' Joanna grumbles.

Pétur swings round. 'The more of you who can help, the better.'

'I'm going,' I tell the other two, who don't move.

I step outside and follow Pétur as quickly as I can. Jón the collie keeps coming back to circle me. Am I mad? Maybe staying at the farmhouse is the best plan, the safest. But, right now, I need to keep busy. Besides, I've said I can cook and help.

I'm walking through the thick snow, Jón bounding around me, the wind moaning.

Behind me, a door slams, making me jump. I put my head down and attempt to keep going through the thick snow.

'Wait!' I think I hear a cry but I don't know if it's the wind or a voice.

'Wait!' I turn. 'Wait for us!'

I see the three figures behind me, scarves flapping.

'We're not staying at the house on our own!' says Joanna, out of breath.

'Do you think he was kidding about the elves?' Meg looks terrified.

'It's best we stick together,' I say.

'Otherwise we could die.' Joanna repeats Pétur's words.

Pétur comes back to join us, smiling.

'Did you say there was electricity at the school-house?'

'We have the means to get electricity there for moments like this.'

'Can we charge our phones?' asks Meg.

Pétur is thoughtful. 'Yes.'

'Oh, thank God!' Her eyes brighten and there's even a hint of a smile.

'But it won't be any good,' he adds. 'In weather like this, you won't get any signal.'

She deflates like a burst balloon.

There is still snow in the air, but nothing like last night. It's as if someone has laid a thick layer of royal icing over everything.

'Grab a shovel. You'll need it – and a head torch,' he says, pointing to the shovels and torches in the porch. We do as instructed.

Joanna looks as if she can't tell one end of her shovel from the other. 'What does he want me to do with this?'

'Use it,' says Meg, matter-of-factly.

'Switch on your head torches.' Pétur starts towards the barn again.

Jón weaves in and out between us, lumps of snow clinging to his coat, rounding us all up.

We follow Pétur towards the big dark barn where he and I fed the sheep and horses earlier. Again, I'm exhausted by the time we reach it, shuffling and pushing through the deep snow, which is making my calves and thighs ache, digging a path as we go.

Pétur attempts to pulls back the sliding door, next to the smaller door we used earlier this morning, but with the snow that's gathered there, it's not easy. He starts to dig at the runners with a shovel and I join in. He tries the door again and this time it shifts and pulls back. Inside the sheep are huddled together, freshly fed, looking contented and warm.

'We were lucky. The barn has stayed firm. Only a couple of years ago, when my brother was here visiting, the neighbours' barn roof was ripped off in a storm. The sheep escaped. The whole village had to turn out to round them up. I'd had my leg in plaster from an accident and wasn't much use. Luckily my brother and his now wife found the last of the missing animals.'

'How did they manage that?'

'On horseback, of course.' He points to the far side of the barn where half a dozen small horses gaze at us, clearly surprised by our second visit.

'Right!' I laugh.

'You're not serious!' Meg says. 'They went out on horses?'

'Of course. These are Icelandic horses. They have served as transport since the Vikings first arrived.'

'They don't seem very big to be carrying Vikings around!' says Joanna.

'All Icelandic horses are short and sturdy, sure-footed and very strong.'

'Well, I've never been on a horse, and I don't intend to start now,' I say, under my breath.

There is calm in the shed. Clearly the snow and the wind aren't worrying these creatures. I look around the barn for our transport, a snowmobile perhaps.

'Right, let's get you paired up with some horses.' He claps his hands together, his dog at his heels.

'Us? On horses?' we say, as one.

'How else? I told you, this is how we get around here.' He chuckles.

Our jaws drop. This may not be a wise idea.

8

'We have just a few hours of light,' Pétur reminds us. He's beside a beautiful black stallion, with a flowing mane and arched neck, standing as tall and proud as he can for a small horse. He puts one foot in the stirrup, swings his leg over the horse's hindquarters and settles into the saddle. If only we could have made it look that easy. Frankly, we were a shambles. 'The more people we have to help, the more people we can reach.'

Pétur helped us all onto the patient horses, but we look like the bunch of terrified tourists we are, clinging to the front of the saddles and the horses' manes as if our lives depended on it. They probably do. We're dressed in hard hats from the tack room at the back of the barn, where I saw rows of saddles and bridles, and smelt the earthy odour of leather mingling with the sweet scent of hay.

'Let's go,' says Pétur. His horse, shifting from side to side and tossing its head, is keen to be moving.

My body is colder than I've ever known it, and I'm frozen with fear in the saddle.

'We'll head for the old schoolhouse,' Pétur explains, pointing. All I can see is snow falling all around us. 'It's next to the church,' he says, as if that makes any sense to us. I can barely see the farmhouse we've come from, let alone any other buildings.

'How far is it?' says Meg, clinging to the front of her saddle.

'On a clear day, ten to fifteen minutes, quicker if you gallop.' He laughs. 'But on a day like this, it could take longer. There, we will meet up with my cousin, then split up and check on the other farms around here. We'll divide up the area, make sure everyone has what they need. If you get lost, head for the church spire. And trust your horse. They know this terrain and area well.'

'Trust isn't something that comes naturally to me,' I say. I'm terrified, yet adrenalin is buzzing through me. My mouth is dry with anticipation, my heart racing – I can hear it pounding.

'Are you sure about this? Should we just wait here for someone to come and get us?' says Meg, to Joanna.

'Help will come,' Pétur says. 'But, in the meantime, we help others. It's how we work around here. When you need help, someone will come. And if you don't, you go to help others. It's how you can be sure that the road will be cleared. So, are we ready to go?'

The alternative is to sit and wait – and people out there need our help. I can't just sit back and do nothing. We move off behind Pétur, who closes the barn behind us, switch on our head torches and follow him out onto the snowy landscape, hearts in our mouths, gripping our horse's manes for all we're worth.

The sight of dawn creeping over the horizon is more welcome than anything I've seen in a very long time.

I'm still clinging to my horse's mane, but so far, despite the land being covered with snow, and fierce flakes driving into our faces, she hasn't put a foot wrong and I'm so grateful to her.

'Okay?' asks Pétur, riding up beside me. I'm so focused on staying in the saddle, he gives me a bit of a start. 'How are you and Carrie getting along?'

'Carrie?' I say, thinking of the woman who drove into us. 'I thought she was . . .'

'Carrie, your horse.' He smiles.

'Ah, yes. She's wonderful. Looking after me well. Is it much further?' I ask. My fingers are freezing into their position, my backside is aching, and Carrie's doing all the hard work.

'Just up ahead. Maybe five minutes more. You'll hear the waterfall soon. Then we'll regroup, take food to the outlying farms. Check on them, their sheep stocks and any other livestock.'

'And you do this a lot?' I ask. My lips are almost numb.

'When we need to. We might be off the beaten track out here, but we're close. We meet up when times are tough, like this, but also when we want to celebrate. Like Christmas or, even bigger, the midwinter festival next month. We stick together. A lot of people don't have families living here any more. They've moved to the city for work and an easier way of life. Some older people are totally on their own.'

'Why don't they move to the city too?'

He gives a half-laugh. 'Because this is their home. A beautiful home at that. Look at it!' He stands in his stirrups and spreads his arms.

I can't see anything, with the snow still in the air. 'How do you know which direction to go in?'

He points to a small tower of snow-covered stones. 'See that? They're here to guide us when the snow comes. They're built on rocks beside the roads – or tracks out here. But they show us the route of a track so we don't fall down ditches or ravines!' He's still smiling, as if this is perfectly normal.

'So, by going from one rock pile to the next, we're following the track?'

'Exactly.'

'What if the rock piles get smothered in snow?'

'Then we're in real trouble. But it's worked for all these years, so I don't see it being a problem today.' He attempts to reassure me with his wicked smile.

I hear the crunch of snow under Carrie's hoofs, a snort every now and again and a shake of her head as the snow settles on her neck, in her mane and on her ears.

'And they show us where the big rocks are too,' he continues.

'Like the one we drove into?' I say.

'Yes.'

'If only we'd known,' I say, relaxing a little, now that I know we're following an actual route, not just hoping we won't fall down a mountainside.

'Some rocks were left where they were when the roads and tracks were built, because they're where the elves live.'

I frown. 'Elves again! You're not serious?!' I tut.

'It's true. I told you. A lot of people out here still believe in the elves. They mustn't be upset so we don't joke about them.'

I have no idea if he's teasing me or not, but a small smile pulls at the corners of my mouth. Elves!

'The ground is levelling, and the schoolhouse is just ahead.' He points to a building a little way off that's finally coming into sight through the dark and snow. 'Let's try the *tölt*!'

'The what?'

'The *tölt*! It is a smooth pace that makes Icelandic horses so special. It is perfect for rough terrain. Sit up straight, keep your heels and hands down. Your horse will look after you.'

'Right,' I say, unsure, sitting up straighter and feeling a little safer in the saddle by doing it. When I push my heels down, I'm more centred and balanced.

'Later we can try the flying pace,' he says, and this time I'm sure he's joking.

'Come on, everyone,' he calls, and clicks his tongue, urging his horse on, although it needs little encouragement. The others all follow.

And we're off at a faster pace and all I can do is sit tall, push my heels down, and hope I'll get there in one piece.

9

'Hey!' Pétur calls, as we reach a building in the middle of nowhere. Carrie starts to slow and I can't believe I'm still on. Snow has frozen on my eyelashes, and the wind stung my cheeks as we travelled faster than I was expecting across the snow. It was terrifying and exhilarating. And so smooth. I held the front of the saddle with one hand, the reins in the other and let Carrie have her head, as Pétur told me. We practically glided through the snow. My nose is red and tingling, my eyes are watering, my breath coming out in plumes. But I stayed on. I'm smiling.

I turn to look at the others. Meg's hat has slipped sideways, but she has one hand on the saddle, the other holding the reins, and I think that's a smile of relief. Frankie is wide-eyed, but clearly pleased with herself. The corners of Joanna's mouth are downturned in horror, but she looks the most comfortable of us all in the saddle. Who would have thought we'd be dashing through the snow on horseback on this trip? Maybe later we'll look back and even think it was fun.

We're outside a single-storey building with a red roof that shows only where large lumps of snow have slid from it. Icicles hang from the guttering and over the windows, huge ones, like spears. Next door there's a black church with a spire and a single brass bell. Between the church and the schoolhouse a pen holds another couple of horses, waiting patiently. It's the equivalent of a car park but a corral for horses.

Then I hear it, just as Pétur said I would, behind the schoolhouse and the church. I thought it might be my blood racing through my body, past my ears, but it's a tumbling, rushing waterfall, with icicles suspended from the rocky edges at either side of it. It's breathtaking.

Pétur jumps off his horse. 'Welcome to the heart of our village,' he says, holding out a hand to the single-storey building.

'Hey!' a man, a little younger than Pétur, comes out of the schoolhouse wearing a big hat covering his ears, gloves and a padded coat. He has a thick beard, with snowflakes caught in it. He strides over to Pétur in knee-high boots and they hug heartily, slapping each other's backs, exchanging a few words in Icelandic, maybe asking how everyone is doing. I seem to be frozen to the saddle of my patient horse.

A short stout woman comes out of the schoolhouse in a woollen hat pulled down over her ears and I'm not sure how many jumpers. She's smiling, waving a tea-towel and wearing an apron over her layers.

'I've brought you a cook, Anna,' says Pétur, swapping to English.

'Fantastic,' she says, clapping her plump hands, red in the cold.

'She and her friends were out looking for the Lights and got stuck here.' He waves to us.

'Their misfortune is our good fortune!' She beams.

I'm still trying to work out how to get off my horse. I may have felt chuffed with myself for staying on, but no one said how hard it would be to get off. My feet are numb, my hips seem soldered into place, and I have pins and needles in my buttocks.

'Come, come, let's get you a warm drink.' She flaps her tea-towel towards the building.

'This is Kristen, my cousin,' Pétur introduces the big man.

'What did you say this place was?' Joanna asks Pétur.

'The old schoolhouse. It's where I went to school, my brother and cousins too. But now we don't have any children in the village so it's closed. We use it for the community and for times like this. A meeting place. If someone is in real trouble, if a roof has been damaged or there is a problem with their geothermal heating, we bring them here. We may not have any children to go to school now but it is still the heart of our community. Most other rural villages have been abandoned. Life can be hard in the winter. But we seem to be able to look after each other well enough here.'

I'm staring at the beautiful waterfall in the slowly brightening morning half-light.

'Are you coming in? Or are you planning to sit up there all day?' he says, breaking into my thoughts.

Although I know it's meant in good humour, I can't laugh. 'I'm just . . .'

'Have you ever tried to get off a horse before?'

'No.' I shake my head.

'I think I've got it,' says Joanna, leaning forward and swinging her long leg over the horse's back. She's off with one simple step. 'You need to swing your leg!' she calls to me.

I feel like a child being told how to brush their teeth.

Joanna pushes me forward from behind and has me lying up Carrie's neck, against her snowy mane, then grabs my leg and throws it over the horse's rear end. I land with a thump in the snow on my backside.

'Next time, try to land on your feet,' she says, brushing off her hands, clearly feeling a good job has been done. She holds out a hand to pull me up.

'Okay.' I grit my teeth.

'Here.' Another hand is outstretched. Pétur and Joanna pull me to my feet. Everything aches, but I try not to wince. 'This way,' he says, and we go into the school-house. Candles have been lit so it feels welcoming in the high-ceilinged room and the kitchen beyond it.

'Now, take off your coats and have a hot drink. Kristen, pour the coffee,' says Anna, to Pétur's cousin.

I rub my hands and look around the kitchen. Pots and pans are bubbling on the stove and, despite my aching thighs and buttocks, I begin to smile. Kristen hands me a coffee and I wrap my hands around it. They hurt with cold, but the warm cup is helping bring them back to life. I hold it to my chest and breathe in the steam deeply. Even its aroma is reviving me. I take a sip of the hot, strong coffee and it hits the spot. I sip again. These people know how to make good coffee, and if their food is as good as the coffee, it'll be great.

'Now, how can I help?' I say, glancing around the well-organized, busy little kitchen.

'Over here.' Anna points to a huge pan and a pile of potatoes. I can't wait for her to tell me what she's cooking.

'*Kjötsúpa!* It's a traditional Icelandic stew, with lamb, potatoes and carrots, vegetables we can keep in store over the winter,' she tells me. 'It is a very simple dish, but the bone in the meat makes a good stock. It brings warmth and comfort.'

'Sounds great,' I say.

'But we need to chop the potatoes and carrots, lots of them!' she says.

I head to the pile of potatoes, feeling like a new young chef again, eager to please with my knife skills. As the meat is seared, ready for the pot, the kitchen fills with its scent.

Meg gets stuck into the washing-up. Joanna stands by the door, unsure what to do.

'You can help me make up parcels to deliver,' says Kristen.

'Oh, yes. Hampers,' she says, and leaves the kitchen quickly.

'I can help with that too,' says Frankie.

'I'll do the bread,' says Pétur, 'and here . . .' He hands Anna some packages in brown paper, having unzipped his backpack.

'A real treat!' Anna clutches them to her chest. 'Petur's smoked salmon,' she tells me. 'Have you tried it?'

'I have,' I say, peeling knife in hand. 'It's just about the best I've ever tasted.'

'And with good reason,' says Anna. 'It is the best.' She opens the packages of the salmon I helped bring in from the smokehouse. She takes a knife, cuts me a piece and hands it to me. Once again, I lift it to my nose and smell the smoky earthiness of straw I remember from earlier already recognizable to me. My mouth waters. I breathe it in, deeply. There's a hint of birch too. I open my mouth and put it on my tongue. It sits there, and I shut my eyes. It's smoky yet delicate.

'Delicious! Without doubt the best I've ever had,' I

say, as I open my eyes. And I've tried a lot of smoked salmon.

Anna beams. 'We're lucky. We have salmon here and they're thriving. But the numbers elsewhere are falling . . . Fewer of the adults return home in the summer . . . a bit like our little community,' she says wistfully. She claps her hands together. 'Now, let's get to it. Can you chop and stir at the same time?' She laughs, her whole body wobbling under the layers of knitted jumpers.

'Nearly!' I say, pushing back my sleeves and getting stuck into the big pile of potatoes, while Anna focuses on the meat.

'Remind me what we're making?' I ask.

'*Kjötsúpa*,' Anna tells me again, and gets me to repeat it. 'A traditional thick soup made from slow-cooked lamb, braised with the bone in to make a rich stock. And stored potatoes and carrots cut roughly into chunks. They will give it body and sweetness.' She smiles, making me smile too, and we set to work.

With the potatoes peeled and chopped, then a mountain of carrots, my arms are aching. I'd forgotten what hard work it is doing the groundwork to feed a large number of people. These days, of course, I have a team working for me. It's been a long time since I've been at the coalface with a vegetable knife and hands wrinkling from cold water, but despite the aching shoulders and arms, there's a smile on my face as I finish the last of the carrots with a swift cheffy flourish.

Pétur comes into the kitchen.

'The woman is great!' booms Anna. 'A real cook! Where did you find her? We need you here every time we have bad weather!' Her sleeves are pushed up, her cheeks rosy from stirring the huge battered pot with a big wooden spoon.

'Ah, she found me!' Pétur grins. Then he frowns. 'Actually, I thought she was from Barty and Son Fisheries and told her to go away.' At least he has the good grace to look a little embarrassed. 'And not very politely.' He lowers his head and gazes at me with apologetic eyes.

'Good job you saw sense!' Anna bustles to me across the kitchen and between us we carry the board of chopped carrots to the cooker, lift it high and add them to the meat and broth.

'Sense? Over our guests or Barty and Son?' he asks, teasing.

'Both!' says Anna, puffing with exertion.

I frown, hot and breathing heavily. 'What's Barty and Son?' I ask, intrigued.

He waves a hand, looking a lot more serious. 'That company will never set foot on my land,' he says crossly, 'no matter who they send.' Suddenly the atmosphere in the kitchen changes, like a cold blast from the outside whisking in, making me feel as if I've stepped into the middle of another snowstorm.

'Okay, okay!' says Anna. 'I know. Enough now. These people don't want to hear about our worries.'

I open my mouth to ask more, but before I can, she says, 'Have you done the bread, Pétur?'

'Yes, buried it,' he confirms, swiftly doing as he's told and moving off the subject.

I have no idea what he was talking about, but clearly that conversation is over and, quite possibly, none of my business. I'm not even entirely sure where we are, let alone privy to local goings-on.

'Buried the bread?' I ask, wondering if he's joking to lighten the mood.

Pétur nods. 'By the geyser. It cooks in the hot earth there,' he says, making me think he isn't joking, although maybe my face says otherwise. 'Would you like to see?' He points towards the door. 'You can help me dig it up if you want.' The awkwardness has passed and he's back to smiling playfully at me.

'I'd love to!' I say, fanning my face with a tea-towel.

'When we've finished here,' Anna says, bustling between us. 'There's lots to do to make sure everyone has a hot meal on their table tonight.'

Pétur throws back his head and laughs. It's a very attractive laugh. In fact, when he's not telling me to get off his land, or talking about some company that'll never set foot on it, he's an attractive man. But I have way too much on my plate to be thinking about attractive men and where that might lead. Nowhere! I have a kitchen to get back to!

'She's allowed a break, Anna,' he says, and his smile is charming. 'And we're only going for the bread,' he adds, chiding while reassuring her and holding out a hand to me, as if to rescue me from the kitchen taskmaster.

'Of course. What am I thinking?' She brandishes a tea-towel. 'Of course. And thank you,' she says, running her hands over her rounded hips. 'Go, go,' she shoos us towards the door, 'but make sure you come back with bread!' She throws back her head and laughs, this time shooing us right out of the kitchen with her tea-towel.

It makes me think of what it would have been like to grow up in a kitchen like this, full of warmth, love and laughter. Mine wasn't like that. It was always full of love, but it was just me and Mum. It was loud and fun. After she died, I found myself drawn to working in the hotel kitchen. It was loud and not much fun but it helped me through that time, getting used to her not being there. The noise seemed to drown the pain. The fun was cooking for my friends, after work, on a Baby Belling in the staff quarters and eating it sitting on the floor of the tiny bedroom I shared with Laura.

Pétur opens the back door, and the snow in the ferocious wind hits me as if I've stepped inside a commercial blast-chiller. I walk out and close the door to keep in the warmth for Anna and the others. I pull my hat down and fumble for the edges of my coat as they fly up in the wind, then try to grasp the two ends of the zip to do it up, but, without gloves, my hands are shaking with cold.

'Here, let me help,' Pétur says.

'No, I'm fine,' I say, my hands fumbling at the zip, my eyes blurring with snow gathering on my lashes. 'Oh,' I say, frustrated.

'Always do up your coat inside.' Pétur states what is obvious to me now. 'Here, let me help.' He moves forward. This time I let go of the zip and hold up my hands. He catches and tames the two zip ends and, his head close to my chest, wrestles them into working together. Despite the bitter cold, I feel my cheeks burn with embarrassment and something else: a quickening of my heart rate, a flush up my neck to join my red cheeks.

Trying to distract myself from my proximity to him, and the effect this is having on me, I stare up at the sky, snow like icing sugar falling from a sieve into a bowl and settling all around, like the swirls of whipped meringue I would make for a pavlova. Such big snow! Will it ever stop?

'There,' he says, standing upright and taking a step or two back. 'Better?'

'Much better, thank you,' I say graciously, hoping my flushing cheeks will now settle. I pull on my gloves and take a deep breath.

'Okay, this way.' He raises his voice and points, grabbing a shovel, towards a little hill. 'Be careful, it could be slippery near the geysers.'

'The what?' I call back over the wind.

'Geysers!' he shouts. 'They're not just something for tourists to visit nearer the city,' he says. 'We have geysers here. And plenty of hot water! Come,' he waves his arm in a big semicircle, clearly delighted to be showing me. I follow him, feeling like a newborn foal trying to find its legs for the first time, as I stumble and try to keep upright through the deep snow behind him.

I'm keeping a close eye on where my feet should be – I can't see them – when suddenly I hear a *whoosh!* rather like a rocket launching into space. My head snaps up and I see a plume of water, like a huge fountain, shooting into the sky.

'Be careful, it's very hot,' says Pétur, putting out his hand towards me, but I don't reach for it to make the final few steps. I struggle up the last bit of the hill to stand beside him, out of breath. 'It's okay to take a helping hand,' he says. 'We all need one sometimes.' He raises an eyebrow and he's half teasing, half reprimanding me. He might have interpreted my not taking his hand as a bit of a rebuff.

'Sorry, I'm just used to, y'know, doing things myself,' I try to explain and feel completely ridiculous doing so. 'I'm not used to being in a situation where I need it,' I say, sounding a lot frostier than I'm expecting to, like Freya in the kitchen, where I'm Chef. 'But thank you.'

'Out here we have to help each other.'

I can't help but be fascinated by the colour of his eyes, like pools of iridescent water. And his earlier words come back to me: 'Or else we die.' I give a nod of understanding. Accepting help has never come easily to me. Maybe it's because I had to fight my way up the kitchen ranks. No one helps you there. In fact, it's the exact opposite: if someone offers to help, you're wondering how they'll try to bring you down. I learnt that early on. Alan was his name. He offered to help me catch up when I was falling behind after being given one of chef's favourite dishes to serve. He added extra salt and ruined it. I know it was him, but he never admitted it. I was put back on chopping and cleaning for weeks. I learnt that if anyone offered to help, you said, 'No, thank you,' and dug deeper in yourself. You always had to watch your back or there'd be a knife in it in no time. No one was on my side when it came to the professional kitchens I'd worked in. It was every man and woman for themselves.

'Now, this is all about timing.'

I have to shake off the memories of being a young woman in the kitchen. Things are different now. I'm in charge. But it doesn't stop you watching your back.

'Freya?'

'Oh, yes, sorry!' Pétur has my full attention, with his ever-present slight smile and the twinkle in his eye.

'What happens now?' I ask.

'We wait,' he says, the smile tugging at his cheeks.

Whoosh! Another rocket of hot water shoots sky-wards, making me laugh.

'It's fantastic!' I shout.

'And useful,' Pétur says, as he picks up the shovel, moves forward and starts to dig.

'What are you doing?' I ask.

'Getting the bread, like I said. And before they shoot again!' He gestures to where the jets of water have abated.

'The bread?' I confirm.

'Uh-huh,' he says, digging up the soil around the hole from which the hot water exploded. Excitement is growing in me, like water flooding a moat around a newly made sandcastle.

'They have been in the ground for twenty-four hours,' he explains. 'It is rye bread. We have hot lava running under our land, creating these pools of hot water. Why not use it?'

Mother Nature, sharing the tricks of her trade! Hot water, reminding me that there's life outside the four walls of the kitchen.

'Here,' he says, lifting a big round pot from the ground with a cloth. 'It's hot!' he reminds me, as I reach out to help. He puts it down in the snow, letting it sizzle and steam. 'Stand back,' he says, and holds out an arm in front of me. This time, I do as directed and suddenly there's another *whoosh*, filling me again with excitement and joy.

'It's amazing!' I shout, over the rush of water shooting upwards, then a second and a third.

When they've settled, he digs up two more of the round pots and sits them in the snow. 'Here.' He picks up the first and cradles it in the crook of his arm, as lovingly as if it were a baby. 'Try some.' He breaks off a piece of the warm bread.

It's crisp on the outside, steaming and soft within. It smells wonderful.

'Like the bread we had last night?' I think of the mushroom soup.

'The same,' he says, with the little smile and the twinkle.

I bite into the bread. Oh, my word! It's heaven. Everything it promised in its smell is there in the taste.

'You like it?' he says.

'I love it,' I say, and smile, as does he. His face lights up at the next *whoosh*, making me laugh. I take another bite of the bread. I can just imagine the dark rye with the light slices of his smoked salmon, maybe a strand or two of dill just to marry the two, lemony, sweet with an aroma of aniseed. I shut my eyes. Just thinking about the heady combination is making me feel grounded, excited and alive.

'Come on, let's get these back to Anna,' I hear him say, and I open my eyes to see him smiling at me. I put the last of the bread into my mouth, wanting to remember eating it here, where it was baked by the hot lava beneath the ground I'm standing on.

Pétur picks up two of the bread bundles and I reach down for the last, trying to repress a giggle, feeling like Baby in *Dirty Dancing*, carrying her watermelon. I'm keen to find out more from this man and what goes on in his world. I watch him heading confidently through the snow, leading me off the beaten track of my life, just for a little while, to somewhere I know I shouldn't go. My head is telling me to be careful, not to get involved, but my heart is giddy with excitement from the shooting geysers and the warm rye bread scent that's wrapping its warmth around me. I'm still remembering the taste of the salmon I ate in the smokehouse and considering the possibilities of an added ingredient or two as we head back to the kitchen.

'I won't ask if you need a hand,' he turns back to say.

I laugh, trip and take another face plant in the snow. Pride just went before my fall. A hand appears in front of my face and this time I take it, letting him pull me and my bread bundle to my feet.

'You have snow.' He points and I attempt to brush it away with my spare hand. He puts his two bundles into one arm and then, hesitantly, lifts his hand. I hold my face up to him, and he brushes the snow from my forehead, my eyes, cheeks and, finally, my mouth. The same excitement I felt on seeing the geysers is fizzing in my stomach. I gaze at him and my head shouts that this can't happen, while my heart is dancing with delight that something delicious is on the way.

'Did you get it?' Anna breaks the moment.

We turn to her and hurry towards the kitchen, with just the briefest glances that say we have unfinished business. Such an unfamiliar feeling and I'm not sure I should be paying any attention to it. I haven't experienced it since Mark and I worked side by side in the kitchen, and couldn't stop throwing each other occasional glances.

But, I tell myself, I'm only here until the road is reopened. Just a day more probably. It's better not to think about Pétur in that way at all. He's an attractive man, but I'm not here for a one-night stand. I'm here because at the moment we're stuck and will leave as soon as we can. I clear my throat, hoping it will clear my head too, and set to work portioning the bread and revelling in its glorious warm smell, which I will never forget and will always remind me of his touch in the snow.

10

⸙

Finally, all the packages are made up. The stew, bread and cake are tied in tea-towels and we load them into bags with flasks of hot coffee.

'Oh, no! Wait! What about the putrid shark?' Pétur says seriously. We stop what we're doing to stare at him in horror. Suddenly he laughs. 'Isn't that what all you tourists think of when you imagine Icelandic food?'

I look at Anna, blush and breathe a sigh of relief that we're not going to be preparing putrid shark. 'Well, I didn't know much about Icelandic food when I arrived. And the hotel serves the worst kind of fake Mediterranean stuff.'

'At exorbitant prices, I bet,' says Anna, tutting.

'Yes!' I agree.

'That is what is wrong with this country. They imported ingredients for the restaurants and tried to recreate what was going on elsewhere. And when the crash came – *boom!*' She claps her hands over her chest, which is covered with flour, her apron having slipped to the side. 'So did the businesses. No one could afford to import ingredients at those prices or eat out.'

'As interesting as this is, we should get going,' says Pétur. 'You know my feelings about food for profit, Anna.'

She rolls her eyes. 'It's complicated,' she says, ushering me and him out of the door, where the horses are ready for us, with bags full of stew, bread and home-made cake.

Meg, Joanna and Frankie are there with Kristen, already mounted on their horses.

'This is excellent. The more help we have, the more food we can carry and the more homes we can cover. Let's split up and get to as many properties as we can before dark. We'll meet back at the farm later. Okay?'

We nod. Only Kristen smiles.

'You deliver food parcels to the farms this side of the village,' Pétur instructs. 'The ones we can't make it to today, we'll head out again first thing in the morning.'

'Do you want to come with us, er . . .?' Pétur hesitates.

'Frankie,' I tell him, as he seems to have forgotten her name.

'Of course. Frankie. Do you want to—'

'Yes,' she says.

But as the other three take off in one direction, Frankie's horse follows them. She is toppling backwards and I rush to help, but she rights herself.

'It's okay, you go with Kristen. We'll manage. See you back at the farm. Stay safe and stay together!' Pétur shouts. Frankie raises a hand. She looks petrified.

I watch them go. Frankie is where Laura would have been. She'd have been smiling at us now. And then I wonder about Frankie. Why was she up here looking for the Northern Lights on her own when the weather came in? She seems nervous, as if something's on her mind. It's none of my business, I tell myself. I'm just delivering food until we can leave again, which will be soon, I hope. I chance a glance at Pétur. My stomach flips and I wish it wouldn't. Tomorrow, with luck, the road will open and then we'll be on the plane home.

'Take care, everybody. The storm hasn't left us yet.' And, with a feeling of trepidation, we set out into the snowy, windy landscape.

11

Finally, I'm back in the saddle. It wasn't a dignified affair. I managed to stand on a rock, then ease myself back onto my horse as she stood patiently still.

Anna waves us off, with instructions of which houses to deliver to and what to give them.

Pétur and I set off in the opposite direction to the others and I feel panic rising. What am I doing out here? I have no idea where I am. What if something happens?

'You okay?' he shouts, as the wind whips viciously at our cheeks. The snow is blurring my vision, making me squint.

I nod, although I don't feel it.

'The horses know what they're doing,' he says. 'Trust them.'

We ride in silence, but for the horses' hoofs pounding through the thick snow. The wind is whistling, the horses' manes flying up as they keep their heads down and move forwards. Not unlike myself, I think. I just kept my head into the wind and went forward determinedly. Just like Laura told me to do. Keep going. And I have. We all have, over the last couple of years, barely taking time to look back and enjoy the good times while we try to forget the bad, when she had finally run out of treatment options. Then I moved in with her, just like we had shared accommodation at the hotel when we were young, determined to cook something she'd like, something to make her smile.

'It's not always like this here!' Pétur interrupts my thoughts, his head down, black hard hat to the snow and scarf partially covering his face.

'Really!' I manage to laugh back. 'And do you always welcome visitors to your village like you welcomed me?'

'Ah, about yesterday you mean, when you first arrived?' He's riding beside me, sitting deep in his saddle, relaxed, holding his reins with one hand as the small black horse marches majestically through the snow, sure-footed and certain, its neck arched and wavy mane catching the snowflakes as they continue to fall. It's getting slightly lighter, I realize. It must be around midday.

'Yes,' I say. 'You didn't seem pleased when I turned up.'

His face seems to tense and I regret pushing him now. It's none of my business.

'Look, sorry, I shouldn't have asked. None of my—'.

'You're right,' he says, 'and I'm sorry. I was expecting someone else when you arrived last night. I shouldn't have assumed.'

Like a sudden thaw, I see him smile again. 'Someone you clearly don't like.'

'Truth is,' he shrugs, 'I've never met them.'

'Oh? Isn't that a little presumptuous? I mean, they might be lovely.'

He shakes his head. 'They might indeed. It's not who they are, but what they want that's the problem.' He bites his lower lip.

'Oh?' The only sounds are the crunch of horses' hoofs on the snow, and the wind carrying it into our faces.

He lets out a long breath and studies the barren land, the mountains and the river on the other side of us.

We ride on in silence and I can feel the cold right through to my bones. 'Where exactly are we going?' I ask, my lips feeling like they're turning blue.

'We have to get round the whole community. The others have gone to visit some of the older people on their farms. We're heading for a community house.'

Clearly he realizes he needs to explain more. 'It's a safe house,' he says. 'It's for people . . . women who need some help in their lives.'

I can see he's serious now.

'It's a fairly new initiative. When the 2008 financial crash happened, lots of things changed for us. Suddenly people were finding themselves jobless, homeless. There was a lot of pressure. In some cases women needed to escape domestic violence, which got worse after the crash, or their mental health was suffering. Lots of people lost their businesses and their homes. We're still picking up the pieces. So many lives were affected. A non-profit organization, based in Reykjavik, was set up to help women, a refuge for women in trouble to have some peace, to get away from the tight-knit community they lived in. Be close to nature.'

'This place is certainly off the beaten track.' I'm impressed by someone's initiative to bring people here for refuge.

'Believe me, everyone in Iceland knows everyone else. It's hard to change direction if everything around you is familiar. This place is somewhere for the women to take time out and get their lives back on track.'

Sitting on Carrie, I notice my toes are now so numb they might have fallen off without me noticing.

'I can see why it would be good to get away from everyday life,' I say. 'Somewhere to pause and take stock of life. It's like the clock's stopped ticking. Like you've stepped out of everyday life, just for a while. It must really help.'

'It does.' He smiles. 'It's working well.'

'You must be proud.'

'I am.' A red house, with corrugated sides, white window frames and fascias with snow halfway up the windows, has come into sight. 'We'll deliver some food and head down to the beach.'

'So, people come and stay here for a while?' The little red house has a smiling face, with its two windows for eyes and the porch for a mouth.

'Yes, for as long as they need.'

'And where do they go from here?' We're surrounded by the vast expanse of snow, with mountains in the distance.

'Mostly back to the city. There's nothing for them out here. But they have a chance to pick up the pieces of their lives and put them back together. Some never come back. Others are more regular visitors.' He gives a half-smile.

'It's a shame there isn't more for them out here,' I say.

'Just to have time out and feel safe is what it takes sometimes.'

'But you have so much going on out here, with the farm. Isn't there a chance for other people to move here and work?'

'There's not a lot they can do. As you've seen we have to do a lot of things to make life work here.'

'I don't know how you manage it all!' I say. In my own life I focus on what leaves the kitchen every night and again the following day.

'Well, it really works hand in hand. With the sheep, the wool goes for jumpers, which Anna and her family make. The meat is smoked in my smokehouse. We save some for ourselves, swap some for other produce with our neighbours and sell some. It's the same with the salmon. We keep some, swap some and sell some. Out here you have to turn your hand to many things to make life work. It's not as easy as just having an office job.'

'But what about your jewellery business? Don't you wish you could just do that full time?'

'Well, maybe,' he says. 'As I told you, I am going to London, to take part in an exhibition and maybe to stay on.'

'What will happen to the farm? Will you sell it?'

'I don't want to. It is our home. My brother, the opera singer, was on tour, with his partner. He met her working in the UK so someone had to stay here and run the farm. I don't want to have to give it up but if I go to London and there is no one here to look after the animals . . . It's hard. This is our home. Like the salmon.'

We've reached the red house and Pétur calls. He jumps off his horse, landing on his feet in the snow, then ties the reins to the fence.

'I'll go and see if everyone is okay and take the food to the door. Do you want to come or stay here?'

'I'll come,' I say, 'if I can get off Carrie.' My feet are blocks of ice.

'Here, let me help,' he says. He steps forward and this time I have no choice but to accept his help or be stuck there. He takes my foot from the stirrup, then gently rolls it to get it moving. It hurts. 'Now lean forward and swing your leg over the back of the horse.'

'It hurts – it all hurts!' I say.

'Slowly lower yourself down, and bend your knees when you land.'

I do as he instructs and this time I'm not falling into the snow, like before. I can feel his body behind mine, and as I slide off the horse, I can feel his warm breath and see it on the snowy air. I'm down, but my knees buckle and practically give way.

'Oops,' he says. 'It's okay. It happens if you're not used to being in the saddle for a long time.' He catches me under the arms and holds me there, while my feet and knees are trying to recover.

'Um, thank you,' I say, with unusual hesitancy in my voice.

'No problem. Like I say, out here we help each other.' He waves to a young woman opening the front door. 'I'll leave the food on the front porch. They'll feel more comfortable that way.'

We pull out a couple of flasks of stew and bread.

'Maybe we should have put this in plastic containers and left them here,' I say, thinking we'd have to get the flasks back.

'We don't allow any plastic in our town,' he says firmly. 'It's our way of doing our bit not to pollute the waters. We do everything we can to protect them.'

'Oh.' That's the most sensible thing I've ever heard and I wonder why we all don't think like that. 'Of course.'

'If everyone put a bit more thought into where their food comes from and the conditions it needs to thrive, well . . .'

'. . . the world would be a better place,' I finish. He nods and smiles again. Not as widely this time. This one is like a smile he keeps for special moments. And colour rushes into my cheeks. Quickly I take the flasks from him.

'I'll take them, if that might be better,' I say, holding the flasks against me.

'Sure. Just check everyone is okay and that they have everything they need,' he tells me and takes Carrie's reins from me. 'Check they have heat and water. There is an oil system that kicks in when the power goes off to keep the water pumping and the heat on. They may not have lights but should still have heating and hot water.'

I turn to the house and see a face at a window. Pétur

waves and I walk – well, shuffle – through the snow towards the porch.

The door is open slightly.

'Hi, I'm Freya,' I say to the crack between door and frame, and to the blue eyes staring at me. 'I'm . . . I'm staying at the farm with Pétur. We just wanted to see if you were okay. The road in and out of the town has been blocked by an avalanche.'

'Blocked?' says the woman behind the door, which opens a little more.

'Yes, an avalanche last night. Are you all okay? Everyone here who should be?'

'Yes.' She opens the door wider. 'We're fine. No one missing.'

I look into the house, which is minimal in furniture but warm, and two other women raise a hand from the kitchen.

'We've brought some food. Stew, bread, and there's cake too,' I say, handing over a tin.

'*Takk, takk.* Thanks,' says the nervous woman, taking the tin from me, but not managing the flasks as well.

'Shall I bring them in?' I ask. 'Put them in the kitchen?'

She looks at the other women, who nod and beckon me in.

'Shut out the cold,' one jokes, and I smile, stepping inside, with a glance back at Pétur, then shutting the door with my foot.

'Shall I take my boots off?' I ask.

'Please.' The woman waves to their outdoor shoes by the door and I unlace mine, then slide them off.

I follow her into the surprisingly warm kitchen, undoing my coat. 'It's warm. That's good!' I say.

'We are lucky to have heat, even if no power,' says a woman.

I walk in and place the flasks on the table, with the bread. 'So, there's stew and bread,' I repeat, 'and cake.'

'Thank you,' they all say.

'And hot coffee.' I point to the flask.

'Would you like something to drink?' says one of the women. 'Some coffee?'

'Thank you, but no, we have others to get to.' I think of Pétur waiting outside. I look around the kitchen. It's as clean as a whistle, everything in its place.

'We're grateful,' says another woman. 'We only have this in the cupboard.' She holds it open. 'A food delivery was due yesterday. The people who run the house usually come up from the city once a week with supplies. They didn't come. Now we know why.'

'Thank goodness for this,' one says.

'It's made at the schoolhouse. They have emergency supplies there.' It's amazing what you can make when you need to be inventive. I think, my mind starting to turn over. 'Do you mind if I look?' I point to the cupboards.

'Go ahead.'

Their store cupboard is basic: flour in a jar, sugar, dried herbs, like dill, and spices, such as ginger. There's butter and some dried berries. I close the cupboard.

'Erm, I have to go now, but maybe I could come back tomorrow. We could make something from what you have here. I could show you, if you like.'

They turn to each other for approval, then nod.

'Okay.' I smile. 'And in the meantime, enjoy the stew and bread.'

'Thank you, we will,' they say. '*Takk!* Be safe!'

'*Takk!*' I reply, and they smile.

I pull on my boots, my mind turning over what to do with the ingredients in their cupboard.

'All okay?' asks Pétur, as I join him by the horses.

'Fine,' I say. 'They're all well but low on food.'

'Okay,' he says. 'We'll head on to the next.'

He hands me my reins and gives me a leg up, depositing me in my saddle.

'*Takk!*' I say, and grin.

'You're welcome.' He flashes that smile, then mounts his horse, which is shifting from side to side, ready to be on the move.

As a small farmhouse comes into sight I see a small figure waving to us. It makes me smile. Pétur, though, doesn't seem happy and urges his horse into a faster pace. Carrie follows. As we draw closer I can see it's a woman and she's not waving to us in greeting but frantically.

Pétur jumps off his horse and I follow as quickly as I can, tying both horses to the fence. 'What's happened?' he asks in Icelandic. Her husband has fallen, she tells Pétur, who translates for me as we follow her to the side of the house.

'Silly fool,' she says, as we lift him to his feet, then walk side by side with him into the house and sit him in his chair. 'He went to check the shed. I told him to leave it,' she chides affectionately.

He has a graze on the top of his head. 'I couldn't get up.' He chortles. 'Old bones!'

'And I couldn't lift him. Heavy bones!' she says.

I help him take off his boots and his big coat, and hang them up.

Pétur makes sure the heating is working, checks the shed and the chickens, then tells the couple to stay inside where it's warm and he'll be back tomorrow. I pour them coffee and serve the stew with bread on trays. They're delighted and tell me I remind them of their daughter, who is working in the city.

'She must worry about you,' I say.

'She knows there will always be someone to look out for us here.' She gazes at Pétur, then at me, with a hint of sadness in her eyes. 'We'll be sorry to see Pétur leave us. But he has a big future ahead of him. We are proud of him.'

We leave with our saddlebags full of jars of home-made rhubarb jam 'for the community', she tells me.

As we ride slowly away from the farmhouse, the light is fading even though it's only mid-afternoon.

'I need to do one more visit while I'm out this way,' Pétur says to me. 'Are you okay for a bit more?'

I nod. These people need the help. They need this food. It's important we came out to check on everyone. If we hadn't, who would have helped the last couple back on their feet, literally? Would the safe house have known why the food delivery hadn't arrived?

We head on in silence.

'I'd like to go back,' I say eventually.

'I told you, the road's blocked, but as soon as it reopens we'll get you to the hotel.'

'I mean to the safe house. I said I'd help with some cooking. They don't have much in their cupboard and their delivery didn't turn up because of the weather.'

'Oh, I see, sure. Tomorrow okay?'

'Yes. I'm presuming you don't think we'll be out of here by the morning.'

'Even if the road opens, we still have to rescue your car. It could take time.'

The horses plod on through the snow, and the path we're travelling along narrows. There are rocks to either side of us, like a ravine.

'You're doing brilliantly. Nothing to be scared of,' he

says, as the track starts to incline down. 'Lean back,' he tells me. 'Let your back take the movement.'

I copy him as the horses head downhill. He is riding with his reins in one hand, the other on his thigh, watching me, interested.

The snowy path opens up and we're heading towards a clearing – the beach.

I try to get my bearings. I look back the way we've come, but it's like we're in a snow-globe that's been shaken. 'Where are we?' I call, over the wind whipping up from the shore.

'At the harbour. That's my fishing boat.' He points to it, lurching, swaying and covered with snow, next to two other boats, moored to a wooden jetty. 'We fish from here,' he says, 'although we don't take boats out in weather like this, except in emergencies. It's too dangerous.' I turn my head from side to side, trying to get the lie of the land.

'The church is back that way with the waterfall by the schoolhouse.' He points. 'We've followed the river from the old school and my family farm on the other side of it to here.'

'Okay.'

'And that way will take us to the mountains and an even bigger waterfall,' he says.

'And where are we going now?' I can't see a house.

'Over there.' He points.

At first I can't see anything. I squint against the snow.

There's a mound, like a little hillock, and smoke coming out of a narrow, cylindrical chimney. Around it, the snow has melted. Below the mound there is a small wooden door and a window, half covered with snow, a golden glow flickering inside it. It's a tiny speck of life in this massive wide-open snowy space. Suddenly I feel very small in the huge landscape as I look around, the dark sea and the waves rolling onto the black sand of the shoreline in stark contrast to the snow further up. I turn to the mountains, and the waterfall cascading down them, tumbling furiously into the river towards the dark sea. The cliffs across the water in front of us seem to have faces carved into them, glowering at me, and beyond them is the sea. Freezing cold. And then nothing.

I suddenly feel light-headed. My breathing quickens. The snow feels like the walls of a prison. The huge ragged cliff faces seem to be closing in. They're all around us and I feel trapped. Although I'm freezing, I'm starting to sweat, pulling off my riding helmet.

'Take deep breaths,' I hear Pétur say. 'Sometimes the enormity of Mother Nature's actions can make us feel very small. We're used to this.' His voice is reassuring and calming.

'I may be having a panic attack,' I say, through short breaths.

'Breathe in,' he says. 'Pick a spot and focus on it.' I do. 'And out.'

I slowly release a breath and keep looking straight ahead.

In front of us black shingle leads to the sea. It's dark and terrifying. I stare at the small jetty and the three boats.

'My best friend and I fished for salmon and smoked it. But he left when he had a family.'

'And you? Do you have family?' I breathe out a plume of steam, like the smoke of a dragon's roar.

'Yes, but not here. Come, we need to check on Knútur.' He gestures to the underground hut. 'Are you feeling better?'

I nod.

'Sometimes the elements can take your breath away, literally. It's normal. We often forget how big the world is outside our own.'

I'm starting to breathe normally, perspective coming back into my vision.

'We still have stew and bread and cake?'

'Yes.' I'm doing a mental check of our stock of food and my sense of normality is returning as I run through what we have left in the saddlebags. I sense that he knows this is my safe place, thinking about meals to be served. My breathing and my nerves are settling. I'm beginning to feel like me again. Well, a version of me that has realized how close I am to Mother Nature here. It's terrified me, but also made me feel alive.

'It will be good for him to have a warm meal.'

He guides his horse down to the hut, slides off and I follow him. He ties them to a tall dark rock, like a standing stone, and tells them he won't be long. I breathe in the scent of smoke from a fire, and walk with him to the door.

12

'Knútur!' Pétur puts his gloved hand to the wooden door and bangs on it. I stand back, the salty snow in the air tickling my lips.

'Knútur! It's me, Pétur!' he shouts, above the sound of the sea crashing onto the black sand.

The door slowly opens and I step away as a chink of light creeps out.

Then a bent figure, in blankets that are ragged at the edges, hobbles out of the low doorway and slowly straightens. A man with a long beard holds his face to the cutting wind, frowning, evidently wondering what or who has dared to disturb him. I take another step back, my heart starting to race, and hold my breath as elves and trolls roll around in my head. Then he seems to recognize Pétur and smiles, showing the gaps where teeth should have been.

He holds out his arms, the ragged blanket edges blowing in the wind like fronds of seaweed, and hugs Pétur heartily, slapping his back.

'Good to see you, and with a friend?' he says, and I'm hoping I'm not in for the same kind of hug.

'This is Freya. She's helping me check on everyone. The road is closed by an avalanche. Just checking you're safe and well.'

'I'm fine. That's sad, another avalanche. But it's always good to see you. Come in, come in!' He welcomes us into his home. I hesitate, but Pétur nods for me to follow. As I step inside I feel as if I'm entering a hobbit's home.

Inside, a fire burns in a small stove, with a flue leading up and out through the chimney and a pile of dry driftwood from the shore to the side of it. It's still cold in the hut but it's dry.

There's a chair by the fire, covered with more blankets, a table with a candle in a jar on it, flickering away. Other than that, there is very little – a long tree trunk that looks to be a bench, a blackened kettle beside the stove and some bowls stacked unsteadily there too. The ceiling is low and branches hang there, with another couple of candles in jars.

'We've brought you some lamb stew, bread from the geyser and Anna's cake,' says Pétur, taking the flask from me, the bundle of bread and cake, and putting them on the table.

Knútur shakes his head, and I wonder if we've done

something wrong. Then he straightens as best he can in the low hut and I see tears filling his eyes. 'I have nothing to offer you,' he says.

'We don't need anything, Knútur. Just to know you're safe and that you have a hot meal today,' Pétur tells him, putting a hand on his arm.

'*Takk, takk,*' he says, eyes still full of tears. 'I wish I could repay your kindness, everything you have done for me,' he says, and I'm guessing he's talking about more than the stew and bread. Pétur puts his other hand on the old man's shoulder and squeezes gently, then pats it. I feel my eyes prickle too.

Then Pétur rummages in his pocket, slides out a bottle and puts it in Knútur's hands. 'Something to keep out the cold,' he says.

Knútur clasps it, then wrings Pétur's hands. '*Takk, son, takk.* Your father would be proud of you.'

This time it's Pétur's eyes that fill with tears. 'Oh, and these.' He pulls some candles from his other pocket. 'Light makes everything feel better,' he says.

'It does, it does. *Takk, Pétur.*'

'Stay safe, Knútur. You know where I am if you need anything.'

'I have everything I need, everything.' He smiles through his beard and moustache, his eyes on the flask of stew and the bottle of firewater.

'Goodbye, young friends,' he says, as we turn to leave, and he is already pouring firewater into his mug.

We step out into the falling snow, into the bleak, dark shore-side, and I don't know whether to be glad we've helped, or wretched for the old man living in a shelter on the beach in this weather.

'Does he live here all year round?'

'He does,' Pétur replies.

'Isn't there anywhere else he can go? It doesn't seem right.'

I'm firing questions and we rejoin the horses, our saddlebags empty except for the rhubarb jam and eggs we were given.

We untie the horses before Pétur says any more. 'Knútur chooses to live like that,' he says simply, as he swings into his saddle. 'No one is forcing him. We've offered to help find him accommodation, but he won't stay in it. He is at ease where he is.'

'But it's freezing,' I say, not really understanding.

Pétur sighs. 'Knútur doesn't like to feel he is a burden. So he won't take help.' I put my foot into my stirrup and this time, with a bounce, I swing into the saddle by myself and feel a little leap of satisfaction. We guide the horses up towards the snow-covered road. 'Knútur grew up here – he was my father's best friend,' Pétur tells me, as the horses walk purposefully side by side. What little of the daylight there has been is seeping from the sky. 'He left here and went to set up in business in Reykjavik. But life dealt him a series of blows. He took out bank loans to start in business at a time when tourists were beginning to come to the area. He set up a grocery store, importing goods. But it was hard to make a living. And then, one day, his son became very ill. There was nothing they could do to help him. As he waited for the ambulance, his son died in his arms. After that, the business never reopened, the bills mounted. Nothing mattered. His wife, who also needed to grieve, became a stranger to him. He was so wrapped up in his own grief that he drank to keep reality at bay. His wife went back to her family and he found himself homeless. The dark days and nights can be desperate times and drink seemed to be the only thing that helped him through. One day, my father saw him in Reykjavik and cried. But he knew that Knútur had to make his own choices. He told him he would always be there for him if he wanted help. Eventually, he made his way here. We put him up in the farmhouse, but he never stayed more than a night, always coming back to the seashore. It's where he's found peace with himself. We keep an eye on him. We helped to build his hut and he's happy there. And no one will move him.'

'How do you know?'

'Because the town is in agreement,' he says simply. 'No one will move him while he chooses to live there. Nothing can be done on that land.'

I look at Pétur. The snow is settling on his riding hat and the horses' hindquarters. This is a good man, I think, a really good man. It's not often you meet one, these days.

He smiles his lazy, laughing smile as we reach the top of the path and turn left around the huge stone.

'It's said trolls that aren't home by sunrise are turned to stone,' he says, nodding towards the rock. 'Now, come on. It's dark, and I'm hungry. Let's try the *tölt* again and get home.'

He clicks his tongue and we're off. I sit deeper into the saddle and cling on. By the time we see the lights of the farmhouse I'm smiling even though I'm frozen, sore and exhausted. It's been an amazing experience.

'Do you think the road will reopen tomorrow? It's Sunday,' I ask, as we slow and head to the barn.

'I can't say.'

'Our flight is the day after tomorrow.'

'We can hope,' he says, as we arrive back in the barn where the sheep are warm and waiting for dinner. He jumps off his horse and I do the same, my legs numb, pins and needles setting in. I put the reins over her head, pat her profusely and thank her for bringing me back safely.

13

'I have more salmon to check in the smokehouse,' he says, as we leave our horses happily eating hay in the barn.

'I'll come with you,' I say, then add, 'if that's okay.'

'Of course,' he says, and we set off towards the little smokehouse.

'So, it turns out you really can cook,' he says. He opens the door and the warmth pulls me in.

I look at the rows of fish. 'Yes. You could say I cook for real. I'm . . . I work in a restaurant. I run a kitchen. I've worked in kitchens all my life. You could say they're my . . . I was going to say happy place. My safe place anyway.'

I watch as he carefully takes down a salmon and inspects it. 'We all need one of those,' he says. 'For me it's my workshop. I started to get interested in creating things at school. I didn't know I was going to end up as a jeweller. I just decided one day to have a go. I wanted to make a gift for my girlfriend and didn't have any money. It was her birthday, so I made some earrings. My art teacher was impressed and persuaded me to do more, helped me get into college. We lost our mother as I was finishing. My brother was becoming a big name in the opera world. I stayed here to help out on the farm, but the workshop has always been my sanctuary.'

'And now it could be your time to make a name for yourself in London?'

He shrugs. 'Maybe. Depending on who will look after this place.'

'But you have other family, don't you? Could they?'

'Yes,' he says, but no more. 'And then, of course, there is the community, and my cousin's offered.' He's nearly finished taking down the salmon. 'What about you? When did you find the kitchen was your safe place?'

I give a small smile. 'When my mother was ill. I'd taken a job in a hotel as a pot-washer. I watched and learnt and wanted to cook things for her that she would enjoy when I got home, flavours she could recognize that would bring back memories.'

He smiles and I can't help thinking how attractive that smile is. 'It's good to remember the places we loved by food,' he says.

'And then, after she died, I was determined to become

the best chef I could be, make it to the top. I threw myself into work. My friends were there for me. We've stayed close ever since.' I take a deep breath as if the smokehouse, with the smoke wrapping around me, is a safe space in itself. 'When Laura was diagnosed, the only way I could think of to help her was to do what I'd done for Mum, cook. Cook her flavours she could taste, when the chemo stripped her tastebuds and made her feel sick, and then, towards the end, to remind her of the memories we'd made, the places we'd gone to. I wanted to create them for her. I love the way I can make people smile with the flavours I marry together.'

'And you stayed cooking?'

I nod. 'It's what I do.'

'Good luck with it.'

'And you with the jewellery.'

Neither of us makes the first move to leave. The atmosphere in the smokehouse is so comforting that I could stay here for ever, I think, as he hands me another slice of freshly smoked salmon. This is a happy memory indeed. I smile at Pétur and, as he looks at me, something shifts in me, like a memory being locked in, with his face beaming at me.

We return to the farmhouse. I slip off my coat and boots, hat and gloves by the door and make my way up the open wooden stairs, while Pétur heads along the corridor to his room. I hear him turn on the hot water in the bath. Jón sits out in the corridor, on guard. Looking out for trolls, I imagine.

Upstairs, in our room, Joanna is sitting on her bunk, Meg and Frankie staring at her.

'Joanna?' I say, suddenly concerned. 'What happened to you?' I go to sit by her but she doesn't look at me, just straight ahead, her eyes glazed. I'm worried.

She looks like she's been pulled through a hedge backwards. She seems to be in a state of shock and I'm not sure she's heard what I've said.

'Joanna?' Meg comes to sit on the other side of her and puts her arm around her shoulders where I wrap a blanket.

'There were sheep,' she finally says. 'Everywhere!'

'Frankie and I delivered to a row of small cottages and Kristen and Joanna went on to the farm,' Meg explains.

'We had to round them up! They'd got out of the barn! Kristen was checking the pregnant ewes. I'd never been that close to a sheep in my life.' She looks dazed.

'Have a hot bath,' says Meg, patting her arm.

'Something to eat and drink,' I say, as we guide her to her feet and towards the bath. I turn on the taps, letting the warm water run over my hand just for a moment, then step back. Meg and I help her peel off her clothes and leave her in the steamy bathroom, still cold and in shock.

'This place is desolate,' says Frankie. 'It makes you

wonder whether anyone would hear you if you screamed.'

I think about the book Meg was reading. 'Three go up a mountain, only two come down . . .' It's like a movie trailer playing in my head.

'I'll organize the food we brought back from the schoolhouse. It's in the kitchen,' I say. 'Come down when you're ready,' I tell Meg, and nod towards the bathroom. 'We all need to eat. Or I can bring something up if you'd rather.'

'I'll help,' says Frankie, carrying the lantern, lighting the darkening stairwell as we climb down and enter the big open-plan kitchen. She sets the lantern on the table, while I get to work gathering the flasks and some bowls.

'How come you were here on your own, Frankie?' I ask, as I serve stew from a flask and chunks of bread at the table in the window.

'Here,' I say, as I hand her a full bowl. 'Pétur says to help ourselves to anything from the kitchen but I said we'd be fine with this. He said he's going to the work-shop to try an idea and we should just make ourselves at home.'

'Absolutely,' she says. I hand a bowl to Meg and take another for myself, my hands shaking with cold. I breathe in the smell of warm stew and swing my legs over the bench, letting my feet warm on the under-floor heating. I sniff the steam rising from the bowl

I'm cupping with both hands. It's peppery, sweet from the carrots and meaty from the lamb and the clear stock. I take a spoonful and let the potato dissolve on my tongue in the hot stock then chew some carrot.

I sigh, then take a bite of bread.

Frankie is talking.

'Sorry, what were you saying?' I swallow quickly, not meaning to be rude, but I was lost in the moment, in the flavours.

She clears her throat and I look at her face in the lantern light.

'You asked me why I was here on my own,' Frankie says quietly.

'Yes.' Meg and I nod. Meg is now sitting opposite me, dipping her bread into her stew.

I pick up the lighter next to the candles on the table and light them. The room fills with a golden glow as the light outside disappears into darkness.

'I . . .' Frankie swallows, and I'm not sure she's going to finish what she's started saying. The orange light from the candle creates a warm glow in our cabin and she carries on: 'It was something I promised myself I'd do.' She joins us at the table.

We nod, understanding.

'My partner died,' she says, and without thinking we put down our bowls of stew and reach out a hand to her, one on her knee, another on her arm. 'We didn't have any children. It was just me and him. He was a popular man. He loved life and his work. He took over his father's fish stall and built it up into a well-known business, supplying fish to restaurants, hotels and shops. And one day, that was it. He just had a heart attack and died.'

'I'm sorry,' we both say.

'I thought, coming out here, I'd . . . I'd feel he was here too. I thought I was walking in his footsteps but . . .' She stops.

'Go on,' I say gently.

She shakes her head, tears in her now haunted eyes.

Joanna appears from the bath, still looking like she's spent a night in *I'm a Celebrity*, and the door bangs shut behind her, making us jump. It reminds me of the Yule Lads and their tricks.

'Come on, let's eat up.' I say the only thing I can think of. The only way to help people feel better. 'Who knows? The snow may stop and the road may be cleared tomorrow and we'll be able to leave.' And with that, we eat up and, sooner than necessary, we head upstairs to get ready for bed and curl up in our bunks, believing the sooner we sleep, the sooner tomorrow will come, just like kids on Christmas Eve. In my dreams I'm trying to perfect rows of cakes I have to copy, over and over again, screaming, but no one can hear me – or the door banging in the wind.

14

'Looks like the Yule Lads are on their way down from the mountain one by one and still causing mischief,' says Pétur the next morning, as the snow and wind continue in what feels like the middle of the night, as we gather in the kitchen. 'The door to the smokehouse was undone and banging all night,' he tells us, as we lay out the bowls and spoons.

'The Yule Lads?' I say.

Meg and Joanna look worried.

'You have hooligans out here?' says Joanna, frowning.

Pétur laughs. 'I'm going to check the sheep,' he tells us.

It's still dark outside, like the middle of night, and the snow is creeping up the windows, settling on the sills.

'Light the candles in the window, on the table,' he says, handing me a lighter, 'and in the living room.

Light makes everything feel better.' I remember him telling Knútur the same thing yesterday. I do as I'm told. The little tea lights suddenly start to throw out a golden glow from the lanterns in the window and he's right. I feel less anxious and it really helps keep the bleakness at bay. My thoughts turn to Knútur. I wonder if he's feeling safe in his little grass-roofed hut. The candles, the food and the firewater must have cheered him.

We help ourselves from the bowl of *skyr* in the fridge – thick and creamy, like Greek yoghurt, with a slightly sour taste, sweetness too – with a dollop of the rhubarb jam we were given yesterday.

Once the bowls of creamy *skyr* have been scraped clean, we put the leftover bread from yesterday on the table, slice it on the board there and spread it with thick butter. We eat it with a jug of strong coffee. For once, Joanna makes no comment about needing to watch her weight and just enjoys the food. Now Pétur's back, covered with snow, and there's still talk of Yule Lads.

'Um, about these Yoof Lads?' Meg asks.

'Yule Lads,' Pétur corrects her. 'They come down from the mountains every year, just before Christmas.'

I wonder what stories he's going to tell now.

'They're mischievous. Their mother, a troll, comes down from the mountains, hunts out naughty children and makes a stew with them,' he says. 'There's never a shortage of food for her at this time of year.' He pours coffee for himself and tops up our cups. 'And then her thirteen sons come, one each night. The children leave out a shoe on the windowsill, hoping for a small gift if they have been good. If not, they get a piece of coal.'

'The Yule Lads?' Joanna asks. 'They're nice, right?'

'Oh, not really. A little rough, you might say. There's Gully Gawk, known to hide in barns and steal the froth from the milk buckets. Spoon-licker steals spoons to lick. Pot-licker steals pots of leftover soup. And I'm sure Door-slammer was here last night.' He laughs. 'There's Window-peeper and Doorway-sniffer . . .'

I shudder – and remind myself it's all made up. Then there's a bang, a door slams in the wind, and the four of us jump.

Pétur chuckles. 'I told you, they've yet to go back to the mountain! They're still making mischief.'

'Fun story,' says Joanna.

'Of course, they're not the same as the elves, the hidden people,' he continues.

'The hidden people?' I ask, as he packs his rucksack. 'You're joking, right?'

He shakes his head. 'Many people in Iceland believe in elves. Roads have been prevented because moving rocks might upset them. And if they're upset, very bad things can happen,' he says. 'Elves generally mind their own business, but if you upset their dwelling places, bad things will happen. So they say,' he says.

'What kind of bad things?' asks Frankie, suddenly interested.

'Problems on the construction site, machinery breaking down, someone hurting themselves, freak accidents. Anything that will delay work on an area where they live.'

'And,' she swallows, 'do they live around here?'

Pétur smiles his big smile.

'Maybe,' he says, and closes his rucksack. 'Whether they do or not, people don't want to risk it. This is our landscape and we don't want it demolished. Maybe they saved you from a worse accident than there might have been when you drove into their rock.'

'Or maybe they were unhappy we were in their neck of the woods and created the crash,' I say, teasing him now.

'Maybe,' he says. 'They don't like anyone who threatens their home. Anyone looking to work where elves might be has to make a deal with them.'

'A deal?'

'Uh-huh. They have to offer them something in return, a dwelling or a promise not to disturb their rocks. It's not worth upsetting them. If the work is deemed necessary there isn't usually a problem, but if not, problems can occur. It's just how it is. You don't upset the elves. Don't threaten their dwellings. That way we all live happily side by side.'

With that he swings his rucksack over his shoulder. 'I have more farms and houses to visit,' he says.

'What about the road? Is it going to be cleared today?' asks Meg, standing.

'Yes, we need to get back. Our flight is tomorrow,' Joanna says.

'We'll know when it's been cleared,' he tells us.

'How?' Meg asks.

'People will come,' he says.

'That's it?' Joanna says, slapping her hands to her sides. 'Surely we must be able to find out. We need to get to the airport.'

'Sorry.' He adjusts his rucksack and slides on his head torch. 'From experience, if the weather is this bad, and they haven't been able to open the road here yet, there won't be any flights.'

'No flights?'

'But I have to – we have to get back!' Meg exclaims.

'In this weather, the runway will be like an ice rink. I'm pretty sure nothing will fly until things settle and they can clear it, like the road into this area. I can't tell you any more. I need to get to more houses to check on everyone and deliver more food in the meantime.'

Joanna is lost for words and Meg is on the verge of tears again. Frankie clenches her hands. 'The last time it was this bad, how long was it before the road opened?'

'Honestly?'

I brace myself for the answer.

'The last time it was this bad we were snowed in for a month.'

'A month!' we shout.

'It may not be the same this time.' He holds up his hands, clearly worrying about messengers being shot. 'But they will come,' he says, 'and you will get out . . . eventually.'

'But it's nearly Christmas!' says Joanna.

'I'm afraid snowstorms don't run by the Christian calendar,' he says.

Christmas. Meg has her wedding to get to. Joanna has a big Christmas to organize for her husband, his kids and grandkids, and I bet there's a schedule to be kept. And I have to be at the restaurant for the Christmas menu. How can I have taken such a risk? Now I may not be back to deal with everything. Who will step in? I don't know if I'm worrying that no one can do it, or that too many people will want to step in and my job will be gone by the time I'm back. I daren't catch the others' eyes, in case I burst into tears, so I stare into one of the flickering candles on the windowsill instead.

'Now I have to check on the animals and get ready to visit some more homes.' With that Pétur leaves, Jón at his heels.

There's silence after the front door closes behind him, and then, 'But no one knows where we are!' Meg wails.

Frankie looks just as worried.

'Maybe help will come and we'll be able to get back to the hotel this morning and contact home,' I say hopefully.

'You said that last night and the night before!' Meg snaps, pulling on an extra pair of socks from Pétur's pile in the hallway.

She's right. When are we going to get out of here? I thought the snow would have stopped by now and we'd be out. But we've been here two nights already. We only have one more night until we're due to fly home.

'We shouldn't have come,' I say, without realizing it. 'The restaurant needs me there tomorrow night! I shouldn't have risked it.'

Meg glares at me. 'And is that what you care about most? More than us, me and my wedding, more than Laura?'

The words hit me like a smack in the face, making my eyes water. 'Of course not!' I stammer.

'Well, that's how it sounds,' she says. 'It's work first with you, and it always has been!'

I try to swallow the lump that's risen in my throat. 'It's not like that.' The memories of when Laura died, and I threw myself into work, rush back to me.

'How is it, then? We had to bully you into coming on this trip. The one thing we said we'd do in her memory. You always have to be persuaded to take

161

time off. It's not people you worry about, it's the restaurant.'

I'm lost for words. Then I try to explain. 'It's just the new menu, Christmas and the new restaurant. There's so much to do.' I hate how pathetic it sounds.

'Well, let someone else do it! This was more important. It's not like it's your own restaurant.' Her words sting.

'I'm the head chef!' I retort.

'But it's not *yours*. It's not your name above the door.' She wrestles with the sock, eventually gets it on and attempts the second. Frankie and Joanna stand and stare.

'It's as good as!' I say.

'Why couldn't you just be upset, cry, get angry at the unfairness of her going? You gave up so much to care for her, and when she died, it's like you had to bounce back immediately. Catch up to where Mark was in the kitchen, after you'd taken time away. Like it was a competition between you. But he got the new job offer, and left you behind. It's like you're still out to prove something to him.'

I'm unable to speak or move. It's not true. I just like what I do. In fact, I love it. Is that really what I did? 'I went back into the kitchen because that's what Laura wanted me to do. She knew it's the one thing I'm passionate about,' I retort.

'Or maybe you were just burying your head in the

sand. Trying to ignore what had happened to Laura. And with Mark, you put all your energies into showing him you were as good as him so you could forget what happened with Laura,' Joanna joins in.

'Forget? I stayed late at work, yes, but that was because I was cooking.'

'But that's it! You were always at the restaurant. Your whole life has taken place in that kitchen. Even your one long relationship took place between the kitchen and the few hours in your flat before you were back at work the next morning.'

'That's not . . .' I trail off. 'It's not about Mark. I just wanted to cook,' I say.

'Then cook, but not to get the best kitchen on your CV, the most stars. Cook what matters,' says Meg.

'I did! I cooked for Laura, for my mum, for you guys.'

'And then you stopped.' Meg stands up.

'I stopped when she died . . .' The words catch in my throat.

'And stayed in the kitchen cooking someone else's recipes,' Meg interjected.

I don't respond. Suddenly I get the urge to run, and that's what I do. Maybe it's what I've always done.

'Freya! I'm sorry! Put it down to stress – the wedding, being stuck here,' Meg calls, as I head for the door, but before I get there, Joanna jumps in too.

'The wedding!' she says. 'It's all we hear about! Not

everyone is interested in wedding favours and balloon arches. For the woman who said she was definitely going to do things differently this time around, you have a funny way of showing it. This is going to be bigger than the Royal Wedding,' Joanna finishes, with a loud sigh.

'Look, guys—' Frankie tries to interject.

'That's rich coming from you! At least I'm working and running a family, two families, in fact, with Tom's lot! I'm not just telling other people what they should be doing with their lives from a very high pedestal.'

I try to block out their words. How has the weekend ended up like this? We're best friends. We shouldn't be arguing.

'That's because you let people walk all over you. Look at your ex-mother-in-law for starters. Why should she get to say what guests she wants at the wedding?' Joanna retaliates.

'She's still the children's grandmother!' Meg retorts.

'But she doesn't have to be your mother-in-law! Stop letting her make you feel guilty all the time.'

I put on my boots, gloves, coat, and pull my hat over my ears to block out any more of the argument, throw open the door and go outside, holding my face up to the snowflakes, letting them cool my burning face. 'Stupid bloody snow.' I stomp off towards the big barn, determined not to let the snow stop me carrying out any more of my plans.

'I told you I'd like to go back to the safe house, if that's possible,' I say, a little more directly than I meant to, when I reach Pétur tacking up the horses. He's surprised by my tone. I clear my throat and take it down a notch or two. 'I mean, I said I'd help them use what's in their store cupboards.' I need a distraction from my anxiety about the restaurant and the huge fight we've just had.

'Sure. We'll pick up some more stew and bread from the schoolhouse and I'll take you there. Anyone else coming?'

Just then the door opens and the other three, pulling on hats and gloves, step out.

'You coming or are you staying here?' he asks them.

'No, I'm coming!'

'So am I!'

'And me!'

'Let's get to the schoolhouse, split up to get the supplies out, then do something fun,' he says to me, eyes twinkling.

'Good idea,' we all say . . . perhaps to splitting up, not doing something fun. I feel as if a knife has been stuck into my heart. How could we have come to this? She would have hated seeing us row. She would have made us laugh, seen the adventure in our situation. Maybe without her we're not the friends we thought we were. She kept us together.

I pull my head torch out of my pocket from yesterday

and turn it on. Jón is leaping through the snow, his patches of black fur making him visible.

'Nice stories,' I say to Pétur, as he waits for me to mount Carrie. 'About the elves and the Yule Lads.'

'Oh, they're not just stories,' he says. 'We might not be sure of their existence, but you wouldn't want to risk being responsible for an accident, would you? Like I say, we look after each other out here. They are the protectors of our landscape, of nature, as we should all be.'

15

'You okay? You seemed . . .' Pétur picks his words carefully '. . . stressed back there. Want to talk?' he asks, once we've helped Anna cook and clear up in the kitchen, then packed the saddlebags. None of us have been speaking unless we had to, and then it was in polite short sentences.

'Yes, fine.' Then I correct myself. 'Not fine. It's just frustrating, y'know, being stuck here for who knows how long, maybe even Christmas. There are things we all need to get back for. I'm expected at work tomorrow evening and Christmas is the busiest time of our year. I have a promotion hanging on this menu and our performance over the festive season. This was meant to be a three-night break and here we are, stuck.'

'It's frustrating, but try seeing the positive side.'

'Which is?' I lower my head from the dark sky and

look at him, a smile tugging at the corners of my mouth.

'There are far worse places to be right now.' He holds out his arms to the darkness. 'You might not be able to see it right now, but it really is a good place to be. The best!'

He smiles, making me smile properly. He seems to have a knack for doing that.

'You love this place,' I say.

'I do, and I'm determined nothing will damage it, or the community,' he says. 'I want to know it's safe before I leave. But back to the question, are you sure you're okay?'

Am I really going to tell this guy about the row we had, the mud we slung at each other? Why not? It's not like I'm going to see him again. And this is not like your regular letting-off-steam situation when you can just turn up the radio, drink coffee and pick at the cooking chocolate. Maybe even swig the sherry that's destined for trifle. I smile at the thought of Laura and me helping ourselves to Chef's sherry in those days at the Grand Hotel, never sure if he'd used it or swigged it himself.

'Phhhhhfffffff.' I let out a long sigh. Beneath me I hear the crunch of snow, but seem not to be clinging to Carrie's mane quite so much as I was yesterday.

'We had a bit of a falling-out. I think maybe we're all just anxious. No one knows where we are. We all have stuff we need to get back for. It's not quite the hot springs and Lights-watching we were expecting.' I remember the noisy hen party at the hotel.

'Life can have a way of being not quite what we were expecting. Especially out here.'

The hairs in my nose tickle as the cold air freezes them. 'I can imagine,' I say, as a chink of daylight appears in the snowy sky. 'Where are we heading?'

'For that pile of stones over there.' He points.

The horses seem to know what they're doing, just like yesterday.

'So, what did you fall out about?' he says, his boldness taking me a little by surprise.

'Um . . . I'm not really sure,' I say. 'I think, well, it goes back a long way. After our friend died, the one thing she wanted us to do was to get on with our lives, not to dwell on the sad stuff. So we did. We went off and threw ourselves into life and whatever it had to offer at the time. It's just that we all went off in different directions.' I swallow. 'We dealt with things in different ways.'

'How so?'

'Oh,' I say, surprised, but everything about my situation right now is a surprise. It's like I'm in a dream. Like I've walked into a wardrobe and out the other side into Narnia. Now I need to find my way back to the wardrobe.

'Well, I suppose you could say that we all grabbed

life by the balls. Meg bought a house with her divorce settlement and helped her kids. She juggled work, putting her daughter through university and looking after her parents. She's incredible. And she met Tom. They're getting married. And she has his children and their partners to deal with. She just seems to take on all their worries. Not to mention an ex-mother-in-law, who doesn't seem to understand that Meg isn't married to her son any more. And then there's Joanna. Well, she remarried and went around the world.'

'And you?'

'I . . . I guess you could say I threw myself into my work. It was, is,' I correct myself, 'my happy place.'

'Your happy place, or your safe place?' he says.

'Both!' I answer quickly.

And we fall into silence, me rattled again. Why does everyone think I'm hiding in my kitchen?

'It's a Michelin-starred kitchen,' I tell him, then regret it, feeling I'm boasting.

'Oh, so it's more than "I cook" then.'

I hear the smile in his voice and remember saying that when he asked what I could do to help. 'Yes. A little like you "make a bit of jewellery".' We smile at the *touché* moment and I feel myself letting go of my irritation.

'Have you always cooked?' he asks.

I sigh again, but this time fondly. 'We all worked together in a hotel restaurant, when we were younger.

When everyone was on their first weddings.' I smile to myself, remembering Meg's first hen party and thinking about the rowdy group staying at the hotel here. That was us! 'We did big events. Meg and Laura waitressed, Joanna was on Reception and I was in the kitchen, getting yelled at by some bullying chef! And I remember thinking, I'm going to be a chef and I will never speak to people like that. After that, it was what drove me. My . . . partner,' I say, not knowing what to call him – we didn't really have a name for what we were to each other outside the kitchen, 'and I worked together for years in the kitchen. But when Laura became ill, well, I took a step back from work. It was my natural instinct just to make dishes she might like to eat. Her tastebuds were more or less dead, due to the chemo, and I wanted her to enjoy eating again. So I would go to her house and make recipes from her childhood, from trips we'd taken in our twenties, food that brought back a memory rather than trying to persuade her to try new things.'

'That's wonderful,' he says, and I take time to think about it. It was a strangely happy time. I spent hours in the kitchen after work.

'But in that time Mark and I drifted apart. He was offered a head-chef job in another restaurant. I didn't hear from him again. He moved on. He didn't take me with him. When I went back to work, I was determined to get back to where I was, where he was, running a team with a star.'

'And you never wanted to set up on your own? Have your own restaurant?'

I let out another long sigh, this time not so fondly. 'I did once . . .'

'But not now?'

Our eyes meet, and I feel a flicker of excitement again. I have the feeling there's unfinished business between us. 'It's been a very long time since I've thought about it. Once I was in the kitchen, in that circle, working side by side with Mark, it seemed that it was everything I wanted. But maybe it was, as you say, a safe place.'

'There's the farm.' He brings me back to the here and now, a long way from my safe place. 'Let's deliver the food and then there's something I want to show you. Hey!' he shouts, and waves to an elderly woman clearing snow from her front door. She stands up straight, delighted to see us.

'Are you both okay?' he calls. She nods and is joined by another woman, similar in age.

'Sisters. They have lived here all their lives,' he says, as they welcome us in.

After coffee and cake with the two women, who are thrilled to have visitors, we leave, laden with pots of dried mushrooms, gathered from their land in the autumn. 'Perfect for the midwinter feast!' he tells me, securing the saddlebags.

'When's that?'

'The first Friday after January the nineteenth. The thirteenth week of winter.'

'And you do what?'

'We celebrate the middle of winter and look forward to the lighter days to come. In darker times, it helps to look for the light. We have a big feast, with all those Icelandic specialities, putrid shark, puffin. We have a dreadful time!' He chuckles. 'We tell stories, play games, sing and dance. You'll find out if you're still here!' And this time I know he's teasing me.

16

'I'll leave you here,' he says, outside the safe house. 'I have a few more houses to call in on. I'll come back for you when I've finished.'

'I think I can find my way back from here. It's just a straight line that way, following the river, isn't it?'

He nods. 'Getting to know your way around like a local.' He gives the tiniest wink. And his smile seems to reignite something in me that I haven't felt for a long time. I have no idea what it is.

We hold each other's gaze and I'm not sure what to say. I just know I can't let him in. I have to protect myself. I'll be gone soon and there is no way I want confusion in my head or my heart.

Suddenly a bright light shines on the mountains, on the snowy peaks in the distance, up and beyond the big waterfall. An orange glow. I catch my breath.

'Is that the Lights?'

'It's the volcano in the mountains there,' he says. Orange sparks and bursts of colour spew skywards among the falling snow, against the white sky.

After taking in the magnificent spectacle, I draw away my gaze and see a face at the window of the safe house. I raise a hand. The owner of the face waves back. I take another look at the molten lava oozing down the mountainside in the distance. Red and orange, it reminds me of a chocolate fondant, turned out on a plate, dusted with icing sugar, and broken to release its gooey centre. It's a wondrous sight and I want to imprint it on my mind, while I'm here in the snowstorm, on horseback, looking up at a volcano erupting.

'Take care of yourself,' says Pétur. He stands in his stirrups, leans over and kisses my cheek, taking me by surprise. 'And thank you for all your help.' The warm, melting sensation in my stomach suddenly feels similar to the explosive volcano.

I tie up Carrie beside a small covered shelter and smash the ice on the water bucket with the sledge hammer I find next to it. Somehow I'm desperate to touch the spot he kissed, and I do very quickly, then pat Carrie, turn and make my way to the front door. It opens slowly. I turn to wave at Pétur, who has waited to check I'm safely in and now rides off on the small black horse. I watch him go, and blush when I turn to see the three women smiling at me.

'Hi, we haven't introduced ourselves. I'm Hildur,' says the first.

'And I'm Margrét. This is María.' The other two raise a hand.

'Okay, ladies. Let's see what you have in the store cupboard and then we'll talk about what we can make.' I clap my hands, keen to take control of my girlish emotions, ricocheting all over the place. I slip off my boots and head into the warm kitchen, feeling every bit at home, back in my safe place.

I open the cupboard doors. 'Flour, butter – oh, and I brought some eggs and *skyr* from the schoolhouse. Might be good to bake something,' I suggest.

'I used to bake a lot,' says María.

'Baking is something that happens in families, happy ones,' says Margrét. 'Recipes passing from mother to daughters and daughters-in-law. I never had that kind of family.'

'I baked growing up,' says Hildur.

'What did you bake?' I ask, pulling out everything I can see.

'Oh, the usual.' She shrugs.

'I have no idea what the usual is here,' I say. 'Show me.'

'Cakes and cookies.' She's smiling. 'My mother always made them with me. But after she died, it didn't happen any more.' She swallows. 'Once I was married, we were more interested in drinking than baking. It seemed to fill the space where a family should have been. We'd drink until there was nothing left. Nothing at all. We lost everything . . . I lost everything, even my husband, to the drink. Even then I drank more. Any way I could get it.' Her hands and voice are shaking.

'Drink,' Margrét says. 'That's when my husband became a really nasty man. I would hide, hoping he'd just fall asleep.'

'We . . .' I pause. 'Sometimes we all look for somewhere to hide when the hurt is too much.' I think of myself, working my way up the hierarchy, determined to succeed, leaving my dreams by the door on my way in.

We fall into silence until, with a sniff, I say, 'Well, we may have a problem with baking.' I've remembered the power cut. 'But we could try a no-bake cake, like cheesecake, with *skyr*. And I brought this from the old schoolhouse.' It's a small camping stove.

Hildur laughs.

'I love *skyr*!' says María. 'Reminds me of growing up. I had it for breakfast every morning before school, when my parents still had the business. Before I managed to lose it for them.'

'There have been difficult times for everyone,' says Hildur. 'You couldn't have seen the crash coming.'

'I thought I was expanding, building the business. I took out a loan. Instead I lost it.'

Hildur puts a hand on her shoulder, as does Margrét. It seems to be the first time they've really talked about what's brought them here.

177

'So, a no-bake *skyr* cake,' I say. 'Let's do it.'

I get them crushing biscuits from the back of the cupboard and melting butter over a pan of hot water. We'll top it with rhubarb jam.

We make flapjacks from porridge oats and dried lingonberries, then attempt pancakes – we even toss them.

'Try one.' Hildur hands me a flapjack.

I bite into it – it's delicious.

'So what brought you here?' Hildur asks.

I chew quickly and swallow. 'I, erm, came to see the Lights.'

'Ah,' they say. 'They all come for the Lights!'

I join in with their laughter. When it dies down, I find myself carrying on. 'It was something we promised we'd do, for a friend. She . . .' I clear my throat. 'It was something she had always wanted to do. We hoped we would do it together, now, when she got better. But . . . she didn't.'

'And she's not here any more?' asks Hildur.

I shake my head as my eyes fill with tears.

'Sorry, sorry,' I say, wiping them away. 'I don't know why I'm suddenly crying.'

'Because you can,' says María. 'It's safe here. The real world is a long way off.'

'On the other side of an avalanche!' says Hildur.

'Wish my ex-husband was under it!' says Margrét, deadpan, and we all find ourselves laughing with her.

'It's her birthday this week,' I continue. 'She would have been forty.'

'She obviously meant a lot to you.'

'And have you always cooked?' Hildur asks.

'I worked in a hotel kitchen. It's where we all became friends. I realized quite young the pleasure food could bring to people and I knew I wanted to be a chef. I would cook what I could for my mum when I came home from school when she was ill. And when Laura got ill, I wanted to take her to happy places with the food on the plate.'

I'm caught up in my thoughts, in the past, remembering the fire in my belly when I started to cook. I think of the girl at our hotel here, her determination to make her mark, reminding me of myself.

'And that's how you got your own restaurant?' asks María.

'I run a restaurant for a Michelin-starred chef. I'm about to open a new one for him.'

'You don't have your own restaurant?' Margrét exclaims. It's as if I'd told her I was an alien from another planet.

'I run the kitchen, put out his recipes the way he wants them.'

'Why?'

'Didn't you want to cook your own recipes?' asks Hildur.

'I . . .' The words catch in my mouth. 'You don't want to hear about me,' I say.

'You have helped us find a happy place again,' says Hildur. 'Where's yours?'

The words hit home. Right now, it feels like here!

'We should try buried bread when this storm is over.' What am I saying?

'Oooh, I wonder if we can make *flatkökur* on this?' Hildur looks at the little stove and then at me. 'Like a rye flatbread. Very good with bread and sliced smoked lamb,' she says.

'It would be good to try,' I say.

'And cookies,' says Hildur, who is clearly on a roll. 'And *skúffukaka*, Icelandic chocolate brownies. When the electricity is back. We'll make cookies and an Icelandic Christmas cake!' she says, with a wide smile, a gap where a tooth or two should be. 'We'll make a Christmas cake as soon as we can!'

17

When I leave the safe house, the women are by the door waving and I have a box of flapjacks in my arms from the plenty we made. They have told me about their childhood, the food they grew up on, the meals that made them smile and, of course, what brought them here. I feel I've made new friends, especially in Hildur, who met me at the door and who came here with nothing when she had run out of options.

As I leave, we're all smiling. I brace myself for the cold, my coat done up and gloves on, before I step out of the safe house and walk down the snowy path. I greet Carrie, patting her, and brush off the snow that has settled on her as she's waited in the covered shelter outside the house. I climb on to her and turn her towards the farmhouse. I know I just have to follow the river. I know where I am. And I know there is one small diversion I can make as I wave goodbye to the women. Who'd have thought it? Me, out here, alone on a horse! That'll be something to remember when I finally get home.

'Knútur?' I call, as I arrive at the little wooden hut. I recognize the tall rock, like a standing stone, outside his hut, but other than that, and the little smoking chimney, there is little to suggest that his home is there. I glance at the harbour, the wooden jetty and the three boats on the water, then look back in the direction of the river, reassuring myself that I know where I am, and towards the waterfall tumbling over the rocks, like liquid silver.

I turn back towards the sea, the black sand and the angry waves. It's bleak here. Loneliness strikes me. Am I really lonely or is it just the effect this place has on me? This dark place at the bottom of the valley seems to drain the energy from me. There's no light here. Perhaps Knútur is punishing himself by living here. The bleakness reveals the emptiness inside me that I barely knew was there . . . until now. I shiver.

'Knútur,' I call again, louder, a shout that leaves me feeling surprisingly better.

The little door to the hut opens and he steps out, unfolding himself to stand tall, clearly surprised to see me.

'Hey!' he says, looking around expectantly. 'No Pétur today?'

'I just came by to give you these.' I hand him the flapjacks. 'I made them with the women in the house at the top of the path.' I point back towards the safe house. 'They seemed to enjoy making them. I thought you might enjoy eating them.'

'You are too kind. Come in, come in,' he says.

I hesitate. 'I just wanted to give you these. I should be getting back before the light goes.'

'Of course, of course,' he says. 'You are very kind.'

'And you're okay? You have everything you need?'

'I do indeed!' He nods and smiles, holding his face up to the wind.

'I'm sorry, I don't have any firewater,' I say.

He turns back to me. 'There are some things in life we should all learn to live without, and appreciate what we have got.' He holds up the tin I've just given him. 'I don't want to be a burden on anyone.'

'I'm sure you're not,' I say.

He shakes his head. 'I'm happy here, living as I do. But I would never want to think that I was any trouble to anyone.'

'I know that Pétur doesn't think you're any trouble at all and just wants you to be happy.'

He holds the tin in his arms.

'Well, I'd better be getting back,' I say. 'I hope to see you before I leave.'

'Thank you again,' he says, and then, 'You'll find your way back? I could take you if you like?'

I smile. 'It's fine. I know where I'm going. Up here, turn at the frozen troll and follow the river back to the farmhouse. And Carrie here seems to know what she's doing.' I pat her neck.

'If you're sure,' he checks.

'I am, really. Now, go and enjoy the flapjacks,' I say, and turn the horse around, sit into the saddle and start to head back up towards the safe house, turn left at the frozen troll and follow the river back to the farm. As I reach the end of the snowy pass, by the frozen troll, I see a figure I recognize and my heart flips. I'd know that outline of black horse and rider anywhere and, right now, he's riding towards me.

'Hey!' he says, as he approaches. 'I was getting worried with the light starting to fade.' His horse dips its head and throws it back, tossing its long mane, as if in greeting.

'I told you I'd be fine and I am.' I feel it now. I might have discovered the lonely hole in my heart in the dark harbour but it seems to be filling, seeing Knútur and now Pétur, and thinking about the women in the safe house.

'All okay at the safe house?'

'Yes. We had a very good time.'

'Good.'

'And then I went to visit Knútur and took him some of our baking.'

'I bet he was delighted.' He beams.

'He was. He's a very humble man,' I say. 'Doesn't want to be a burden on anyone.'

'No. And he's not. Only he doesn't realize that. We just want him to stay safe and well, like the rest of us. There's somewhere I want to go before getting back to the farm. Do you want to come with me? Or do you want to get back?'

'Is it far?'

He grins. 'I promised you some fun, didn't I?'

I cock my head to one side. 'You did.'

'In that case, there's something I'd like to show you.'

'So I'll come with you.' I turn Carrie to ride alongside him in the direction of the volcano.

'I'd like that,' he says.

'We're not going too close, are we?' I indicate the spewing volcano. I can hear the waterfall behind us and see the big icicles clinging to the cliff edges, like diamond daggers.

'No, that is some distance away. This place is perfectly safe.'

18

'Where are we?' I'm awestruck.

'You wanted to see the real Iceland. This is the real Iceland!' It's a pool of milky aquamarine water with steam rising from it. He jumps off his horse, taking hold of my reins as I swing my leg over Carrie's hindquarters and slide off into the snow.

'It's amazing,' I say, staring at it. The rising steam is mixing with the falling snow, like some beautiful dance of fluttering flakes and curling mist. It's sheltered here, cocooned among a curve of small caves in the rocks around it and a small waterfall, creating icicles. There's less wind and the snow is falling straight down, not swirling and furious, settling on the rocks around the pool.

'This is a geothermal pool, a hot spring, just like the lagoon you're staying at, but no one knows about it.

Except us locals, of course.' He gives the briefest of winks and beams. The fizzing in my stomach bubbles again.

'Wow!' I can't stop staring at the extraordinary colour of the water.

Pétur's eyes are dancing with excitement. 'So, you want a dip?'

'Really? Now?' My teeth are chattering.

'Of course! We Icelanders love to be in water. It's part of who we are. I think that's why we love salmon so much – we are part fish!' He laughs. 'It's what we do to relax, to contemplate, to clear our mind, to be at one with nature.'

He ties up the horses at the mouth of one of the caves, takes off their saddles and puts them inside the cave away from the falling snow.

'You go first. I'll look the other way. I know you British are not quite as comfortable with nakedness as we are.'

I start to argue, but can't. 'What do I do?' I find myself asking.

'Get undressed and slide into the warm water. As I said, I will look the other way.'

Butterflies are flying around in my stomach. Can I? Should I? How will I feel if I leave here and don't do it? Like a coward. Then I think of Laura, telling me, 'Do it!'

Quickly, I start to undo my coat, which seems the

most absurd thing to do in these freezing temperatures. I nearly bottle out. But I keep going. This is living, in the here and now. Just like Laura wanted us to do.

But it's freezing. I start to put my leg back into my trousers. What was I thinking of? There's no way I can get naked and into a hot spring in the middle of nowhere in the freezing cold.

'It helps if you just go for it,' he says, with his back to me and I stop midway through pulling my trousers back on. 'On the other hand, if you want to leave now, we can.'

'Are you saying I'm chicken?' I can't help but laugh.

'Maybe!' His shoulders shrug. 'It's fine. Some people live life that way, too scared to feel the fear and do it anyway!'

I freeze. Those were Laura's exact words. It's what she would always say to us. I whip off the rest of my clothes, but leave on my bra and knickers. I'm not quite that brave yet!

I have never felt cold like it. It makes me squeal as I half walk, half hop over the snow along what looks to be a well-worn path into the water, over wooden boards and into the pool. Reaching the water's edge, I hurl myself in and the warm water wraps itself around me, like a great big hug.

'I'm presuming you're in!' He laughs.

'I am, and it's wonderful!' I call, from the warmth of the pool, just my neck and head out in the open air, snow landing on my hair and lashes and on the rocks around me. It's totally amazing.

'Okay, well, if you don't want to look, close your eyes while I undress and get in too. On the other hand, if you want to look . . .'

'No!' I close my eyes tight, enjoying the sensation of the warm water all around my body, as if it's working some kind of magic, making me feel more alive than I have in a long time. More aware of myself, my skin and body. I feel weightless and warm. It's like the most luxurious bath I've ever been in, with added snowfall.

I hear a gentle splash and he's in too. And the thought of a naked Pétur in the water with me has my skin tingling with excitement and my stomach fizzing with anticipation. Although I'm sure he's kept his underwear on. He's just teasing me. Slowly I open my eyes and look ahead, then around me, but he's nowhere to be seen. Where did he go? I can't be here on my own. I'm in the middle of I don't know where in my underwear . . .

Suddenly there's a splash and his head comes up from beneath the surface of the water, taking me by surprise and making me laugh. 'I thought you'd disappeared!'

'Really?' He rubs the water on his face with both hands and pushes his hair back. He's wearing a necklace, a silver charm, on a leather thong. I haven't noticed it before, but I've always seen him in jumpers and a hat. I look at his face, his gunmetal grey hair, the silver highlights around his ears and brow, like the icicles and the cascade of the waterfall. His shoulders are broad and solid, just peeking out from the water, surrounded by spirals of steam.

'It's good to get your face wet,' he says. 'Try it!'

I hold my breath, close my eyes and drop my shoulders, neck and head under the water.

'Now.' I hear his voice but my eyes are still shut. I rub my hands over my face as I resurface. 'This time grab a handful of the mud when you go under!' I open my eyes and look at him. 'Like this!' he says, dips under the water and comes up with two handfuls of light grey mud from the bottom of the pool and rubs it on his face.

'You're not kidding!' I laugh.

'It's good for the skin.'

I hold my breath and dive down, then open my eyes to see where I'm supposed to grab the mud from. It's blurry, with that milkiness to the water. In front of me I can see the outline of his body, if not the detail, but it's enough to make me feel something I haven't felt in a very long time. Desire. I push myself deeper in the water and grab two handfuls of the soft mud from the bottom of the pool. Then I come up for air.

'Rub it on your face and shoulders. Do you want me to help?'

'No!' I say quickly, unable to think of his body so close to mine. I hold the mud in my palm. It's white, more like clay. I dab it on my face, tentatively at first. Then, watching Pétur, I rub it into my cheeks, my forehead, my chin, then down my neck and shoulders.

'How does it feel?' he says, the mud drying in patches on his face.

'It's amazing,' I tell him as I sit back and lean against the rocks, him on the other side of the pool. 'Like a face pack. And the water's amazing too.'

'It's what makes the water so blue.' He holds up a handful of the white clay. 'Water is what we're all about here in Iceland. It's why it is so important we keep our rivers unpolluted. Salmon need cold, clean waters to survive and thrive ... Okay, if the mud is dry, wash it off,' he says, and dips his head under the surface again, then comes back up, water tumbling from his chest, shaking it out of his hair, roaring with reinvigoration.

I dip under the water, rub my face, then flick back my head as I emerge and let out what I think is a similar sort of roar.

We sit in silence and take in the falling snow and rising steam around us, watching them dance gracefully.

The small waterfall is almost made up of icicles, like a sculpture that would be at home in an ice hotel.

'And is this where you find inspiration for your jewellery?' I say, more of a statement than a question. I'm enchanted by the place.

'What do you think?'

'It's beautiful!' I say.

As the snowflakes settle on his shoulders, they melt, leaving his skin gleaming as they run off into the steaming water. It's so warm. 'But mostly I'm inspired by the river and the sea, the life blood of the village. The fishing.'

The charm on his necklace glistens. He holds it between his thumb and forefinger. 'The king of the sea, the salmon,' he says. 'That is what makes this place, the cold, clear water for them to swim in. If anything were to threaten that, this place would die with them. I need to make sure it's safe before I can leave.'

The snow falls and in the distance the volcano is erupting again.

'And what about you? Where do you get your inspiration from to cook?' He interrupts my thoughts while I'm imprinting this place on my mind, to remember always.

'These days I work with an executive chef. We plan the menu, based on developing his ideas for ingredients,' I say, and splash water onto my face. He's looking at me, I can feel it. I rub more water over my face to remove any traces of the mud.

'But that's not what you love to cook. That's not your inspiration,' he says, and suddenly I feel as exposed as I would if I stood up and ran around naked in the snow. 'When did you first know you wanted to cook?'

I'm taken aback, and also taken right back to when I first began to cook.

'I was eight when my mum became ill. I stayed with her as long as I could. I would cook for her. It started with toast and tea. It was the one thing I could do to make her feel better. Honey sandwiches next, just like she'd made for me when I'd been home from school and poorly. My boiled eggs were a triumph!' I smile. 'I even drew smiley faces on them like she used to do when I was feeling sad.'

He doesn't say anything and I know he's wondering what happened next.

'I went to live with a foster-family. They were great. I got the job in the nearby hotel. By the time I left the family and moved into the hotel, I knew I wanted to cook, to be a chef. The best I could be.' I remember the steely determination I felt then to make cooking my life. I wanted to work for the best and become the best.

He nods.

'That's where we all met, me and my friends. At the hotel where we worked when we were in our late teens and early twenties. By thirty, we had settled into our lives. I was the only one still working in hospitality and catering. Meg and Joanna had married. Laura worked in publishing.'

'But not you? You didn't marry?'

I know I'm at that point where I might as well finish the story. Like I say, it's not as if I'll see him again. I swirl my hands in the warm water, watching the ripples they make.

'There was someone. We worked in the kitchen together. At first we didn't get on at all. He was very full of himself when he arrived. I was put in charge of showing him the ropes.' I almost laugh at the memory. 'He thought he knew it all! But, as time went by, we worked well together and our lives just seemed to meld into one. Kitchen life, and life after the kitchen in our accommodation. It worked. There's not much time for dating when you work in a professional kitchen.'

He doesn't say anything.

'And then Laura, our friend, got ill and I just went into autopilot, like I had with Mum, making meals she'd enjoy, to make her happy. Her sense of taste left her but I wanted the food to bring back happy memories. That's what I love to cook. Food that takes you somewhere, whether it's boiled eggs with smiley faces on them or something that prompts a memory, a place, a time.' I splash more water on my face. Now I've started, I can't stop.

'I was still working in the restaurant at the hotel but

it was hard. There was a lot of competition for Chef's compliments, a lot of rivalry, even between Mark and me. Especially between him and me. We were lovers in the bedroom, but rivals for Chef's attention and the next rung on the ladder.' I take a deep breath. 'But Laura became my priority and I stepped back from kitchen life, taking time out to look after her. I stopped staying after work, creating dishes to impress Chef. I turned up and did the minimum so I could get back to Laura. Mark said he understood and at first I felt supported by him. Time went on, and when it got near the end, I moved in with Laura, so I could be there and cook for her. A lot had changed by the time we got into our thirties.' I sigh.

'It's often the way,' he says.

'Meg and Joanna were both divorced. And Laura was gone.'

'And Mark. Your partner?'

'He took a lot of my ideas and showed them to Chef, and eventually he got his own restaurant to run with another chef who'd heard about him and his ideas on the grapevine. I never heard from him once he'd left. I heard he moved in with his sous-chef.'

'So you threw yourself into the kitchen and your work?'

I sniff and rub away tears with the water. 'It's a good place to be, a head chef heading a team for a Michelin-starred restaurant owner,' I say. 'I just felt I had lost time,

time I needed to make up to be where Mark was. I didn't want him to think I'd given up. I wanted to show him I was as good as him. He'd dropped me when I needed someone most. Cooking was what I knew how to do. It was what I'd done before, when Mum died, so I threw myself into doing what was asked of me.'

We stare at each other amid the rising steam and falling snow.

'I've worked hard.'

For a moment he says nothing. Then, 'Just not on the food you love.'

The volcano gushes in the distance and I don't reply. I can't. I have no idea how to. But he's right. I'm not cooking the food I love. It's more about trying to hide from the hurt I felt, from Laura leaving me, feeling used and discarded by Mark. I wanted to show him I wasn't going to disappear quietly. I earned Chef's respect. I climbed to the top of the mountain, but now I'm there, is it really the mountain I want to be at the top of? What mountain do I really want to climb? Where do I really want to be? Not with Mark. He just filled a hole in my life, between sleeping, waking and going to work. Will I ever have time for something more in my life?

'You hungry? Or do you want to get back to your friends?'

I think of Meg and Joanna. The last thing I want right now is a repeat of this morning's argument. I feel so alive and I'm tingling all over. I felt the fear and did it anyway.

'I think the longer I'm away the better right now.'

'Let's get dried and dressed and I'll make us something to eat.'

'Really?'

'Of course! Although now I know I'm cooking for a Michelin-starred chef, I'm a little worried.'

My stomach bubbles with excitement again. I wish it was just the food I'm excited about, but there's no denying how attractive I find Pétur . . .

After we've dried ourselves, with small towels Pétur brought with him, and dressed, Pétur sets up a little camping stove, from his rucksack, like the one I took to the safe house.

'How does *plokkfiskur* sound?' He produces a battered frying pan, also from his rucksack.

'Like something I've never heard of!' I laugh. 'It's not the putrid shark, is it?'

'No, it's like a fish stew.' He takes ingredients from his rucksack. 'You get the pan hot.'

'Yes, Chef!' I say, and tip the front of my bobble hat. I put the pan on the stove and crouch by it. He hands me butter and I feel a jolt of electricity as our arms touch. I do what I always do, focus on the frying pan as I add the butter, then let it melt and foam.

He hands me an onion he's chopped on a small tin plate. I add it to the pan to sauté.

'Where did you learn to cook?' I ask.

'Like most of us here, from my mother. My father was a cook too. He enjoyed cooking the fish he caught.'

'And . . .' I'm staring at the pan as the onions slowly turn translucent. He hands me flaked cooked fish and potatoes. '. . . you never married?'

He takes a moment, checking the pan before replying. 'No, I never married,' he says, and I wonder if he's going to elaborate. 'Here,' he says. 'Now add milk.' He hands me a small glass bottle. I pour in the contents and let it warm.

Then he walks over to the pool and puts two eggs into a small net bag and lowers it in on a piece of string.

'Boiled eggs!' I giggle. 'Brilliant!'

'How's it tasting?' he asks, pointing to the stew. He dips a spoon into the milk and holds it to my lips. He stares right at me and I can't take my eyes off his, like I'm learning everything I need to know about him in those eyes, kind, trusting.

I lean in and sip at the hot milk, as he tilts his head.

'Well?' he asks, and for a moment I forget we're talking about the stew.

'Oh, um, needs seasoning.'

He hands me salt and pepper. 'I'll leave that to the professional,' he says.

I add it and taste again, then hold the spoon out for him to try.

'Perfect.' He smiles. 'My daughter's favourite.'

'Your daughter?' I'm stopped in my tracks. 'But I thought you said . . .'

'Not married, no. But I do have a daughter. She works in the city, for the organization who set up the safe house.'

'Wow!' I say, taking in this information. He has a grown-up daughter. I watch as he ladles the stew into two tin mugs and hands me one.

'You must be very proud of what she's done,' I say, holding the spoon he's given me.

'I am.' He stirs his helping.

'And her mother?'

'She lives in the city too,' he says.

I find I'm taking time to digest the information. He has a grown-up daughter and an ex he had a child with. I mean, an ex, but is she an ex he wishes he was with or one who left him? I've never had a child so I don't know how these things work. Do you always regret you're not with the child's other parent? Suddenly, it's a layer of complication that isn't about letting myself give in to the attraction I'm feeling. He has a life outside the bubble we're all stuck in right now. There is life outside here that we will be going back to at some point, however much I'd like to stay here. He hands me some rye bread cooked in the geyser, and a boiled egg. He's drawn a smiley face on the shell, making me think what a wonderful father he must be. There is more to his life than just us, here, now. The bubble will burst eventually, I think, as I eat my stew, but creamy milk, flaking smoked fish and potatoes, eaten with a spoon from a mug, will always remind me of here and now, and of feeling free of the kitchen, Mark, and the hurt of the past couple of years.

19

After we've eaten, Pétur pulls out a notebook and a pencil from his top pocket. I watch him as he makes a couple of sketches while I clean the pan in the snow and wash our mugs.

I pack everything into the rucksack and he puts his notebook back into his top pocket. Then we remount the horses and ride back to the farm in the cold night air. I've never known cold like it. But inside I'm glowing, from the warm-water swim, the comforting fish stew and the smiley faces on boiled eggs cooked in the hot spring.

Our head torches light the path in front of us, the snow still falling. We take our time, letting the horses find their footing down from the mountain and their way across the snowy tundra to the farmhouse. Pétur hands me liquorice in a packet – 'Call it dessert!'

'Look!' He points. 'An Arctic fox.' It darts out, spooking the horses and me, its eyes flashing yellow in our torchlight, but quickly goes on its way and we settle again into a steady rhythm. It's freezing cold, but it's magical too.

My skin is still tingling from the hot spring and the cold trek as we reach the farmhouse. We remove the horses' tack and bed them into the warm barn for the night.

'How did you enjoy your day?' he asks.

'It was fabulous,' I say, carrying Carrie's saddle to the tack room and handing it to him to put up on the rack.

'Thank you for your company,' he says, holding the saddle between us.

My heart suddenly races and my cheeks flush. He's standing close to me. I can smell the leather of the saddles and the sweetness of hay. Right now, I want him to put his lips on mine. The anticipation is actually aching in me. But, with huge effort, I pull myself away, leaving him to put the saddle on the rack.

He pats his top pocket. 'I'm just going to my workshop to drop this off,' he says.

'What is it?'

'My notebook. I carry it with me in case I want to jot anything down,' he says. 'Want to come with me?'

Just a little longer in his company, I think.

*

Having fed Jón, and locked the shed, we walk through the snowy dark night to the workshop where he finds candles and lights them. He pulls the battered notebook from his pocket and puts it down on his work bench, lit with his head torch.

'So this is where the ideas begin to take shape?' I ask, looking around.

He nods and opens the notebook. 'It's about the sights I see, the way this place makes me feel,' he says, picking up a bangle he's clearly working on. 'This place has always inspired us as a family. My grandfather used to paint it.' He turns to a picture on the wall behind him of the waterfall by the schoolhouse.

'Your grandfather did that?'

'Yes, and nothing much has changed around here since.'

I look down at his notebook, the pencil sketches there, and run my hand over them, the things he's seen and noted down, snapshots of life. And then, around his workbench and in the glass cabinet the ideas translated into silver, as cold and shimmering as the snow and ice, as fiery as lava from the volcano we watched.

'I can see from just these pieces how much you love it here,' I say, picking up a brooch inspired by the snow-capped mountains. 'What about the girlfriend you made the earrings for? What happened to her? Did she like them?'

'She did!' He smiles. 'My daughter's mother.' And I

feel something that resembles jealousy. Surely not. I barely know this man, or his ex-girlfriend, who clearly still has a place in his life.

I look down at the notebook. 'You'll miss it when you go away?'

'I will,' he says.

'Can't you stay?' I say suddenly, realizing the hole he will leave with his departure. 'Can't you set up a shop here, bring in people to work for you?' I ask.

He shakes his head. 'I can't see people coming all the way out here to shop, can you?'

'Or the smokehouse – bring more fishermen and expand the smoked-salmon business. Or run holidays from here. Let people see the hot spring I've been in today. Let them breathe this air, offer horse-riding, fishing. It's worked for other places, like the hotel we're staying in.' I can suddenly see all the potential as I hold the brooch. 'I mean, you're needed here. What if there's another avalanche? Who will organize the food for everyone or look out for Knútur?' I'm wondering if I've made any sense.

Then he looks at me, his eyes shining in the candle-light. 'The villagers will still look after each other, whether I'm here or not. No one is bigger than this place . . . only Mother Nature.'

'But surely it would be good to have more families, more young people to fill the school and bring up children here.'

He nods. 'It would. People living here and respecting the area would be wonderful. Maybe better than more tourists impacting on the countryside.' He looks at his work bench and taps his notebook with a pencil. 'It's what makes this place special. It's why I find inspiration here.' He bites his bottom lip. 'Just not right now.'

'No inspiration? Is it me? I can leave. Sorry. I'm talking too much!'

'It's fine. I'm just trying to think of a centrepiece for my exhibition. I can't quite . . .' He taps the book again with the pencil.

'It's me, isn't it? I'm putting you off. I'll go.' I turn to leave.

'It's fine. I'm sure I'll think of something,' he says, and comes out from behind his work bench. 'Let's just hope I think of it in time. Come on, let's go inside.'

We start to move towards the door and as we reach it I realize I'm still holding the brooch. 'Oh! Sorry!'

He looks down at it in my hand. 'Ah,' he says. 'Hoping to take a bit of this place with you when you go, huh?' He smiles, takes it from my palm and holds my gaze.

With all my willpower, I say, 'Thank you for letting me in here again. Goodnight, Pétur. I hope you find the piece you're looking for. I'll leave you to it.'

'Goodnight, Freya,' he says, as I head out of the workshop, pulling my coat around me, making for the farmhouse, feeling him standing at the doorway to the workshop and fighting not to turn back to put my lips on his.

I creep in. Everyone is in bed. It's early, but so dark. I struggle into my bunk and lie there awake, thinking about the hot spring. My skin feels clean, refreshed, reinvigorated. I'm thinking about the ride back after fish stew, boiled eggs cooked in the springs, eggs that had been given to Pétur when he was checking the farms, and more of the delicious geyser bread.

I wonder what to tell the others about where I've been. How do I describe the hot spring, the simple supper and the dark ride home, putting my trust in my horse and the piles of stones left by villagers to help others find their way? I can't help but feel something inside me has stirred and shifted and I'm searching for something that feels just out of reach, something I didn't know I was missing until now, something that feels a lot like home.

I can hear the others' breathing. They're not asleep. But no one seems to know what to say. This morning's row is still in the air, raw and painful. I wish they could have been with me at the hot spring. Or maybe it was being with a near-stranger that made me feel I could talk and revisit the past as I did. The past I have spent the last two years trying to shut out so that I can move on like Laura wanted. But there were good times in the past too. It wasn't all about sadness. Without the good times we wouldn't have the happy memories that I'd loved to recreate in my dishes for Laura, to remind her of the fun we'd had.

Suddenly, feeling younger, freer and happier than I have in years, I realize there's only one thing to say. We're here to celebrate Laura's life after all. And I know she'd be egging me on to say it.

'Truth or Dare?' I say, into the darkness of the bunk room.

With only a moment's missed beat, the others burst out laughing.

20

'What's Truth or Dare?' asks Frankie.

We sit in our sleeping-bags, pulled around our waists. Meg lights the candles and I find the bottle of firewater from our first night, pour shots and hand them round.

'I say, "Truth or Dare?" to someone and they have to decide which they want to do. Answer a question truthfully or do a dare. It was something we did years ago,' Meg explains.

'And you can ask anything if it's a truth!' says Joanna.

Frankie looks terrified and part of me is wondering if this was a good idea, but it seems to have put the row behind us. And that's good. Life's too short for rows. Besides, I'm sure it was all down to tension. We should be leaving tomorrow and there's still no news about the road being cleared. Meg's Tom will be worrying about her, Joanna's husband too. And I'm due at work. We're cut off from the outside world and have no idea if anyone knows we're safe.

'Here's to Iceland. It's not what we planned, but it has been an amazing adventure,' I say, raising my glass. 'To friendship!'

'To Laura,' says Meg.

And we all drink.

'Right, who's going first?'

'Freya!' Joanna and Meg say together.

'Why me?'

'Come on, Truth or Dare?' Joanna insists.

'Okay.' I take another sip of the firewater.

'Truth!' Joanna eggs me on.

'Truth, truth, truth!' Meg chants.

'Okay, okay!' I say. 'Truth!'

'Whoop!' Meg claps, Joanna beams, and Frankie looks relieved.

'What have you and Pétur been up to all afternoon?'

I sip the firewater to hide my blushes and practically choke on it.

'Nothing – I mean, not nothing, but not that thing!' Laughter is bubbling out of me, like the geyser sending water skywards.

There's a knock at the door and it opens a crack. I blush as if my cheeks are on fire.

'Hey! What's going on?' Pétur sticks his head through the door. 'I was just checking on the sheep. Thought I'd see if you were all okay too.'

'Of course! We're fine,' says Meg.

'Come in!' says Joanna, sipping her firewater. 'And close the door!'

'Join us!' says Meg, ever the mother hen.

'Do you mind?' He looks at me and I wish my cheeks would stop burning.

'As long as you're happy to play Truth or Dare,' Joanna says.

He slips into the room, closing the door behind him and pulling up a chair at the round table with the candle on it. He takes off his hat and shakes his silver quiff. Meg pours him some firewater.

'So, what is this Truth or Dare?' He sips.

'You can choose either to tell the truth when you're asked a question or you can take a dare.'

My cheeks pink again as he catches my eye.

'That sounds fine,' he says. 'Whose go is it?'

'Yours!' says Meg.

'And Freya's!' adds Joanna.

'Wait!' I wish I hadn't started this. It was supposed to be fun, not some kind of ritual humiliation. At least Joanna and Meg appear to be enjoying themselves. Frankie still looks dazed. I take another sip of firewater, then find myself laughing.

'*Soooo* . . .' says Joanna.

'What took you two so long today?' Meg cuts in.

Pétur looks at me. 'Maybe we should let them into our secret?' His eyes twinkle.

I blush more.

'We'll take you tomorrow,' he says. 'After we've visited the community centre.'

'So if you're not going to answer, you'll have to do a dare!' Joanna chortles and we all join in. I take another big slug of firewater. I'd rather do a dare than tell them truthfully what I'm thinking about Pétur and the time we've just spent together. That's my happy memory to take home with me.

21

The next morning – at least I think it's morning – my head is banging.

'Come on, sleepy heads. Time to go!' says Pétur, cheerily, around the door. As one we groan. 'Truth or Dare?' he jokes.

'No!' we all shout and a pillow flies across the room at him from Meg's bunk.

He dodges it. 'Time to get moving if we're to let you in on our secret.'

Again, I find myself blushing and I don't know why. I want to say it's not a big secret. But it so is. It's a beautiful one. A hot spring, surrounded by snow, with steam rising off warm milky blue water that seems to massage away your worries.

'Breakfast at the community centre. Leaving in ten!'

We pull ourselves out of our bunks, like the young

festival-goers we once were, only this time we can barely walk from the aches and pains, the thumping headaches and night sweats.

We dive on the bottled water he's brought in and drink plenty. 'A roll in the snow might help,' he says, and we groan, remembering last night's antics.

Joanna looks suitably embarrassed when I remember her Truth or Dare turning into a mix of Marry, Kiss or Kill and chants of 'Kiss, kiss, kiss!' as she chose Kristen as the one she'd kiss, marry and kill. Meg has a bald line in her eyebrow, where it was shaved in a dare and I'm not sure she's remembered that yet. I'm not looking forward to her reaction when she does and realizes she's going to be a bride with bladed eyebrows. Frankie took the dare to do the naked roll in the snow. After that she seemed to relax into it. Until then she'd seemed worried and I suspect she didn't want to talk about her partner.

We travel in silence to the community centre, heads thumping with every step the horses take, but the fresh cold air and falling snow seem to help. The route is becoming familiar now.

'Something's burning!' I smell it on the air before I see any smoke and, without thinking, I give a little 'click, click' with my tongue and tap with my heels, as Pétur showed me, and I'm off at a lick, sitting deeply into the saddle.

'Wait for me!' Pétur shouts, over the sound of the

waterfall behind the schoolhouse. He's beside me. I can see smoke from the kitchen. The horses step up their pace.

Without thinking, I throw my leg over Carrie's hind-quarters and stumble backwards in the snow, but right myself, handing my reins to Pétur, and shuffle as fast as I can through the deep snow towards the kitchen.

From the doorway, it's chaos. There's smoke and mess everywhere. Anna is on the floor, coughing. 'My back. The sciatica. I can't move!'

'Okay. Turn everything off!' I say, putting my face into the crook of my elbow as I grab a cloth to remove the burning pan from the stove, take it outside and plunge it into the snow, where it hisses. Inside, the smoke is lingering. Pétur joins me as we throw open the windows, and Meg is with Anna, comforting her.

Pétur and Meg lift Anna carefully into a chair. She's trying to be brave but we can all see she's in a lot of pain. 'Let's get you home,' Pétur says.

'No, I must cook! The villagers won't eat!' she says insistently.

'Unless we can rescue it,' I say, almost to myself.

Pétur and Meg carry Anna outside and to her nearby farmhouse.

'Can you make something else to deliver?' Pétur says on his return. 'Meg is helping Anna to bed.'

'Meg's used to looking after others,' I say. 'She seems to be the only one in her family who does.'

'A bit like Anna! Meg's very kind,' he says. 'Her new husband will be a lucky man. Finding love is hard enough. You have to take the chance on it when you do. It's a brave person who commits to another for the rest of their lives.'

I find my eyes locked into his gaze. It takes so much willpower to tear them away. 'I just hope she and Tom can. They have so many other people in their lives,' I say, opening cupboards.

'I've found staying out here much less complicated!' he jokes.

'Ah, but soon you'll be leaving for London. Who knows what complications life will hold for you then?' I joke back.

'Indeed!'

I can't help wondering what his eyes are saying to me.

'Hey!' I hear Kristen call from outside the school-house, breaking the moment.

'Hey!' Pétur calls back. He pulls his eyes away from mine and goes out to greet him. I follow.

'My helpers are a little weary this morning.' Kristen laughs.

'You're right about that, but we have a bigger problem.'

'What's up?' Kristen gets off his horse and stands in the snow.

'It's Anna,' Pétur tells him.

'Anna? What's happened?' Kristen flicks the reins over his horse's head and leads him to the enclosure. I take my reins from Joanna, who's holding the horses, and we follow Kristen and settle them.

'Her back. Sciatica, so she can't move. We found her on the floor in the kitchen. She's at home now. Cross.'

'I bet she is!' Kristen smiles fondly. 'And can you cook today?' he asks me.

'I think I can remember what Anna did,' I say, running her dishes through my head.

'Great. Let us know what you need us to do,' says Pétur.

I go into the kitchen, switch everything on and check the fridge for ingredients.

I pull on Anna's apron. It's a ritual I've come to love: once an apron goes over my head I'm where I belong. In the kitchen. I push up my sleeves and form a plan.

'We need to be leaving at eleven to get the meals delivered in daylight,' Pétur says. He glances into the pans. 'Looks like she was making the fish stew we had yesterday. Think you can do that here?'

I remember us cooking it on the camp stove. 'No problem. I can replicate that to a pretty close likeness. Frankie, Meg? I'll need you to help.'

'We're here!' says Meg, and Frankie is smiling too.

'Frankie, you start peeling potatoes. Meg, can you

make a start on that washing-up, then get the dishes ready to serve into?'

I give out instructions, completely at home. 'Here, like this. Keep the tip of the knife on the board when you're chopping, and when you're on potatoes, make your hand into a bridge, and cut under it. With the onions,' I point, 'keep your fingers like a crab, with the tips tucked in. That should work quicker . . . and safer.'

'Oh, wow! Yes!' Frankie says, and starts chopping for all her worth.

Again Joanna looks totally lost in the kitchen. I look around for a way in which she can usefully help and not get in the way.

'Why don't you go and help Kristen? He's going to check on more sheep,' Pétur says, and smiles naughtily.

Joanna doesn't need asking twice and disappears to ride out with Kristen.

'Pétur, can you check the bread? Assuming you've put some in?'

'Of course, Chef,' he says, and my stomach is fizzing and bubbling again, reminding me of a geyser about to blow.

By the time Pétur arrives back with the bread I'm tasting the *plokkfiskur*. 'It needs thickening,' I say, adding flour. 'Here, try.' I hold a spoon to Pétur.

He leans forward and sips, holding my gaze. 'And more pepper,' he says, smiling.

'Frankie? Can you fillet that fish?' I ask, impressed by her chopping skills.

'Sure I can,' she says, and indeed, she seems to know her way around a fish. I have no idea why I didn't think she would. So far the only thing I know about Frankie is that she's here on her own, trying to work out how to grieve for her partner. But she did say he was a fishmonger. Maybe that's what we're all doing here. Working out how to grieve, not just to move on, to allow ourselves to look back at the good times as well as the sadness.

Without any more words needed, we get down to cooking the fish stew Anna had planned. Between us, with Pétur dividing up the bread, Frankie chopping and stirring, Meg on washing-up and coffee-making, we'll have meals made up and ready to go on time.

It's like I'm back doing service at the restaurant. It's what I know how to do.

'Try it now,' I say to Pétur, holding out a spoon of the steaming, creamy stew. 'I want it to be just like Anna's.'

He holds my gaze again, leans in and instead of taking the spoon from me, sips from it. My insides are shifting and slotting into a different place. It feels like a much more comfortable fit.

Pétur grins. 'It's just like Anna's.'

And I'm delighted. So is Frankie. 'Well done, everyone!' I say. 'Frankie, you were great.'

'Let's get these delivered!' Pétur says, as we head out
of the schoolhouse.

'And make sure Anna gets some,' I say, hoping for
her approval.

'And then we can show your friends our little secret,'
adds Pétur, with that naughty grin.

22

'Oh, my God!' Meg holds her gloved hands over her face, covering her nose.

'What is this place?' Awestruck, Joanna is watching the steam rise from the baby blue waters. Snow, like a soft white blanket, is draped around the edges of the pool and icicles hang from the frozen waterfall, sparkling like a curtain of white lights.

'It's a natural hot spring, like the one at the hotel, but without the other guests.' I beam, looking at their excited faces.

'And we can use it?' Meg asks.

'Of course,' says Pétur. 'It's here for everyone. Come on!' He guides them over to tie up the horses. 'Help yourselves.' He holds out a hand to the beautiful steaming water. It's still snowing, but here, out of the wind, among the rocks surrounding it, we've stepped out of the relentless weather, just for a while.

Meg doesn't need telling twice. While Pétur is making sure all the horses are fine Meg strips off her layers and, quick as a flash, steps into the warm water, her eyes brimming with tears. 'This is beautiful! Just how I imagined it would be. All we need now is the Lights.' The sky is still a blanket of white, flakes falling determinedly.

I join her, stepping carefully over the rocks and lowering myself into the water.

'Come on, Joanna!' she calls, waving to her.

'Oh, I don't know . . .'

'I'm going to check on Anna, find out how the *plokkfiskur* went down,' Pétur tells me. 'I'll come back in a bit.'

Frankie joins us in the water. 'Oh, this is fantastic!'

Joanna looks at the three of us. Then, suddenly losing her inhibitions, she strips off in a mad rush and joins us with a splash and a long 'Aaaaah.' For a while we just sit and enjoy the silence of the falling snow. Then I show them how to dive down for mud and use it as a face mask.

'Grab a handful of it,' I say, 'and scoop it onto your body. It's the best exfoliating rub ever.' Meg is rubbing the light grey clay over her arms, her shoulders and then her face.

Once again Joanna is hesitant.

'It's the same as they'd be putting on you at the hotel,' I tell her. 'You're just picking it up yourself.'

She follows suit and we all have mud packs on our face and tilt our heads back to the falling snow, shutting our eyes and enjoying the moment of shared silence, each of us with our own thoughts.

'Truth or Dare?' Joanna asks. I open my eyes and see the others tilting their heads upright.

'Again?' Meg says.

'Actually,' Joanna says, 'I'll go first.'

Why not? We shrug.

'Truth!' Joanna says quickly before she's even asked.

'Okay,' Meg says. 'In the words of Mrs Merton, what was it that first attracted you to the millionaire Tony when you first met him?' She smiles and I can't help joining her, as do Joanna and Frankie. But Joanna's smile is accompanied by tears.

'Joanna! We're only teasing! He's lovely!' I say, feeling bad about teasing her. Maybe she's tired, worried and just wants to know when we'll be able to go home. She has Tony, his grown-up children and their own kids to get ready for Christmas.

'If older!' Meg tries a gentle tease to lift the mood. 'But you've made it work, second time around. We're just jealous! I'm hoping I get it right this time with Tom.'

I see Joanna's tears plop in circles into the water. 'I mean, you're the one who's got life sorted. There's never going to be a second time for me,' I add. 'Not after . . .' and we know I don't need to say it but I finally can, '. . . Mark.'

Joanna looks slowly up at us, the corner of her mouth pulling her cheek, the mud pack drying and crinkling there. 'He left me. Months ago. And before you say it, no, not for another younger model. In fact, someone much plainer, the same age as him. Said he wanted a quieter life.'

None of us knows what to say.

'Said he'd found love at last. I thought he loved me. But, of course, it wasn't love, was it?'

'Oh, Joanna!' I try to take her hands but she waves them away.

'He must have loved you a bit,' says Meg, clearly desperate to say something to make her feel better.

She shakes her head. 'He didn't. I was just another trophy to be bought. I organized his life, his clothes, his social life, his kids. I was just a hired hand with benefits,' she says. She takes a deep breath. 'Marry the first time for love and the second for money,' she repeats her mantra, 'so my mum used to say. Fat lot of good it did me. I don't have a bean right now! Sorry. I – I know I owe you all money.'

'Don't even think about it!' I say.

'No, our treat!' says Meg. 'Whatever needs paying for, we'll sort it.'

'I can't take money from you.'

'Just a loan. We'll work it out,' says Meg.

'It's just . . . I got so used to how things were. Things got paid. And now I have no idea how to start up again on my own. I mean, I have credit cards. But I need to start making some money. Making a life for myself.'

'Me neither,' Frankie suddenly says, and we all turn to her in surprise. She wipes her nose. 'I know how you feel.'

None of us says anything.

'My partner died. We weren't married, but he left everything to me. No one is happy about that. Not his family or his business partners. I don't care about the money. I just want him back.'

'We know,' says Meg kindly. 'We've been there.'

'I just don't know where to start to pick up the pieces. I thought coming here might help. And I'm so sorry I crashed into you. This is all my fault.'

'Not at all!' Joanna reaches out to her. 'We were all chasing what we thought would help us. You and us, chasing the Lights.' She looks at us. 'Thank you for your support, all of you. I'm sorry. I should have told you both sooner.'

'Yes, you should!' I say firmly but kindly.

'I was just . . .'

'Too proud?' asks Meg.

'Embarrassed. You all thought I had this perfect life when I was envying your lives. You with your family, Meg, and you with your job, Freya, a new restaurant to go to, Michelin stars to your name.'

'Not actually my name,' I remind her. And the words

seem to be on a loop in my head. *Not actually my name, my name* . . . I sigh. 'Life was never going to be everything we wanted it to be. We can't have it all,' I say, feeling the hole in my heart again where I would have loved to have a partner, a family maybe, but somehow I missed that turning on life's high-speed Journey.

'Come on,' I say. 'Let's wash off these mud masks, get dressed and head back to the farmhouse. I'll see if Pétur will let me rustle up some dinner in his kitchen. I've got my eye on a few jars of his pickles.'

Joanna's tears fill her eyes again. 'Remember when you used to cook for us after we'd been on a night out? We'd come in sozzled and you'd have batter ready to make pancakes.'

'And a pot of tea!' Meg adds.

'Maybe looking back isn't the worst thing we can do,' I say quietly, enjoying the memories flooding in, the good ones along with the bad: the last few days of her life when Laura left hospital and I moved into her house, juggling the restaurant, the carers and being with her.

Frankie is sitting quietly, thoughtful. I can't help but wonder what she's thinking.

'Come on, let's get dressed – quickly!' I say, dashing out of the warm water into the falling snow. Then I stop to stare at the incredible setting we're in, on the edge of a hot spring, the mist rising off it as hot air meets cold. I hug myself and shiver but don't move, wanting to drink in the moment, the warmth of the water, cold snow on my skin, good friends, new and old. My skin is tingling and it seems as if the aches and pains I've carried around for the last couple of years are being massaged away.

'Look, one thing we've learnt is to appreciate what we have when we have it.' I turn to the group. 'Yes, we're stuck here. I know you should be looking forward to your wedding, Meg, and I should be working, but there's nothing we can do. And there are far worse places to be stuck.' I smile. 'And we're together. We should just make the most of it. Yes, it's looking like we won't be back for Christmas. But there'll be other Christmases. This one, we should just make it the best we can. One to remember. With people we care about.'

'You're right,' says Meg.

'I know who I'd rather be with!' says Joanna.

'Thank you for letting me be part of it,' says Frankie. 'Right now, I can't think of anywhere I'd rather be. I've only just met you but you've cared more about me than anyone back home.'

'We should make Christmas decorations,' says Meg.

'And drink hot chocolate!' I say.

Once we're dressed, Pétur meets us and we ride back to the farmhouse deep in our own thoughts. There, I move into the kitchen and do the only thing I know what to do: I start rustling up something to put a smile on their faces. A favourite I used to make for Laura when her sense of taste had left her and she really didn't feel like eating. This always got her to eat a little and made me feel I was doing something to help. Pancakes!

Joanna lights the candles in the windows and on the kitchen table. The room looks magical.

I head straight to the kitchen and pull out the ingredients for *pönnukökur* – Pétur tells me the Icelandic name for them as I whip up the batter and pour it into a hot pan, with bubbling butter. As the underside mottles, then goes golden and crisp, I toss it, to the delight of everyone at the table, just as I did in the safe house. I make as many as the batter allows, then serve them with sweet lingonberry jam, a dollop of creamy *skyr* and a sprinkling of cinnamon.

'That should get Christmas started,' I say, putting the pile of pancakes in the middle of the table and smiling as everyone tucks in. Pétur looks up at me and winks. We may not be where any of us is supposed to be right now, but it could be where we need to be. The kitchen, in the golden candlelight, filled with paper snowflakes Meg and Frankie have been cutting out while I was cooking, and with the smell of warm butter, laughter, stories about the Yule Lads and trolls, feels warm, welcoming and very much like home.

23

The snow continues to fall through the night; one day passes much like another. We've got into a routine of travelling to the schoolhouse and delivering meals, but there is still no sign of the road being cleared, no sign of the outside world, and any hope of getting home for Christmas has slipped away. We're stuck here and, right now, that's as much as we know. Days and nights seem almost to blend into one with no let-up, and the wind continues to whip around the farmhouse, making me toss and turn. Memories I'd pushed into the very recesses of my mind come back to haunt me. By morning, in the pitch black, I'm up and dressed, ready to get to the schoolhouse kitchen.

I double- and triple-check the lights in Pétur's kitchen to see, hoping against hope, if there is electricity but there's still nothing. Tomorrow night, Christmas

Eve, will be one of the biggest nights of the year in the restaurant. I've been preparing for it for months. I have no idea what will happen if I'm not there. This is something we didn't plan for. Christmas at the restaurant has people paying high prices for a highly organized and executed menu: the taster menu all this week until tomorrow, Christmas Eve; a Christmas banquet on Christmas Day, of seven courses. And on Boxing Day, another long lunch of layered glazed pies, mini Scotch eggs, game, garnished with many different mousses, veloutés and foams. Very different from the warming, spicy soup I'm going to make now, ready to deliver to the villagers and check they're all safe and well. Each one will be delighted to see us and grateful for their food parcels, so far from the picky diners at the restaurant, all thinking they're a critic and looking for faults. It feels so good to cook for people who eat for the flavour, the smell, not just for how something looks on the plate.

There is nothing I can do about the restaurant right now. But I can do something here. I leave a note on the kitchen table. It's been so long since I've left a note for anyone. Nowadays it's all done on text or WhatsApp or whatever. But I find a piece of paper, and a pen, from where Meg and Frankie were making snowflakes, and tell the others where I'm going. Then, for the first time, I slip out into the dark before the others are up and go over to the big barn, where I pull back the door, just like I've watched Pétur do. I find the saddle and bridle and tack up Carrie, then lead her out into the snowy morning, switch on my head torch to light the way, and we're off to the schoolhouse.

By the time the others arrive I'm well ahead in the kitchen, enjoying its warmth and peace. I've chopped dried mushrooms and onions, and am gently frying them to make a thick, creamy soup, just like we had on our first night when Pétur brought us in from the cold. Outside, the snow is still falling relentlessly sideways in the wind. I'm wondering what to cook with the soup, maybe dumplings or perhaps rye bread. Or even a sort of tortilla, Icelandic-style, with eggs, potatoes and dill, maybe a stir of *skyr*.

'You left early,' says Meg, appearing in the kitchen, letting in a cold whoosh of air.

'Couldn't sleep,' I reply. 'I was thinking about what to cook, so I came to get on with it.'

I see Meg glance at Joanna and Pétur.

'So, Chef, what's on the menu?' he asks, smiling.

'Don't call me that!' I laugh, and feel that shift inside me again.

'Why not? You are!' he says, leaning over the pot, breathing in the steam rising from it. He is fresh from the bath, with the scent of pine on him, making my skin tingle.

'I think . . .' my thoughts are turning over in my mind,

the restaurant, the kitchens I've worked in, the sharp elbows I've had to develop to work my way up, '. . . I think it's because I'm a cook more than a chef.' I hear the words come out of my mouth and they may not make sense right now to me or anyone else but it feels like the start of a journey, setting out on the right road having been lost for a while.

Pétur says nothing, just looks at me, and I find myself wanting to say more.

'A cook, who wants to please people with their food, make them smile, give them back memories, make new ones. For me, being a chef has been about learning to execute a dish to perfection. It's been about learning to perform under pressure, learning to take the pressure and not snap. When Laura died and I took time away from the kitchen, I felt I had to keep up with everyone else when I got back. Especially Mark. I threw myself into becoming a chef. But actually . . .' I'm assailed by memories of shouting chefs, wielding knives and abuse when service and their instructions weren't executed to perfection. Where was the food? Where was the love expressed on the plate? '. . . I'm a cook first and foremost, and I think I've forgotten that. I want to enjoy the experience, the thought, the preparation, and for people to enjoy what they eat. The kitchen is not a place that should be filled with fear. It should be a place filled with love.'

My heart lurches as Pétur smiles at me, taking a

spoon, dipping it into the big pot and, eyes twinkling, raising it to his lips. 'Well, I know everyone is going to love what you've cooked here this morning,' he says. 'This is fantastic!'

'Thank you,' I say happily. And decide to make the Icelandic tortilla to go with the soup.

Once the bags are packed with soup, bread and a slice of dill-flavoured tortilla, I plan to drop into the safe house to see how the women are doing, and since I'm going that way, I'll take Knútur some food too.

'I'm going to check on Knútur, take him some more soup,' I say.

'Somebody has a fan!' Pétur grins and winks playfully.

My stomach flips. Seeing that someone has a hot meal for the day makes me feel good, better than every plate of food I've sent out from the restaurant kitchen.

'Here, take this,' he says, reaching into his bag and giving me a bottle in a paper bag. 'Tell him I said to stay warm and safe.'

'I will,' I say, feeling a warm glow inside.

'I'll come with you,' says Frankie.

'Sure,' I say, glad of the company and glad she's feeling she can.

'And you'll be okay?' asks Pétur.

'Fine. I know the way. Follow the stones, past the elves' church and the frozen troll.'

'Exactly! You're sounding like a local!' he says.

The horses walk slowly and steadily through the thick snow that has fallen overnight.

'It's an amazing place, isn't it?' says Frankie, marvelling at the snow lying thick and untouched around us.

'It is.' I gaze at what I first felt was bleak, but now, since the snowfall has lightened, it's beautiful. Like a picture postcard.

'If cold,' she adds.

'You didn't come dressed for it!' She's wearing clothes Pétur has found for her. They're far too long in the legs and arms but she was lucky he had enough to help us all out. I'm wearing one of his jumpers. I know it's his. I can smell it. A smell I've come to really, really like.

'I didn't think it through. I just picked up my warmest coat, the long woollen one I wear at home in the winter. Clearly not good enough for Iceland.' She giggles. 'And I had no idea I was going to end up stranded somewhere so cold.'

'And remote,' I add.

After a while of travelling in comfortable silence I decide to ask Frankie what's been on my mind. 'You said you'd lost your partner. I was just wondering how come you decided to travel here on your own.'

She sighs. 'The truth is, I came on business. It was supposed to be get in, find out what's going on, fix it and leave.'

'And did you?'

'I don't think so. I don't think I have the answers at all.'

The horses' hoofs crunch through the snow.

'I thought I'd be in and out and back in no time to report,' she says. 'My company . . . well, my partner's company want to start bringing in salmon directly from Iceland. But they haven't managed to seal the deal yet. They need some finer details sorted before they can go ahead. In particular, they need to find a unit here in a place where they can access the sea and the road.'

I sense that she's trying to tell me something.

'Looks like the elves had other ideas,' she half smiles, 'and there's no way Pétur and the villagers are going to let a company set up and affect the landscape.'

The penny drops. 'What? Are you from that company Pétur was talking about?'

She takes a deep breath and nods.

'Why didn't you say anything?' I ask, more sharply than I meant to.

She sighs. 'You saw how he reacted when he thought you were from the company. I didn't know what to do. He knew the company were sending out a representative. They want to talk to him and the other villagers about buying a plot of land so they can have access to fish and to the road. It's just one parcel of land. It would make all the difference. But he's refusing to speak to anyone. And he certainly wasn't expecting me. Besides,' she says, 'I thought trying to find out a bit more about the area and the people would help me find the fix.'

We follow the river as it rushes and tumbles around the rocks, between the snow-covered banks.

'And has it?' I ask, guarded.

She shakes her head.

'You've seen how beautiful this place is,' I add. 'Pétur doesn't want anything to change. I can understand that.'

'But I actually think what the company has in mind could really benefit the area. I just need the chance to explain it to him.'

'So you decided to keep your identity a secret,' I say, feeling more than a little deceived.

'Just until I could see it all for myself. But now that I have, I really believe that what the company is suggesting would bring this community back to life. Young people are leaving. Without the likes of Pétur and his cousin, who will look out for the older ones?'

She's right. If Pétur is going to London, who will look after the older community if this sort of thing happens again? And Knútur, who will look out for him? Pétur needs to go to London without worrying about them all.

'Look, what I told you was true. My partner died. I got his share of the fishmonger's, his business. The biggest share. He wanted to farm the fish he sold, know exactly where it came from. Bring salmon from here to his customers. I thought by coming here, finishing what he planned, I would feel closer to him.' Tears trickle down her cheeks, and I feel bad I've upset her. 'I thought I could do some good by showing the locals what we could do for them. I really thought I was helping them to see why the village would benefit. And if I could do that . . .' she gulps, '. . . perhaps the board, mostly his family, would understand that I'm an asset not just . . .' She tails off and chews her bottom lip.

'So what exactly does your company want to do here?' I ask, interested and keen to lift her spirits. What if they could do something for the village, do some good?

'This place is famous for its salmon. You've seen it, tasted it. We want to sell more of it. Breed it here and sell from here. The potential for it is huge. Imagine if everyone could buy salmon from this village, these waters, at reasonable prices.'

'Okay,' I say slowly. 'So you want to create a salmon farm in the village?'

'Yes. Ever since my partner holidayed here with friends, fishing, he thought this place would be perfect. And so did the other shareholders. You're a chef. You've tasted it.'

'I'm a che— cook,' I correct myself and like it, 'not a

business person. But surely a company moving into the area would bring jobs, more families. It would help the area, wouldn't it?' I'm processing exactly what she's saying.

'Yes!' she says, perking up. 'If we built a salmon farm here, there would be lots more work. The economy and the area would thrive.'

'And if the salmon is anything like the salmon I've tasted here,' immediately the smell and the taste of the smoked salmon come back to me, 'it's sure to be a winner.'

She nods. 'If only we could make all the residents of the area see that. One in particular, Pétur.'

I frown. 'I know it's good to have local support, but why do you need his agreement? Does Pétur own this land too?'

'The land belongs to the community. This is the problem. The harbour. They all have to agree on how it's used. Without it, we can't get access to what would be the salmon farm.'

'Ah, and Pétur is a keen opponent.'

'Others can see the sense in it, what it would bring to the community, like Anna. I get the impression she thinks it's a good idea. She has family in the city and would love to see families growing up here again. But Pétur has a lot of sway around here.'

She takes a deep breath, the two of us sitting in our saddles as if we were sharing a car journey and this was

237

all perfectly normal. 'It's complicated. But, like I say, we need that parcel of land to get access from the sea to the road. Without the villagers selling a small piece of land to us, it can't happen. But we need everyone on board. If Pétur thought it was a good idea, the rest of the village might agree to sell us the plot.'

'So why don't I tell him, make him realize how good it would be for the area?'

She shakes her head. 'I'm not sure he'll listen. Pétur clearly likes things as they are. He's made that very clear. We've tried to get him onside, but he refuses to listen or help. In fact, he's making it really hard.'

'So, he needs to see how you could improve the community,' I say, as I start to see how this place would benefit from more people and jobs.

'The company, my partner, offered to improve the roads around here. Make sure there are other routes in and out so this wouldn't happen again.' She juts her chin towards the snowy silent road in front of us.

'But Pétur's all for increasing salmon stocks,' I say. It's the one thing that does matter to him. Maybe that's why he's so against the idea. He doesn't want the competition, I think, remembering the fishermen who stay with him every summer. But this place would be wonderful if more people lived here. The school could reopen. Access would improve. 'So, you need to sort something out with Pétur, get him onside, so the village will agree to the access for your salmon farm.

Then you'll have proved your worth to your partner's family.'

She nods.

'And this place gets an injection of life, jobs and families.' I see the sense in it. I take out a piece of liquorice that Pétur gave me and hand the packet to Frankie. She helps herself and passes it back. It's sweet, soft, salty, malty and chewy. I just know this should go into a recipe. Maybe with ice cream.

Frankie's nose is red with cold. She sniffs. We're heading towards the harbour and Knútur's shack.

The horses walk on down the darker path towards the even darker sea. I don't know how Knútur lives here, although he seems to be existing rather than living.

'Could you talk to him maybe? Pétur? It seems like you two are pretty close.'

'Oh, no, we're just . . .' My cheeks burn. 'Do we?'

'Oh, yes.' She smiles and my stomach leaps, leaving me half excited, half terrified of how I feel about this man. But while I can see that what Frankie is saying makes sense, clearly Pétur isn't interested in listening to it. Or he's made up his mind. He might be laid-back in most things, but he's clearly quite stubborn when it comes to the village. I can't do it, I think. I can't risk spoiling the friendship we've developed in this short space of time.

'It is an amazing place,' says Frankie. It's as if she's seeing it for the first time with very different eyes.

'Yes, it is,' I say. I'm slowly falling in love with it and it will always have a special place in my heart, but what if it becomes another ghost town? If they don't have the salmon, they don't have anything here. The buildings will slowly be abandoned, as in so many other remote villages. I want to help protect this place, keep it as it is, alive, with a community at its heart.

But Pétur's clearly made his decision about what's right for the community. He must have his reasons. It's not my place to try to change his mind. I have to trust that what he's doing is the right thing.

'I'm just here to help with the cooking until we can leave,' I say firmly. 'Sorry, I can't help.'

24

The horses pick their way down to the shore, where the snow is less, but mixes with the black sand and snakes viciously around in the biting wind. I say biting, it's stinging and slapping too. It's so cold it feels like shards of glass on my face.

I take my feet out of the stirrups, turning my ankles to get them moving before I dismount, my toes and feet practically screaming with pain as they hit the ground. I take a moment and breathe in the cold air, which seems to hurt my lungs too, as if the shards are filling them.

There's no sign of Knútur.

I pull the reins over Carrie's head and tie her to the single standing stone, just like I did with Pétur. Even his name seems to create ripples within me. I look out at the dark, dark sea, the waves crashing on the shore, and remember the lows that come after the highs. The highs of sharing time with people you love and the lows when they're gone.

I think about how I'll feel when I'm back home and this is just a memory. It's why I can't fall for Pétur. I've loved people and lost them, and it's broken my heart: Mum, Laura and then Mark. But with Mark I managed to fall out of love. I've done it before so I can do it again now. I can't let myself fall for Pétur like that. I'll be gone from here and I don't want to leave with my heart in two. Besides, he has family, a daughter. When the snow thaws there are other people in his life to consider.

I have a life, a sorted life, and this is just a blip. Soon this will be forgotten and I'll be back in my comfort zone, doing what I do best, cooking, running a well-organized kitchen and menu. If I still have a job when I get back.

I go to the door and glance over my shoulder at Frankie, who is still frozen in the saddle. 'It's going to hurt. Just do it. Like ripping off a plaster,' I say, and I watch as the pain hits her feet when she lands and her knees buckle beneath her. She rights herself and is soon coming towards me, encouraging her joints to start working again, and loosening up with every step.

'Now, let's find Knútur,' I say. I bang on the wooden door, my teeth chattering.

I hear a shuffle, then a creak, and the door opens a crack.

'Knútur, it's me, Freya,' I say. He doesn't say anything and I wonder if the door is going to shut again. 'Pétur's companion,' I say, wishing the words didn't feel so warming, knowing that it will only be harder to leave here if I'm starting to feel we have something between us.

The door suddenly creaks all the way back. 'Pétur's partner!' he says, his long beard blowing in the wind. He is dressed in layers of tatty woollen clothes. 'Come in!' he says. I nod to Frankie to follow me as I duck my head and step into the shack. She shuts the door behind us, looking around, agog.

'Knútur,' I say, realizing how different it is in here from the last time I visited. 'It's freezing.' It's even colder than it was last time. He coughs, a chesty cough, and waves a mittened hand.

'The wood, driftwood, it's not easy to find when everything is covered with snow,' he says, reaching for his chair by the dead fire. Everything in here feels dire and depressed.

'I'm going to find you some,' I say. He can't stay here with nothing.

'I'll come,' says Frankie.

'No, you keep Knútur company,' I say, worried about his coughing.

He coughs and splutters. 'You won't find much,' he says, catching his breath. 'You know the joke? What do you do if you are lost in a forest in Iceland?' I admire

243

his ability to joke right now. 'Stand up!' He gives a mighty laugh that sets him off coughing again. 'You see? Because we have no forests! This island used all the trees so there are none. The new forests are very young, with small trees, so if you are lost in a forest, stand up! Because it won't be a tall one!'

I laugh with him. 'Stay here. Frankie has soup and bread for you. And an Icelandic tortilla,' I say. 'I made it specially. I'll go and find some wood. Oh, and Pétur sent this,' I say, pulling out a small bottle of firewater.

'He is a good man.' He takes it and holds it in both hands.

I step outside again, and I'm not sure there is any difference in temperature, except maybe the vicious wind, driving itself into my bones. I have no idea how Knútur lives like this.

I head towards the water's edge where the snow peters out. I run my toe through the wet black sand there. As black as the water. I look across the small bay and see birds huddled together for warmth on the jagged rocks on the cliffs opposite.

I look down and start my search, kicking at mounds to shake off the snow. Sometimes it's just rocks and stones, but I uncover some wood. Eventually I find what I'm looking for. A big piece of driftwood, poking up from the black sand. A fallen branch, carried here from the mountains, down the river and ending up on the beach. I look at its beautiful outline and think of how I could make something look like it on a plate. A driftwood sculpture almost, in black sand with a snowy backdrop. There's something unworldly about this place. Something that could make me think that the talk of the hidden people, the elves, might almost be true. It has a magical feel. It's a world where humans live with nature; they don't try to work against it.

I pull at the branch. It doesn't want to move.

'It's for a man who needs heat,' I find myself calling to the wind, and give another tug. This time it frees itself and I tumble backwards. The big dried-out branch comes with me.

I push open the door of Knútur's home with the branch and get to work snapping and sawing it with the small blade he has. I breathe a sigh of relief when the flames in the fireplace start to build and give out a little warmth.

'Are you sure you have everything you need, Knútur?' I stand away from the fire.

'I do.' He's pouring a good drop of firewater into his tin mug. The blaze is now throwing up orange flames, like the ones from the volcano across the water. The shack seems altogether cosier.

'Go easy on that stuff and make sure you eat,' I tell him, with friendly concern.

He gives me a gappy smile.

'*Takk, takk*. Thank you very much,' he says. 'You are kind, just like Pétur and the others around here.'

Frankie is still clearly wondering how someone lives like this.

We say goodbye, as Knútur looks like he's about to tuck into his soup and bread, a smile on his face. 'Just like my mother would cook,' he says, dipping the bread into the hot soup, letting it drip back into the bowl before he bites it.

And I leave feeling as warm inside as he looked.

On the way back to the farm, I check on the women in the safe house. They open the door wide and welcome me. I introduce Frankie and explain she's here with me. They welcome her just as warmly, their previous wariness gone. They are all in the kitchen, making more flapjacks.

'You'll be ready for Christmas now.' I smile and they laugh.

'You want some soup?' they ask, and I notice how much more comfortable they are with each other.

'You made soup?' I query.

'Yes. With the preserves in the cupboard, the lentils.'

'Of course! And I'd love some.' I turn to Frankie, who nods, clearly in need of warming up.

We help lay the table. I light more candles that I've found in one of the kitchen cupboards and put them on the table and in the windows. This place is cosy, despite the otherworldly feeling outside. I think about the geysers, the waterfall and the hot spring. Most of all I think about the shack by the little harbour, the feeling of being at the end of the earth. As if I went any further I'd drop off the edge. Right here and now, though, I feel really safe.

There is laughter and talk around the long pine table, and eating.

I tear off a hunk of bread I've brought from the schoolhouse and wipe it around my bowl, soaking up the last of the soup clinging to the sides. I'm smiling at the patterns it makes, as if I was the younger version of myself: I loved the tinned tomato soup my mum would put in front of me for tea, the Spam fritters, the Findus pancakes, singed at the edges . . . maybe burnt on the bottom. She wasn't a cook, my mum.

'This is fantastic!' I say.

'You suggested it the other day when you looked through the cupboards,' says Hildur.

'A hug in a bowl,' I say.

'Is this the sort of thing you would cook for your friend when she was ill?' she asks.

I find it feels good to talk about Laura, and I'm happy that Hildur has remembered her. 'I used to cook my own recipes. I'd stay after work creating ideas for Laura, then taking them to her late at night when I'd finished. Or sometimes first thing in the morning before work. I loved it. It was all I ever thought about, the tastes and memories I could put on the plate. I would tell my partner what I was thinking of making. Pillow talk for a couple of chefs.'

'Did you marry?' asks María.

I give a hollow laugh. 'No. We didn't.' I plan to stop there, but as the candles on the table flicker, the day outside darkening, I find myself continuing. 'Mark and I would cook together and there was a healthy rivalry between us. I would stay late after work and so would he. He would try my recipes when I'd cooked them . . .'

'Sounds like a plan, a chef as a partner,' says Margrét.

I shrug. 'We would vie for Chef's attention. We thrived on it. The thrill of being noticed by Chef or a customer. But when Laura was ill I stepped back. I wanted to spend as much time as I could with her. Not in the kitchen. Well, not that one. I cooked for her as much as I could. It was what I felt I could do,' I say, trying to find a place to stop.

No one says anything. I realize I can either say nothing or say something. I take a deep breath.

'When I got back to the kitchen Mark had filled the space I'd left. He'd been promoted and poached by an even better-known restaurant. He was now rubbing shoulders with top chefs. And I wasn't on his radar. I wanted to prove I could catch him up. I worked as hard as I could but he'd left me way behind, professionally and emotionally. He'd moved on, and I don't think I've stopped trying to catch up.'

Angry tears jump into my eyes. Tears I haven't felt before. I was so busy being angry, angry with him, angry with Laura for dying, that I just ploughed forward, determined to 'live my best life'. Maybe, I think, with a jolt, I've been living someone else's best life. Not mine. I've been living Wilfrid my boss's best life, riding under his coat tails . . . 'For too long,' I hear myself say.

'Sometimes you have to take time to realize how far you've come,' says Hildur. 'We are very different women from the ones who first arrived here.'

'When I lost my business, I lost everything. I had failed. I couldn't see a way out,' says María.

'When my husband got angry, I stopped fighting back and just hoped it would pass soon,' says Margrét.

'I drank way too much,' says Hildur.

'But something must have changed for you to get out and help yourselves,' I say.

'When you reach rock bottom, when you think this is where life has taken you, it's hard to start clawing your way out,' Hildur says. 'But one day something clicks and you take a tiny step in the right direction.'

'You just have to start and get on with it,' says María.

'Sometimes it's hard not to feel stuck,' Frankie says, and we turn to her.

'Sorry, I shouldn't have said anything.' She lowers her head.

No one else speaks.

The soft golden candlelight seems to be pulling us

closer, and she carries on, as if she's feeling safe in the space.

'My partner died. I thought we had years ahead of us. I took over his share of the company and threw myself into it. I was determined to finish what he'd started.'

We nod.

'I had dreams, once,' says María.

'I still do,' says Hildur. 'Of my own home, where I feel safe like I do here. My own money.'

'I'm dreaming of that too.' I have no idea where the thought came from.

'You still have a dream?' asks Hildur, gently.

I run my finger across the last traces of the soup at the bottom of the bowl and lick it. Right there, I think. At the bottom of an empty bowl. A bowl of food that puts smiles on people's faces.

'I'm dreaming of that *skyr* cake we made earlier,' says Margrét, and we stand to clear away the plates.

That soup is a dish I will never forget. Sitting here, with these women, realizing that life is precious. Sometimes you need to stand still to see how far you've come, or if you've got stuck. I look at Frankie. Is that me? Did I get stuck too? Too determined not to look back, I kept moving forward and forgot what I had, all the good bits.

Eventually we step out into the dark night. We switch on our head torches and make for the horses. I pat

Carrie's neck, tell her we'll be home soon and promise her extra hay and feed.

We wave goodbye to the women at the door and set off towards the farmhouse, following the stone piles that now feel familiar, the frozen troll and the elves' church. I wonder if they brought me here for a reason. To take a look at how far I'd come, but maybe to give me a shove too.

'This place is full of amazing people,' says Frankie, as we leave the safe house.

'It is,' I say, thinking of everyone I've met through this wild adventure – the women in the safe house, Knútur, Anna and, of course, Pétur.

'That's the thing . . . What will happen to them all if this town can't survive? They need to see what my company could do, how we could help them not just to survive but thrive. Bring back a real community, jobs, for families,' she says. 'Open the school, improve the infrastructure.'

We turn into the farmyard and let the horses guide us to the barn, where the sheep gently baa. We're home and they know it.

Everything Frankie's saying seems to make complete sense.

'Hey! Okay?' Pétur's voice makes me jump, and my stomach flips, like the lava from the volcano, hot and explosive.

Frankie catches my eye. I close my eyes with a small

251

nod. I understand what she's saying. It's the least I can do to try to help this small community.

'I'll try,' I tell her. I'll try to talk to Pétur. Perhaps I'll feel I'm doing something to help the community and thank them for looking after us.

25

Christmas Eve

Kristen is shaking his head.

'She still can't move and is very cross about it!' He shakes his head some more. 'I think she may actually be Gryla, the Yule Lads' mother. I took her breakfast before I came here and she was furious. She told me she was fine and then she tried to get out of bed and discovered she couldn't. Honestly, she's just like an ogress!'

Pétur is smiling fondly at the thought of the village matriarch, clearly unhappy to be bed-bound.

'But it's Christmas Eve. Avalanche or not. And she wants everyone to have a meal to share at home. It is the start of Christmas.' Kristen is suddenly serious. 'People put up a tree if they have one and, come evening, families enjoy a meal together and there will be singing, presents too, new clothing and a book. And, of course, sweet things. It's important we start Christmas with a good meal.'

'Can you help?' Pétur turns to me. 'Can you cook something for us to take out?'

'Well . . . what have we got?' I look around the kitchen in search of ingredients, with fire in my belly that I haven't felt for a long time. Like a gas hob that's been dormant, it has now been ignited and is burning clear and bright.

I think of the women in the safe house, the memories the food brought back, the good ones. I thought I was helping them but, actually, they were helping me back to the old Freya who loved to create, starting from scratch with simple ingredients and putting something lovely on the table. Like magic. The ideas are tumbling in, filling me with excitement and passion.

'You just need to work with what we've got,' says Pétur, and I stop to look at him. It's like he can see my mind whirring and working overtime.

'Remember, it's about the memories,' I hear Laura's voice. 'Just do what you do!'

I smile.

I look at the bottle of firewater.

I remember my first real flavours of Iceland. I think about Pétur's kitchen, the rows of preserves and pickles in their jars. I think about the safe house, the jars of flour and beans, the buried bread, the gloriously soft smoked salmon and the *skyr*, tart yet creamy.

'Can I help? Can I get you anything?' says Pétur.

'There is something,' I say. 'Could you bring me some of the smoked salmon?'

'It's done,' he says, and leaves to go back to the farmhouse.

Very soon I'm cooking, working it out as I go along. Behind me Frankie is helping.

'Here are the onions,' she says.

'Great. Can you stir the sauce for me?'

'Where did I put the whisk?'

'Here,' says Meg, clearing up after us.

'Thank you.' As we work, we start to sing, a few little carols that get us into the Christmas spirit. I can't imagine ever singing carols in the kitchen at home, but we should. Everyone is enjoying themselves.

'Okay, done!' I say, and stand back to regard the dishes ready to go out to the families trapped in the snow. Flaking salmon with a splash of firewater, creamy mashed potatoes with a stirring of *skyr* and a sprinkling of smoky cheese over the top. Fish pie made with love, I think, tears prickling once more at the joy of making food I care about for people to enjoy. This is what I'd want to eat on Christmas Eve, snowed in. Chunks of smoked fish, in a creamy sauce with capers, topped with peaks of potatoes, crisp and browned on the top, fluffy just below the surface.

Pétur hugs me. I'm surprised by how my insides spin and melt at the same time. I can't move until he stands back – I mustn't let myself fall for this man.

'My mother used to make just the same,' he says, and breathes in deeply, enjoying the memory for just a little longer. 'Okay, now let's split up and get them delivered. *Takk!* Thank you,' he says to me again. 'It means a lot.'

I remember Laura tasting my food, tears in her eyes, thanking me for the memories I'd made for her.

'Now, will you travel with me?' he asks, his eyes sparkling.

'Sure!' I smile.

'I want to tell everyone who made their dinner today! The award-winning chef!'

'I'm just a trained chef. None of those awards were for my food. This is me!' I say. 'I'd rather be a great cook.' And I feel that shift inside me again. This is me, I repeat in my head, and feel something change. I just don't know if it's for the good. But I think of Laura and know exactly what I want to cook. I want my food to make others happy. Nothing else. I feel like I've stepped out of the darkness into the light. Out of the kitchen and into the outside world again.

We have delivered the fish pies to three houses, all grateful and keen for us to stay and eat with them. We thank them but tell them we have to keep moving.

'Hopefully the storm will have passed soon,' says a grateful resident.

And maybe, when the snow and clouds clear, we'll be able to see the Northern Lights. We've been so busy getting ready for the Christmas celebrations that I haven't thought about them for a while. But it would be amazing to see them, to fulfil Laura's dream, even though it hasn't worked out as we planned.

'Where are we going next?' I ask.

'We can go to the safe house and Knútur. Kristen and the others will go to the farms and check on the sheep.'

We travel a little further in silence, listening to the horses' hoofs on the virgin snow from overnight. There is still snow in the air and I can tell the clouds still have a few more flakes to sprinkle, like the crumbs in the bottom of a bag of crisps. 'You know, this really is a beautiful place,' I say to Pétur, 'just like I told Frankie yesterday.'

He's looking around as the day lightens, now the snow has eased. 'It never leaves you. It's what made me want to craft jewellery. It's this place. I want its beauty to be reflected in what I do.'

'Your work is exquisite,' I tell him, thinking about his workshop, full of ideas, half-finished pieces, drawings on the wall that have been ripped from the notepad he showed me and that he carries everywhere.

'I don't think I would have been a jeweller if it hadn't

been for this place.' He taps his top pocket where I know his little notebook will be. The horses carry on rhythmically through the snow, the little flakes starting to fall harder, erratically, in different directions. The wind has picked up, flicking them into my face.

'You know,' I say, slowly forming my thoughts in my head, 'if more people settled out here it would be wonderful to see the school back in use, the church.'

He nods. 'I agree.'

'So, how come you don't want the salmon farm? The salmon from here is amazing. The farm would bring jobs and families to the town,' I say quickly.

'So, you've heard about the salmon farm?' But before I can explain how, he goes on: 'I understand what you're saying, more people and jobs are exactly what we need. But . . .'

'Why not think about allowing the salmon farm, letting them have access?'

He takes a deep breath. 'First, because this community promised that all the time Knútur wanted to live where he does, he can. The salmon farm needs that piece of land as access to the water. They can't have it because Knútur lives there.'

'But there are other places he could live. Warmer ones!' I think of his cold cabin and am keen to check his fire is still lit. 'Or does it suit you that he lives there?' I say and feel bad for even thinking it.

He gives a gentle laugh. 'Believe me, if Knútur wanted

to live somewhere else, we as a community would make it happen for him. He's happy. He wants to be there.'

'But . . .'

He looks sideways at me. 'You're a chef,' he says. 'You should know the difference between a farmed salmon and a wild one.'

'Yes, but there is a place for both in the food chain, surely. An all-year-round supply of salmon?'

'Sadly, you cannot have your cake and eat it, so to speak.'

'Why not?'

'The farmed salmon often escape from their enclosures and carry a virus that kills off our wild salmon. The numbers across the world are falling as it is. Here, we still have the salmon returning every year to spawn. We're the lucky ones. We have to look after the fish we have. Live sustainably. Catch and eat what we do. Find a way to get even more wild salmon to make their home here. Preserve what we catch and what we have.'

'So what you're saying is, if the salmon farm were to set up here, the wild salmon would die out.'

'Exactly,' he says. I bite my lower lip and look ahead, scales falling from my eyes like light snow. 'I am hoping there is another way.'

I can see why the jobs would make sense to save the village, but not at the expense of the wild salmon that return here. That can't happen! What was I thinking?

That isn't helping the community and the village: it will kill it.

My heart starts to race. Frankie will have to rethink and talk to the board of her company. If they go ahead with their plans it could be disastrous for the area. I'll talk to her, I tell myself, as soon as I get back. I just hope she understands the situation before it's too late. This area doesn't need some kind of project to rejuvenate it: it needs to be left as it is.

'You seem very interested in our fishing affairs,' he says idly, but with a hint of questioning.

I wish I could think of a way for the two to work side by side. But maybe some things, I think, snatching a glance at Pétur, my stomach leaping like a salmon from the water, just aren't meant to be. And it's not just the salmon farm and the wild salmon living side by side that I'm thinking about.

There is a sudden flurry of snow. Just when I thought Mother Nature might be done with us.

'Are you saying there's no way for salmon farming and wild salmon to live side by side? Think of all the good it would do for the area.'

'If only it were that simple! But it isn't. We need to make sure our waters stay as clean as they can be. For all our sakes. All the time the salmon keep coming home, our habitat is living in harmony. If the salmon start to decline, it affects all our wildlife. We and

Mother Nature will no longer be living harmoniously. Nothing must happen to upset that balance.' He stares at me and it's like he's looking into my soul. But I still can't help wishing more people could eat the salmon from here, the taste of the clean water they've grown up in, the fresh air and snow-capped mountains. I'm imprinting many of the scents, sounds and landscapes into my brain and my memory box, because if what Pétur says is right, there really is no way that the salmon farm can come here.

'You take the pie in – they'd like to meet you,' I tell him, as we arrive at the safe house on our way back to the farm. 'I'll go and check on Knútur.' I nod towards Hildur, who is standing by the door, waving. I wave back and point to Pétur to explain he's coming in.

'Knútur's a lucky man to have your affection. Be careful or I will be jealous!' He smiles a wide, beautiful smile, his teeth as white as the landscape around us. His eyes, like the hot spring we bathed in, make me feel as warm and alive as I did then.

'They make amazing flapjacks in the safe house,' I say. 'You won't get to leave without trying some.'

'I shall be delighted!'

I turn Carrie away, smiling over my shoulder.

'And watch out for Kertasníkir, the Candle-stealer. It's his night to visit!' I hear him call after me with a laugh, making me smile, then I give a click, click, and ride away from him, sitting deep into the saddle, trusting in her surefootedness and holding my face to the cold but brightening sky.

As I ride towards the beach, the wind has died down. Usually it picks up as I come down this path between the rocks at either side of it. But today there's a stillness about the place as I arrive on the sand, covered with patches of snow. I jump off Carrie and lead her so I can pick up firewood as I go, stopping every so often, to stuff it into my practically empty saddlebags. Just one pie left, for Knútur.

I pat Carrie every time I stop for bits of wood. I feel a sense of calm. It seems that the storm may actually be passing. And I feel like I've found a part of me that has been missing for years, finally cooking again from my heart instead of with my head. Not matching flavours because they automatically go together, cooking to make people smile. I know the flavours I want to put on the plate, the flavours of this place, like I'm coming home. I know what I don't want to make any more, but I have no idea of what I can do about that.

'Knútur,' I call, as I knock on the door of the hut. 'Knútur!' There's no smoke coming from the chimney. I pat Carrie and tie her reins to the standing stone. There's no smell of smoke, so the fire's been out for some time. I tut. 'Knútur!' I call again, and bang on the door. I stand and wait, stamping my feet in the snowy black sand.

Still there's no reply. I wonder if he's asleep.

I knock again gently and call his name. Nothing.

I look at the big wooden latch and the door. It's open, ajar.

I pull at it, my heart starting to pound, wondering what I'm going to find on the other side.

'Knútur?' I say, my mouth turning dry.

26

'Pétur! Pétur!' I can barely say his name.

'What? You look like someone's died.' He's in the safe house, sitting at the table with the women, drinking tea and eating flapjacks. In any other circumstances, I would have loved to see him joking and holding court. But not now.

'It's Knútur!' I say, out of breath, my lungs stinging as they drag in cold air. My chest is tight, panic rising.

'Freya! What is it?' He stands and holds my arms.

The women all look at me. I take a huge breath.

'It's Knútur. He's gone.'

27

'I've looked everywhere. There's no sign of him.' My lungs burn as I try to drag in the warm air, bending, my hands on my knees to help me regain my breath. Focus, I tell myself and slowly straighten. 'The food from yesterday is still there, half eaten, the spoon in the soup. The fire is dead, and I lit it before I left yesterday. He's gone and, by the look of it, he's been gone some time.'

I'm suddenly frightened. My eyes sting as I watch Pétur's face turn from listening to concerned.

'Okay, take it easy. Maybe he's just gone to look for firewood or a walk.' I know he's not convincing himself – or me.

He grabs his coat off the back of the chair and pulls it on, then his waterproof trousers and his snow-boots.

'Tell me again. When did you last see him?'

'Yesterday, when I went with Frankie.'

'The woman from the salmon farm.'

'You knew?'

'I'm not stupid. I thought she might have learnt a thing or two while she was here. Just don't tell me you left her alone with him.'

He sighs.

I can't reply.

His eyes tell me everything I need to know. 'Come on, we have to find him,' he says, and it's what he doesn't say that worries me more.

'Where is he? And why has he gone?' I say, my throat tight.

'What has Frankie got to do with him disappearing?' asks Hildur.

'Her company are the salmon-farm people,' says Pétur. 'They want to buy that patch of land where Knútur's hut is to build their farm. She's obviously spoken to Knútur of her plans and how she thinks it will help the community. He will feel like a burden.'

And I'm suddenly even more terrified. 'What will he do? Where will he go?'

'I'm not sure, but Knútur doesn't want to feel a burden. He is a fragile man. Damaged in many ways. But he has been able to live life quietly where he is. This was the one place he felt he could live in peace. But now he clearly thinks he's not welcome here,' says Pétur, angrily.

'We have to find him,' I say, even more panicked than before.

'I'll help!' Hildur says. I don't know what to be more surprised about. The awfulness of Knútur missing, that it may have something to do with the salmon farm, or that Hildur is joining us to look for him. These women haven't been out of the house since they arrived.

'And me,' say the others, and I suddenly feel so proud. These women, who have stayed behind closed doors since they got here, safe from the outside world, are now offering to help find someone else in need, someone who was once as fragile and broken as they were. I have no idea if the tears in my eyes are for Knútur, the women's bravery or what I may have done to this community by interfering where it wasn't my business.

'Don't worry, we'll find him,' says Pétur, as we leave the house.

'Where do we start?'

'We'll get the villagers to come out and search,' he says seriously. 'We have to head back to the school-house and the church. We'll gather there and split up. I'll take out the boat and check the shoreline.'

'A boat? We could take a boat out of here?' I say.

'As long as we don't go very far or meet any icebergs,' he says, and I understand how dangerous this could be. 'I wouldn't be thinking of it if it wasn't an emergency. Let's get to the boat. We can check along the shoreline for just a kilometre or so, to see if he has gone for a walk or is lost in the storm.'

'And if not?'

'If not, we'll go to the church and ring the bell. Call out the community.'

The bell is rung only in very special circumstances.

'Ready?' shouts Pétur, over the engine noise of the boat as it rumbles into life. Pétur's collie, Jón, takes up his post in the wheelhouse towards the stern.

I nod, shivering, as I stand on the little wooden jetty near Knútur's hut.

'Unhook the rope and throw the front one into the boat, then go to the stern, throw in the rope and jump on board,' he instructs. The other three women are on the shore, waiting to see us off. They look as nervous as I feel. My hands are shaking and I have no idea if it's the bone-freezing cold or fear of messing this up.

'Okay, ready when you are!' he shouts, giving me the thumbs-up. I go to unhook the rope from the metal post on the jetty. It catches and I try again. Still it catches on the post. I take a deep breath, and imagine I'm back in the kitchen, focusing on the job in hand. This time I slip it off its mooring post and toss it onto the deck in an ungainly but effective way. As the nose of the boat starts to swing out, I slip and slide, in an attempt to run to the rear. The water under the jetty is dark, so very, very dark. Black. I can't see a thing down there. Just a whole load of the unknown. Terrifying. I grab the rope with my still shaking hands and attempt to unhook it from the post holding the boat, now drifting nose out. My hands are shaking, teeth chattering. The wind has picked up, tormenting me. The boat is swinging round and I know Pétur is willing me to release it.

'Come on, Freya!' I hear Hildur from the shore and, with one almighty pull, bring the rope over the post and throw it onto the deck.

'Jump!' he shouts.

'Jump, jump!' the others yell from the shore.

Suddenly a wave of what-ifs washes over me. What if I fall? What if— It's dark down there. And I feel a huge lurch of fear in my stomach.

'Jump!' I hear Pétur's voice. There's no joking this time and the fear seems to wash away. I jump and land on the deck, once again in an ungainly way, but I'm on board.

'Is this safe?' I ask. 'I mean, how come you didn't suggest we leave here by boat?'

'Like I say, it's only something we'd do in an emergency.'

'Like now?'

He nods. 'We have to keep an eye open for icebergs. We'll go very slowly,' he says.

I catch his eye as he starts to steer the boat from its mooring at the jetty and as I gaze out to sea, I can't help looking back at him. When I do, he's looking from the sea and catching occasional glimpses at me. My heart is thundering with fear. But I trust Pétur. If I'm safe with anyone, it's him. Oh, God, this can't be happening. I can't be falling for him. I'm leaving here as soon as the snow clears. There's no way I can still be here for the midwinter festival. I have a restaurant to get back to, a life. If it's still there. This is just . . . I have no idea what it is, a sliding-doors moment, when we got stuck for a while, but know we have to go back. People will be worried, Meg's family, my boss . . . And it hits me like a kick in the guts. That's it. My boss, wondering why I'm not back at work. I love my job, the life I've made for myself. But, actually, does any of it belong to me? My flat comes with the job. And those words: did you never want your own name above the door? When did I settle for making someone else's name? I know when . . .

The boat moves forward swiftly in the dark water and Pétur gives me an approving and reassuring nod as he guides the boat away from the jetty. Opposite there are huge cliffs, towering over us. I cling to the side of the boat as I go to join Pétur in the wheelhouse.

'If he's on the shore anywhere, we'll spot him,' says Pétur, scanning around him. The others are going to look around the area on foot. But, right now, Knútur's nowhere to be seen and I wonder how far he could have got.

I turn to look behind us and see the women splitting up to start their search.

'We'll find him,' says Pétur, and I only hope he's right. 'If he's here, we'll find him,' he adds, and I wonder what he means.

'What are those?' Huge white birds are following in our wake.

'Gannets,' he says. 'Hoping to find fish.' He steers the boat, looking this way and that, waiting to catch sight of Knútur. 'And over there,' says Pétur, jerking a thumb at the dark sea, the little birds bobbing there, 'are the puffins.'

Some are standing on a rocky outcrop, with their brightly coloured bills and orange, clown-like feet, as we sway, tip and dip along the shoreline, moving out of the bay into more open waters. If I wasn't so worried about Knútur, I'd be captivated. I feel like I'm in a whole other world. 'They stay out at sea for the winter, but come the spring they will nest on the rocks and bring up their young. It's unusual to see them at this time of year,' he says. And I know I'm seeing something quite incredible. The gannets behind us pull in their wings every now and again and dive like bomber planes into the dark depths. The puffins, despite the cold, seem to be smiling.

My hope for Knútur starts to waver as we move further along the coast.

I look at Pétur, wondering what on earth we're going

to do. He shakes his head sagely. Just then something catches my eye. Something in the water. My heart lurches and my stomach leaps up to meet it. I look again. Nothing. I go to the edge of the boat and cling to the railing. I see a movement. I squint into the dark water.

'There's something here!' I shout. Then there's a splash. Pétur spots it and I move as quickly as I can on the lurching boat to the other side and cling to the railing there. The wind is more vicious on this side.

'What is it?' I say. What if it's Knútur? I don't say it but I know we're both thinking it.

There is silence. Nothing. I hold my breath. Pétur cuts the engine and the silence is deafening. The boat swings from one side to the other, my stomach with it. Pétur comes to stand beside me and I can feel his body next to mine, close and comforting.

Suddenly there is a shot of water from the dark depths, like a fountain of freezing salty sea water, spraying us. I let out a shout of surprise and then, even more surprisingly, laughter.

'Ah, I think we have a visitor,' says Pétur, his face relaxing a little. 'Not what we thought it might be.'

'What is it?' I'm worried all over again, the icy cold water droplets falling off my hat.

'Watch!' He leans into me and points. I can smell the salty sea water on him, the cold snowy air and something else, something that is just Pétur. The smell of his home. A smell I won't forget. I follow where he's pointing with his thick black glove and something large and black appears just under the surface of the water and disappears again, like a submarine, barely surfacing. I don't move, and hang on to Pétur's arm in shivering anticipation. There it is again, this time just surfacing and bending to dive again. I watch, and when I think it's gone, a big wide tail flips out of the water.

'A whale!' I exclaim. I'm not sure whether I'm thrilled to see it in the wild or absolutely terrified.

Pétur nods. 'A humpback.'

We fall into silence again. Another blow hole full of water goes up and the body rises, then curves up and over into the water, the tail apparently waving to us as it dips under the water.

'It's gone under the boat,' says Pétur.

And this time my stomach knots and I'm scared. An animal that size only has to flick a fin to turn the boat over. Suddenly the dark depths seem even more terrifying. Who knows what else is down there?

'He has a friend!' says Pétur, pointing. A second tail flicks up from the water. I feel totally helpless, yet privileged to see this. I'm incredibly small and vulnerable, yet entranced. My eyes are flicking between the sprays and the shore in case I spot Knútur. The two whales seem to be swimming under the boat again, and this time I can see their dark shadows as they duck under, turn and reappear on the other side of the boat. My heart is thundering. 'They're playing,' Pétur assures me. I watch in wonder as the whales rise up, double back on themselves, then dive long and slow under the boat, twisting and crossing and reappearing elsewhere until, finally, their bodies break the surface and their tail flips are further away from the boat. Having stayed and played for a while, they move off. I watch them go, and find myself raising a hand to them. It was just a moment when our lives crossed, thrilling and terrifying, and I can't help but look at Pétur, knowing my time here will soon be over.

I look back at the shoreline. Still no sign of Knútur.

Without words Pétur restarts the engine and heads back to the jetty. I'm watching the ripples in the dark water for a sign of the whales returning, but they don't. I just wish Knútur would. As we moor up, I clamber off the boat and towards his hut, hoping he's come home while we've been out looking for him.

'Knútur!' I call, but I know, as I push open the door, he's still not there. A chill creeps over me.

28

'Where have you been?'

Meg, Joanna and Frankie jump up when they see me. 'We've been worried sick – you've been gone for ages!'

'I was with Pétur and Hildur and—'

'Our phones were working! We had to find some sheep that had got out of one of the barns, on a high-up mountain.'

'I've messaged Tom!' Meg beams.

'I've messaged the office,' says Frankie.

'I've . . .' Joanna shrugs. 'I checked on the caterers for Christmas. I'm guessing as long as Tony and his kids have Christmas organized, no one will notice I'm not there.' She exchanges a look with Kristen, who gives her a warm smile.

'It's Knútur! He's gone missing,' I say quickly.

'Missing?' they all say.

I nod. 'He's gone. We have to find him! Everyone needs to meet at the schoolhouse and we'll go out in pairs, a search party.'

'But why? I thought you said he was happy where he was,' says Meg.

Joanna starts pulling on her boots.

'Pétur thinks he may have been . . .' I look at Frankie, '. . . persuaded to leave.' I can't decide if I'm furious with her or myself for thinking she knew how important it was to the village for him not to leave.

'What?' She looks horrified. 'Not like this! I told him we'd build him a new house, whatever he wanted, wherever he wanted.'

'He was where he wanted to be! He had everything he wanted! His memories of his son!' I say angrily. 'Here, he felt he was with him every day. It's all he needs! He was content. But now it looks like he feels he's holding back the village by not stepping aside to let Frankie's company move in on the land. So he has . . .' It catches in my throat. 'So he's left. We don't know where he's gone or what will happen to him. Pétur is worried. His mental health . . . Knútur's fragile.'

I step outside, feeling sick.

I think of the dark waters. Please don't let him have done anything stupid.

The snow has stopped altogether now. I hear a crunch of feet behind me.

Pétur is pulling on a rucksack over his big coat.

'What's happening? Where are you going?'

'To ring the bell at the church.'

Without any more words, I climb back onto Carrie and ride with him. At the schoolhouse, he walks towards the church and goes inside. The sound that follows breaks the silence in the snowy, locked-down world.

Clang, clang, clang, it rings out. Clang, clang, clang. He keeps ringing until Anna appears, leaning heavily on the shoulders of the couple from the neighbouring farmhouse.

'What's happening?' She looks worried, clutching the door frame, pain etched on her face. As Pétur said, that bell is only rung in a real emergency, when they need to get all the villagers to come to the schoolhouse.

'It's Knútur,' I tell her, a big ball in my throat. 'He's gone missing.'

'Oh, no! And in this weather!' Her hand flies to her mouth.

'Why? Where?' she asks, looking at Pétur as he comes out of the church and walks towards us, his face no longer relaxed and an unexpected twitch in his jaw line.

'Moving on by the look of it.'

Across the snow I can see figures appearing, on horseback, on foot with snow poles and snowshoes. The elderly couple who gave us the rhubarb jam, her riding the horse, him leading. When a fair-sized group has gathered, Pétur holds up a hand to quell the concerns and questions on everyone's lips.

'A member of our community has gone missing,' he says. 'As you know we look after each other out here, so I want you all to go home, check your barns and sheds and the local area for Knútur.'

The villagers agree.

'Why has he gone?' asks the woman whose eggs we ate at the hot spring. 'He loves it here.'

Pétur takes a deep breath. 'I think he may have been persuaded. As you all know Knútur wanted never to be a burden on this community and, least of all, to feel he was standing in the way of the community's future fortunes.'

'Wait! This is my fault,' I say, and walk over to stand next to Pétur. There is more murmuring. 'I was told there was a salmon farm interested in setting up in the area. I could see the reasoning behind it. The jobs it would bring, the families who could move here.'

I can see Meg, Joanna and Frankie standing among the villagers. I take a deep breath and carry on: 'But I've seen this place, its beauty, how you all care for each other.'

'Wait!' says Frankie, moving through the crowd and coming to stand beside me. 'I'm Frankie Oliver.' This time she takes the deep breath and begins to speak. 'My partner owns, owned,' she corrects herself, 'Barty and Son Fisheries, the company that wants to build the salmon farm here. I came here to try to find a way of persuading you all to let the salmon farm come.'

I see Pétur look at her sternly.

'I thought I was doing something good. That by offering you a financial settlement, a new home for Knútur, for him to leave the beach hut, that I was doing the right thing for everybody. I thought if I could persuade Freya it was a good idea, she would help me get Pétur and the rest of you onside.'

'How much financial settlement?' pipes up the older man and gets his wife's elbow in his ribs.

'I realize now I was wrong. This is not the right place for the salmon farm. The salmon farm could affect the wild salmon that return here every year. And now I can see why they do!' She attempts a smile. 'And I can see how the farm coming here would destroy what you have. And I'm sorry. But most of all I'm sorry that I made Knútur feel he was a burden. I know none of you feel like that and all support each other. You have a sense of belonging. This is your home. You are very lucky indeed. I thought coming here would help me find my place in the world. Maybe it has. I know it's not to destroy this one. I've been looking down the wrong path and I need to find a new one. Now, let's please find Knútur and bring him home.'

'Já, já!' I hear the villagers say.

I look at Frankie and feel her pain as she wipes away the tears. She never meant this to happen.

'Okay, everyone, split up. Stay in pairs or more, and if you find him, ring the bell to let us all know,' says Pétur. People start to talk among themselves, pair up and make plans for the area they can cover near their homes.

Anna comes over with the help of her neighbour and takes Frankie's hands. 'Sometimes we have to take a wrong path to find the right one,' she says to her. 'Come on now, you stick with me. I need help,' she says, leaning on her shoulder.

'What about Pétur? He looks so angry,' Frankie says.

'Freya, you go with Pétur. If anyone can put a smile on his face, it seems to be you,' Anna says.

I don't question it.

'I'm coming with you,' I tell him, still feeling bad that I had my own part to play in this drama.

He mounts his horse, ready and raring to go. It dances to and fro as Pétur checks his girth. 'You stay here with the others and help to get the schoolhouse decorated for the Christmas feast.'

I frown and feel suddenly worried. 'Look, this is my fault. I should have realized the salmon farm was a bad idea.'

'I told you why it was bad for the area. I told you,' Pétur repeats. 'I thought you agreed, that you understood.'

'I know, but this was before I . . . before I realized what would happen to the salmon.'

'But this is why Knútur has left,' Pétur says angrily. 'He thinks he's standing in the way of "progress" for the village. He will feel he is a burden.'

Tears are rolling down Frankie's cheeks. 'Yes, I made him an offer. It was before I understood why it was all so wrong for here. I thought by offering him a new home, us buying the land, the community would thrive.'

'And the wild salmon will die!' says Pétur, angrily. He glares at me. 'I thought I could trust you! I thought you understood. I thought you all did,' he hisses. 'We could have lost a member of our village, all because of greed and people who think they know best.'

I try to speak, but tears catch in my throat. And then, without asking him, I tell him, 'I'm coming to help find Knútur.'

He opens his mouth to object.

'I'm coming. This is down to me. I need to put it right.'

His flash of anger seems to pass and he nods. 'Okay. But it may be difficult.'

'Where are we going?'

He looks at me, steadily. 'To see if he's attempted to walk over the mountain to get back to town.'

'I thought you said there was only one way out of this place!' This time it's my turn to show a flash of anger. I'm furious that I've been stuck here, furious at all the memories it's dragged up, furious that I've had my head in the sand, ignoring the pain of Laura dying, and furious at the years I feel have been stolen from me when I buried myself in someone else's kitchen, earning them Michelin stars. And I'm furious at having been instrumental in Knútur leaving.

Knútur had it right. He was happy with his memories, holding on to them, not trying to forget, like I've been doing.

I look at Pétur angrily. 'You said there was only one way out of this place and it was closed because of the avalanche.' A sense of betrayal and mistrust overtakes me, just as it did when Mark stepped into my shoes and rose up the ranks, leaving me behind.

'There is only one route out,' Pétur replies. 'Only one that's safe.'

We stare at each other, both aware of what's at stake.

'No one's made it over the old route in years. It's treacherous. You should stay here.'

'In that case,' I say, not missing a beat, 'I'm coming with you.' My heart is pounding so loudly that I can't hear if he argues.

'I'm coming,' I repeat. 'This is down to me and I'm coming to help find Knútur, whatever we might find.'

29

'You don't need to do this,' he says again, securing the saddlebag Anna has handed him to his horse, patting him and checking the girth once more. Kristen is adding another saddlebag to the other side.

'I do,' I say. 'I need to make sure nothing has happened to him.' My anger has been replaced with a sickening fear of where Knútur might be and whether or not he's safe.

'What should we do?' says Frankie, standing next to Meg, Hildur and the other women.

I look at Pétur. He can think only about Knútur and the journey right now.

'Check around the safe house, and my farm, then wait there for any news. They'll ring the bell,' Pétur says.

'We can't just wait!' says Meg.

'Then help Anna,' I say. She's rubbing her back. 'Get ready for Christmas. It's tomorrow. Cook. Everything we talked about in the kitchen, Hildur. Meals from your growing-up, the good times!' I try to smile. 'Make the Christmas cake!'

'Stay safe!' she says.

'And, Frankie,' I go on, 'lots of smoked salmon. With *skyr* and dill as a dip.'

'And *hangikjöt*, smoked lamb!' Pétur joins in. 'You'll find all you need in the storeroom at the farm.'

'With rhubarb jam,' I say.

'Make sure there's enough for everybody!' Pétur says firmly, an instruction more than a request.

'You can do this, Hildur,' I tell her, 'you and the others.'

She takes my hand. I know she's telling me she will, and at the same time thanking me. 'I'll be back to help soon.' I clamber back onto Carrie and thank her once again for looking after me. I ask her to do it this time for Knútur as I lean up her neck and rub her ears.

My hands are shaking. We have to find Knútur before something happens to him ... .

'Ready?' Pétur looks at me and Carrie. My heart is racing. I might be scared but this is something I have to do.

He nods to the gathered group who quietly wish us well and tell us to come home safe. Pétur raises his hand to them and we set off. It's no longer snowing and the wind has dropped as we set off across the snow into the unknown. Suddenly I feel like doing something that matters, not just existing, hiding in my kitchen. I'm taking a risk, because I care about what happens here. I care about these people. It's not like putting up someone else's plates of food with precision, day after day, thinking it's important. Compared to this, it really isn't. Who knows what will happen here today? At least I'm alive, and I just hope Knútur is too.

We ride silently, mostly uphill, and the path gets narrower and narrower. Every now and again, one of the horses slips in the snow, or stumbles, and each time I catch my breath, praying we'll find him and bring all of us home safely.

'You okay?' asks Pétur, turning every now and again to check on me. 'Don't be scared. Let the horse lead the way. Trust her.' Out here there are no piles of stones to let us know we're on the right route. 'There's a plateau and we'll stop for a break.'

I can't believe that if Knútur has come this way he's got so far. This is a steep climb.

'Lean forward. Try to lift your weight off the horse's back,' he says, standing slightly in the stirrups, letting the horse's legs work beneath him. I do the same, once again patting Carrie and thanking her for her help.

We reach the plateau, where Pétur pulls up his horse and waits for me. The wind has picked up here, wailing around us, and I'm fighting to hear him. When I turn I can see the village we've left at the bottom of the hill. I can see the beach where Knútur's hut is and the sea beyond the fjord, where the whales swam under the boat and the gannets dived. I can see the river, and the huge waterfall as it thunders towards the sea. I take a deep breath. Pétur jumps off his horse and brings me a water bottle. I drink, big glugs, slowing my breathing and refreshing me.

'Are you okay to go on for a bit?' he asks, smoothing Carrie's neck, checking on her as much as he is me, running his hands over her legs checking for any cuts or swelling. He pats her again, happy with her.

'Stretch your legs for a bit,' he says, taking hold of Carrie's reins.

I circle my feet before I dismount, but they still hurt when I do, though not as much as if I didn't. I blow into my gloved hands. 'How much further?' I ask.

'There's another beach just over this mountain,' he says, not answering the question.

So there's still a long way to go. I look around. It's starting to get darker. I have no idea what will happen when we lose the light.

Suddenly there is a crack, a rumble and another *whoosh*.

I turn this way and that to see where the noise is coming from, too scared to scream – no one would hear me if I did.

'Quick! Here!' Pétur shouts. The wind is suddenly whipping up even more around us now.

He grabs my hand, hurrying me and Carrie forward. The horses throw back their heads, spooked. 'Sssh, sssh!' he reassures them.

'What's going on?' I'm scared, really scared. I hold his hand tightly.

If he does reply, I don't hear him over the noise. The placid horses are now tossing their heads, their snow-speckled manes flying, nostrils flaring, shifting their hind legs to and fro in the deep snow.

He heads for the rocks and I have no idea why he's taking us into this small corner. I try to pull back. 'Come on! It's safe here,' he says. I have to trust him so I follow. Suddenly I see a small opening in the rock face. He dips his head into the dark hole and I follow, as do the horses.

Inside, we're out of the wind and it's far quieter. The space inside is much bigger than I was expecting, a sanctuary out of the snow and wind.

'What is this place?'

'A lava cave,' he says, peering outside. He's no longer the fun-loving Pétur I have come to know. He looks concerned.

'What's happening?'

'This is when the storm can be at its most danger-ous. Just before she leaves us. The winds are turning. The snow is drifting and falling.'

'Are we stuck here?'

'No, but it would be safer just to sit it out for a while.'

I shiver.

He goes to his horse and removes the saddle, then does the same with Carrie.

Then he carries over a sleeping-bag, unrolls it and puts it around my shoulders. All the time, we are watching the falling snow, listening to the rumbles and whooshes. 'We're safe here,' he says again.

'A lava cave?' I ask, looking around.

He nods. 'An old volcano,' he says, reaching into the saddlebags.

'What about Knútur?'

'He is used to being outside, living with the elements. He will find shelter. Knútur knows these parts and the weather as well as any of us. He'll stay safe . . . if that's what he wants.'

'What do you mean?'

He takes a deep breath. 'I just mean exactly that. If he wants to stay safe, he will.'

'Oh, my God! No!'

'Look, I'm not saying that's what he's thinking. But all I know is, we can't put our own lives at risk. We have to sit this out for a bit. When it's safe, we'll carry on. No one wants to hear of deaths or injuries,' he says firmly. 'Now we should eat.' He pulls out the packages of food from the schoolhouse kitchen, leftovers from the meals I've cooked there.

'A flask of coffee and one of soup,' he says. 'Bread, cake. We'll be fine. And plenty of water when we get some snow to melt.' He attempts to make me smile again. Pétur, whom I have come to know, to care about, to . . .

'Thank you,' I say.

'For what? Taking you out in a snowstorm and putting your life at risk?'

'For making me stop to think and realize what's important.'

'Out here, you have time to do that. Out here is where you're inspired. You learn to live with nature, take what you need from it and put something back. There is no way I would let this place lose what it's got. The King of Fish lives here and they will always come home! It's the way it should be.'

And suddenly it all makes sense. This place doesn't need a project like the salmon farm. It's doing fine as it is. What it needs is for the salmon to keep coming home, the fishermen, the sheep and people like Pétur to find inspiration here. For life to go on as it always has, with clean waters and fresh air, and for that to be celebrated.

He wraps his arm around me and pulls me in for warmth, tugging the sleeping-bag around and over us. 'It's Christmas Eve,' he says, looking out at the snow being whipped away by the wind. 'What would you be doing at home right now?'

'Me?' I give a small laugh. 'Working.' I wonder how

the Christmas Eve taster menu is being executed tonight. No doubt my place has been filled by one of the many chefs desperate to take over my role. I can see them all, knives out ready to stab each other in the back, anything to get Wilfrid's attention, to knock another out of the running by whatever methods. Working faster, finishing their preparation to 'help' another or even to sabotage a dish, adding more salt, knocking over a sauce. They're all tricks I've seen and experienced as the victim. My response was always to come back working harder, staying later. And for what? To stand at the pass and run the service for somebody else's menu and restaurant.

'And then?' he asks.

'Oh, pfff! Falling into bed exhausted and getting up early to do it all over again.'

'You love what you do, don't you?'

'I do,' I say, 'but I think I may have lost my way. I love to cook. But I stopped cooking for pleasure a long time ago.' I don't want to be someone else's puppet, a cog in a wheel, a big cog, but still a cog. I never wanted to be a chef who thrives on power in the kitchen. I just wanted to put out the best food and see people's faces when they enjoy it. Like Christmas dinner. It's about the togetherness, the sharing, not about foams and micro-greens. I wish I was cooking Christmas dinner now, in the schoolhouse.

'In Iceland,' Pétur's words cut through my thoughts,

'on Christmas Eve, I think I told you we give each other books.'

'It's a lovely idea.' I smile.

'It's tradition so you can curl up, read, eat chocolate, go to bed early and, in the morning, see if the elves have left you gifts.'

'What kind of book would you have?' I ask.

'Probably a new notebook.' He reaches into his pocket. 'Here, I want you to have this,' he says, handing me the one he takes everywhere.

'Pétur, I can't take it!'

'I want you to have it,' he insists.

'But it has all your ideas in it, for your final piece, for the exhibition.'

He smiles. 'I know what I'm doing for my final piece. I have all the inspiration I need. I just had to see what was under my nose. You made me do that. Thank you.'

I take it from him slowly and open it. There are sketches of the farm, the horses, the sheep, the geysers and the waterfall, the river and the salmon, leaping, curling, flying from the water. There are even sketches of elves, snowflakes and then, on the final page, one of . . . me? Just a sketch of my face, but it brings tears to my eyes. It's me as I feel I am. A small smile on my lips. He must have done it after our trip to the hot spring when we cooked.

'Everything that I . . . admire, respect and,' he coughs, 'have come to realize I cannot live without.'

I stare into his eyes, the blue-grey colour of the lagoon, and then, as suddenly as the small avalanche above us continues to rumble and fall, I take his face in my hands, the book falling into my lap and pull his lips towards mine. Together we slide down inside the sleeping-bag, fingers circling and entwining as we grapple to zip it up, our bodies next to each other and our hands exploring, like unwrapping a parcel, layer after layer, until the anticipation becomes too great . . .

'I suggest you leave your hat on, for warmth,' he says. So I do.

30

The wind has settled, as has the snow, and I have never felt more alive. I look at Pétur, his beautiful face next to mine, our limbs entwined in the sleeping-bag, and I want to kiss him all over again, like I did last night as we clung together.

I'm lying in the crook of his arm, staring at his face, his light-coloured eyelashes and the faint freckles on the bridge of his nose, when slowly he opens his eyes, as bright as always. I catch my breath, wondering if he feels the same as me, until he smiles widely and kisses me deeply. There is no need for words.

Eventually we pull away and he says, 'It's Christmas.'

We know it's time to find our clothes and leave the warm cocoon of the sleeping-bag.

'It will be getting light soon. We should push on,' he says.

I know I should move, but I can't. It will be freezing.

'Here,' he reaches for my clothes at the bottom of the sleeping-bag, like he dived for mud in the pool.

My teeth are chattering as the ice-cold air comes in to greet us.

'Oh, they're mine!' he says, retrieving his black boxers from my shaking hands as I try to put them on, anything for warmth.

Finally, I'm dressed. I crawl out of the sleeping-bag and dive into my coat and gloves. My pink bobble hat is still on my head.

'I think that hat will always be my favourite now,' he says, and I want nothing more than to climb back into the sleeping-bag, but we have more important things to think about. I'm feeling bad that for the last few hours Knútur has been the last thing on my mind.

'We should get going,' I say, feeling guilty and blushing.

'There was nothing we could do for him in the dark,' he tells me. And he's right. But now it's starting to get light – we need to get on.

I slip off my pink hat and pull on my riding helmet. The label of my roll-neck jumper brushes against my hand – I have it on inside out and back to front. But I'm not taking it off again now.

We set off on our journey, this time downhill on the other side of the mountain. We travel silently, letting the horses find their way along the snowy, narrow path, one eye on the ground, the other on the sheer drop from the cliff edge beside us. One slip and . . . I can't even think about it. I can look only up, in the direction we're travelling.

If we make it through this, if we get back, I'll be a better person, I think. I'll change my life. Be grateful for what I have. Take time to stand and appreciate the good things. I'll travel more, see Meg and Joanna more, and stop thinking about Mark, how he moved on without a by-your-leave.

I will trust again – just let me get out of here alive. Let us find Knútur and I will trust myself and others again. I look down to the small dark beach below as we climb up and over the mountain.

'There are waves you have to be careful of,' Pétur calls. 'You have to stay back from the shore or the waves will suddenly rise and swallow you,' he says, scanning the shoreline. 'Just follow me, you'll be fine,' and I trust him.

My heart is thundering, and I'm not sure if it's because we're so close to the edge or because of what we might see down on the beach as we scan it for Knútur.

Suddenly Carrie drops a rear foot and her hindquarters dip backwards. I grab wildly for handfuls of her mane, find them and cling on for dear life. Behind me there is the craggy edge of a dark ravine and certain death. Snow and stones tumble down it. All I can hear is the rushing of a waterfall below us, pouring over rocks, rushing on its path to the next big waterfall, then on to the sea. I freeze, too terrified to move.

Pétur turns, wide-eyed, but relaxes as Carrie rights herself, finds her footing and carries on along the narrow path, settling into a steady rhythm as if nothing has happened. It may take time for my heart to do the same. I don't let go of the clumps of mane I'm holding.

'Well done. You trusted her. You didn't panic. You make a good team.' He smiles and I relax, just a tiny bit, pat her and thank her once again.

Finally I feel Pétur's horse slow down in front of me and see, past him, the path opening up. We are at a precipice. Carrie draws up beside him and we stand side by side, the horses' breath rising upwards in curls.

Dawn, I can tell, is beginning to break. We gaze at the sky over the precipice, over the dark sea below. The cloud starts to lighten. The snow has stopped falling, and the wind has dropped. If it weren't for the fact that we still haven't found Knútur I'd want to take time to imprint this image on my memory. The clouds shift and slide and small shafts of golden light pour through them, like spotlights onto a huge stage. It's like watching a golden staircase open to the pearly gates and whatever may lie beyond them. I smile at the image, full of joy, serenity and hope in those golden rays.

And then I see something . . . or, rather, someone. And I'm gripped with fear all over again.

31

'Knútur,' Pétur says quietly to me.

I stare at the figure. He's on the tip of the cliff edge. His arms are open wide, his worn coat flapping. He's holding his face up to the shafts of sunlight in the sky, his palms out flat.

'He's alive!' I say breathlessly, part relieved, despite his precarious position. Neither of us moves, for fear of startling him.

'What's he doing?' I ask.

Pétur says nothing at first, then takes a deep breath. 'He's holding himself up to the elements.'

'He looks like he's on a crucifix,' I say. He is silhouetted against the golden glow and, in the distance, the fiery volcano, against the white of the snow, with the sound of the waterfall cascading over the rocks below us.

'He's asking the elements to take him,' says Pétur.

'What?'

'*Ättestupa.*'

'What's that?'

He turns to me and I see pain in his eyes. 'Remember I told you about the people who felt a burden? This place is where the elderly came when they felt they were a burden on their family or community.'

'They came here to . . .?'

He nods slowly. 'In Nordic prehistoric times, elderly people threw themselves off here to relieve their family of their burden.'

This is too terrible.

'We must go carefully,' he says, and slides off his horse.

The snow is thick and I land silently. I barely notice the throbbing in my cold feet. I can hardly breathe as we walk slowly through the snow, my thigh muscles burning with exertion, Carrie standing still where I've left her. I never take my eyes off him, in a bizarre version of Grandmother's Footsteps.

We get closer and I'm thinking, *Not now, not now!* We are so close but just out of reach. I want to rush at him, stop him, but I know I mustn't. I mustn't scare him or put him off balance on the edge of the precipice. I swallow the sickness I'm feeling.

Pétur looks at me and we stop, neither of us sure what to do next. 'Knútur,' Pétur says evenly.

At the same time I step forward, but to the side of

him. I don't know if he's aware that I'm there. I feel so small in this expanse. I know how it feels to be alone. But I also know how it feels to be loved and to love. Laura, Meg, Joanna . . . I miss Laura. I can see her smiling face. She's with me. She always has been. She never left. I just had to let her back in. Tears are rolling down my cheeks as I hold out my arms, just like Knútur, and lift my face to the sky.

And at that moment it flickers with a streak of light, different shades of green, elves at work when no one is looking. The green moves across the sky, and builds as if the first elf has called to his friends. The colours dance across the sky, growing in size and strength, getting brighter and brighter, spreading. I'm in awe of the spectacle overhead now. I reach for the tips of Knútur's fingers. He's here. Alive. And we watch as the Lights move back to where they came from. I've just experienced something magical. This is what Laura wanted to see. I turn to Knútur, and as I do, the snow slips and disappears from beneath my foot. I feel dizzy as I lose balance, arms flailing. I'm fighting a losing battle – this time there's no mane to grab – and I fall.

32

The hand is tight around mine, a big rough hand. I dare not look down or up. All I know is, I've stopped falling. I'm still here. Just. I daren't do anything. I can hear rushing, and I don't know if it's the waterfall, crashing over the rocks beneath me, or the whooshing of blood around my body.

Another hand clamps to my wrist. It's Pétur's. I'd know his touch anywhere now. The touch from last night. A touch that I want to feel for ever on my skin.

I hear muffled voices in Icelandic and then, 'Okay, I have you. Let go of the rock. We've got you, I promise.'

My chest is heaving and I can't let go. I can't.

'You can do this, Freya. This is me. I've got you. I promise. You won't fall.'

I take a huge breath and, with a rush of adrenalin, I let go. I dip and then I feel myself pulled upwards until I'm lying horizontally face down in the snow, with ground all around me. I let my fingers wriggle first. Then my hands and then I'm making big sweeping movements with my arms and legs, like I'm making a snow angel. I'm on the ground, in the snow, not at the bottom of the precipice.

I'm being lifted to my feet and I don't know who to hug first, Knútur or Pétur, so I hug them both, my arms around their necks, my face between theirs. I'm sobbing in big ugly gulps, tears and nose streaming. We say nothing. There are no words. We gaze at each other, tears rolling down our faces for what might have been and what we have realized. We are not alone, and I want to remember this for ever.

'Come, let's go home,' Pétur says. The only words I want to hear right now. 'Knútur?'

He nods.

'It's your home as much as any of ours. You have every right to be there and no one can stop that,' Pétur tells him firmly.

'I don't want to stand in the way of progress.'

'This town thrives on its community. It always has. It has everything it needs,' says Pétur. 'A community that cares about what happens to each other.' With that Pétur directs Knútur towards the horses and settles him on Carrie.

'I'll walk,' I say.

But Pétur beckons me to follow him. On the other

side of Carrie, next to his horse, he stands close to me. So close I can feel his breath on my lips. Then he kisses me, and I think my knees may give out all over again. When he pulls away, he says softly, 'You gave me a scare then.'

I still can't speak, but can't stop looking into his eyes. I can't quite believe I'm here, with him. He reaches down and taps my leg for me to lift it. 'Come on,' he says, and he gives me a leg-up. I hold onto the mane of his black stallion. Then he puts his foot into the stirrup and lifts himself onto the horse's back, into the saddle behind me, wrapping his arms around me, taking up the reins, his body against my back and his thighs around mine. 'Ready?' he says.

'Ready,' I finally say.

He clicks with his tongue and the horses move, solidly, faithfully, forwards. I have never felt more grateful as we step out into the snowy mountain pass towards home.

Knútur is riding slightly in front of us.

We go on in silence until we see the roof of the schoolhouse and next to it the black-walled church, with its white doors and window frames, tall tower and, just poking through where the snow has slid, its red corrugated roof.

'They're here!' someone shouts.

'It's them!'

I see people pointing.

'They've got him!'

The church bell is ringing now.

Everyone comes out of the schoolhouse to welcome us home.

'Merry Christmas,' says Pétur in my ear.

I turn to him.

'Merry Christmas.' I smile and it really does feel like it, like the brightest Christmas I have ever had.

33

'Come in! Get warm!' says Anna, back on her feet stiffly, with two crutches.

'I'm going to take the horses home,' says Pétur.

'I'll come,' I say.

'No, stay here, enjoy being with your friends.' He glances at the sky. 'It looks like the storm has passed. It's going to be a clear day. Enjoy it. I'll be back. But I need to see to the animals. Besides, it's Christmas. There's a feast to get ready!' He gives me his gloriously lazy smile and I couldn't feel happier.

Knútur is sitting surrounded by candlelight outside the schoolhouse on an area cleared of snow. Someone has given him a hot drink, which he's nursing in both hands. He seems content to be back and that's the best Christmas present of all.

Meg and Joanna hug me hard. 'We've been so worried!'

'You were gone! All night!' says Meg.

'With Pétur,' says Joanna, and I can't help blushing. But I'm not sharing those details with anyone. I want to take time to savour every bit of the memory: Pétur and me in the lava cave, alone, in the dark, at night, as the winds turned, the snow fell from the mountains in great crashing plumes, the night we shared a sleeping-bag, in a cold, dark place. It was one of the best times of my life. But I do tell them about the journey, how scared I was, how beautiful it was, serene but terrifying. I tell them how we found Knútur, who then saved my life. Once I've told them all the details, we hug again. I'm happy to be here with my friends. Happy to be alive.

34

'Wow! Someone's been busy!' I say as I take in the outside of the schoolhouse and the fact Joanna has a snow
shovel in one hand.

'Turns out I'm quite good with this thing, sheep and
getting my hands dirty!' She beams at Kristen, who
beams back. The area outside the schoolhouse has
been cleared of snow, banked up neatly at the sides,
with candles resting on black volcanic rocks where
Knútur is sitting.

'Who made the bunting, the greenery arch and the
wreaths?' I'm admiring the wreath on the door, the candles lighting the sides of the footpath leading into
the schoolhouse. A long table, decorated with candles,
twigs, moss and black lava stones against a white cloth,
and napkins, not in fans but, more impressively, in the
shape of snowflakes, stands against a wall. Paper chains

and snowflakes hang at different heights from drift-wood secured with ropes to the ceiling. The candles flicker and the paper snowflakes, twisting and turning from the gnarled, weathered sticks, throw shapes across the big room, making it feel warm, inviting and cosy.

'Did you do this?' I ask Meg, in astonishment.

'At those craft workshops I learnt how to make table decorations and wedding favours,' Meg says. 'At least they came in useful for something.' She shrugs.

Today she should have been waking up with Tom, days away from her wedding and her new life with her new husband. I hug her hard.

My eyes rest on Knútur. 'I'll be back in a moment,' I say, and walk over to him, carrying two small glasses, each containing a shot of firewater. He's sitting on a straw bale, brought from the farm by Joanna and Kristen. I slide onto the bale next to him.

'Thank you, Knútur,' I say, and hand him a drink.

'No.' He shakes his head. 'Thank you for coming to find me,' he says, his voice cracking.

'I could have died if you hadn't saved me,' I tell him.

'We both know I could say the same,' he says.

'They made us who we are, didn't they, the ones we lost? They might not be with us any more, but they made us who we are today,' I say. 'And he would want you to stay where you're happy.'

'And you,' he says. 'Whoever you lost, they only want

you to be happy too.' We clink our glasses gently together.

'To not forgetting. Thank you for making me stand still and remember,' I say, thinking of how wrong I've been getting it all these years. I've been moving on, working hard to forget instead of taking time to remember.

As he chinks his glass against mine again, I see the colour of the firewater start to change, from clear, to aquamarine to emerald, and I see the sky beginning to light up once more. And then we see it, the light falling around us on the snowy ground. It's just a green shimmer across the sky at first.

'They're here! The Lights!' I call over my shoulder to Meg and Joanna.

And once again the Lights come out in purples and greens and dance across the sky, like a private performance just for us.

'Bugger! Forgot the bottle of champagne we were going to open!' says Joanna. 'It's back in the farmhouse. Shall I go and get it?'

'No. Stay, watch. Enjoy them. I don't think Laura would mind. I think she knew what she was doing when she sent us here. It wasn't about seeing the Lights. It was about seeing the bigger picture. Taking time to work out how we want to live the rest of our lives.'

'Well, I know what I'm going to do,' says Frankie, joining us. 'I promise, Knútur,' she sits on the other side of him, 'no one will try to move your home. I'm so sorry.' She takes his hand and he nods, gratefully, forgiving.

'And I know exactly what we're going to cook for tonight. Memories of this place!' I say. 'Smoked salmon, with firewater. And the *hangikjöt*, smoked lamb with caramelized potatoes, rhubarb jam! Let's get cooking!' I step back into the kitchen to make people smile as I put down a plate.

'Let's get peeling potatoes, and that lamb needs to go into the oven,' I say, checking its temperature. 'Hildur, are you okay on cakes and desserts?'

'We've got it all under control,' she assures me.

'Let's get this smoked salmon plated up. We'll need rye bread to go with it,' I say, putting out baskets.

'On it,' says Meg.

'I'll get the lamb in,' I say, 'and then we'll make the sauce, boil the potatoes and put them to caramelize with brown sugar on the hob. How about you lay the table, Joanna? Ready for the feast!'

And we all smile, happy to be part of the festive preparations.

35

'She would have loved this!' says Meg, as we sit outside with glasses of firewater, after a fabulous feast of flat-breads cut and baked to look like snowflakes, just like Anna showed us, smoked salmon with a creamy dill dip, then smoked lamb with the potatoes, a cream sauce and spoonfuls of tart yet sweet rhubarb jam from jars along the table. Everyone is here. Everyone made sure that everyone was here. Anna is still here, though furious at not being able to get out of her chair and work in the kitchen. She's giving guidance, handing on the skills and recipes, but she's having a wonderful time, finally able to sit and soak up the atmosphere instead of cooking for others. Pétur sat next to me, and there were times when I could barely eat, because my gaze kept drifting back to his, like a compass finding its home position.

And now we're sitting on the straw bales, blankets around our shoulders and looking up at the stars overhead. Knútur is well wrapped up and everyone is keen to make sure he has had plenty of food, and his glass is topped up. He's gazing up at the sky too. It is changing colour and shimmering as the Lights appear and disappear, playing hide and seek, fading, then fanning out and fascinating us.

'Better than any firework display I've ever been to,' says Meg.

'Me too! And I've been to some very—' Joanna stops mid-sentence, evidently realizing she doesn't need that façade any more. We love her for who she is, and her ability to use a snow shovel.

'Did you know I wasn't in love with him? Tony, I mean,' she asks, still staring at the sky.

'Of course we did,' Meg says, still looking up.

There's a moment of silence.

'I didn't. Not really,' says Joanna.

I see the sadness etched on her face.

'Not until now,' she adds. 'I wish someone had told me.'

'Well, we thought you were happy. And we were all doing our own things. Getting on with life, like Laura wanted us to,' I say.

Joanna shrugs. 'Or maybe we were just hiding from it,' she says, the candle flames lighting her face, her cheeks rosy from the firewater. 'Your food was amazing this evening.'

Meg and Frankie agree.

'Really amazing,' says Frankie.

'Thank you,' I try to say, but it doesn't come out. 'She always told me to keep going. I thought she meant in the kitchen, where I was. But I realize now what she meant was that I should keep taking risks. Living life. Never leaving for tomorrow what I want to do, never keeping anything for best. It was remembering what we always really wanted that was important. That was what she wanted for us.'

'She wanted us to live life to the full, follow our hearts,' says Meg.

The other two nod.

'All this time I thought she didn't want us to look back, didn't want us to feel sad, didn't want us to cry. But she wanted us to enjoy the ride, and that's something I've forgotten to do.'

And as I'm staring upwards, something feels wet on my cheeks. It's not snow and I brush it away but there's more. Tears are rolling steadily down my cheeks making me want to laugh and cry at the same time.

'She's here,' says Joanna.

'She never wasn't here. She was always with us. Every bit of advice, encouragement, words of wisdom, they never went away. We were so busy "living our best lives" that we forgot everything else. She never went anywhere,' I say.

'It's true. She told me to listen to my heart, to stop putting everyone else first,' Meg says.

'She told me to listen to my heart too,' says Joanna. 'I thought that meant marrying Tony but, actually, that was me ignoring my heart.'

'We didn't need to see the Lights to celebrate her life. We just needed to stop living "our best lives" and take some time out to listen to our hearts,' I say.

The Lights reappear, getting brighter and brighter.

'And she'll always be here. That never goes away. The memories, the laughter and the words of advice.'

'What would she say to us right now?' Meg asks, still with her face to the Lights.

'She'll tell us again, "Listen to your heart",' I reply.

'She'd tell you you're far better off not being Tony's trophy wife. Just start living your own life,' Meg says to Joanna. I catch my breath, hoping Meg's directness won't start another row.

Joanna looks at her and glances to where Kristen is standing, a hand in his jeans pocket. Then her head turns back to us and she nods slowly. 'Even if it's madness? Even if they're younger than you, don't have any interest in material things, just living life in the wild, with their sheep?' she says, not looking at any of us now.

'Especially if it's madness.' I smile. 'If you've found

some happiness, Joanna, you should grab it, with both hands.'

'Same for you,' Joanna says to Meg. 'Don't let families get in the way of being happy together.'

'You're right!' Meg's eyes widen. 'I love Tom. I've always loved Tom. It's just this wedding malarkey I don't love. Or haven't loved!'

'Or his family!' Joanna says it as it is this time. The green and purple glow from the Lights dancing overhead seems to make this a safe space when we can finally say what we mean and know it's said with love.

And we all laugh.

'You're marrying Tom. The children are old enough to deal with it. They have their own lives. And so do you. And your ex-mother-in-law is just that. She doesn't get to call the shots.'

We all laugh and sniff as the Lights recede to the back of the giant stage and the stars pop out one by one, brighter and better and utterly breathtaking.

'That's if we can reorganize the wedding,' she says, worried all over again. 'If we can get our money back on the one that isn't likely to happen. What if he thinks I did this on purpose and just didn't turn up? Stood him up, days before, practically at the altar?'

'Meg, Tom knows you and you know Tom. He knows you would never do that. Just like you know he wouldn't do it to you. You trust each other. Married or not, you have it all. He knows there's a good reason you're not there.' And she smiles.

'I love him!' she says, with every bit of her heart.

'We know,' I say, at the same time as Joanna.

'Look, I'm sorry about what I said, Freya, in our room at the farmhouse. I don't know what came over me. I shouldn't have said those things,' says Meg.

'Forget it.' I wave a gloved hand.

'No, I shouldn't have said what I did.'

I take a deep breath. 'Yes, you should,' I reply, looking at her. 'Because she would've.' I don't brush the tears from my wet cheeks but let them sit there. 'She told me my food was how I showed people I loved them. It was an expression of me, who I was. I should have done that, instead of settling for cooking someone else's recipes to perfection. Every word you said was true. She would have said it.'

'Maybe she did,' says Meg. 'Somehow . . .'

And Laura may be right, but that doesn't mean there's anything I can do about it now. That time has gone. With any luck, I still have a new restaurant to open for Wilfrid.

Joanna is looking up at the sky with tears in her eyes, sparkling as brightly as the stars that are popping out, multiplying.

I put my arm around her, the other around Meg.

'She knew what she was doing when we promised her we'd come here to fulfil her dream,' I say. 'She wanted us to reflect. Take time. Get a bit of clarity.' I think about sitting in the hot lagoon, about nearly falling from the cliff edge.

'We've certainly had that!' Joanna laughs.

'Do you think the elves really did have a hand in it?' says Meg.

We look at her, but none of us is laughing. We're wondering.

'Whatever, whoever, however . . . I don't know. But it feels like something brought us all here,' I say. I wonder what Frankie's thinking.

She holds up her hands as if reading my mind. 'And I promise, nothing more will happen here from my company. I'll make sure all interest is withdrawn. This place needs to stay special.'

I look at Pétur, talking with neighbours, sitting by Knútur, all holding their drinks. He looks at me at the same time and my stomach fizzes up like a geyser. What now? I have to talk to him. See if he meant what he said when he and Knútur rescued me. If so, what now?

Hildur comes to join us.

'I'd better lay out the cakes,' I say to her.

'I'll help,' she says.

'You already have,' I say, as we turn to the kitchen. 'You know, you should really think about a career in cooking,' I tell her.

'Maybe I will,' she smiles, 'once I leave here. Thank you,' she says, 'for helping me find me again.'

'I think this place has done that for all of us.'

Everyone is choosing their dessert, slices of buttery loaf cake, with cardamom and raisins, and *vinarterta* that Hildur proudly brings out from the kitchen to a round of applause and cheers. Seven layers of crumbling biscuit, with a filling of dark prune purée, cardamom and vanilla. Hot coffee is served from big flasks and shots of firewater are handed around.

Outside, I hear a guitar playing. I follow the music, holding a plate of cake and see Pétur, sitting with his guitar. He brought it from the farmhouse when he returned from seeing to the animals on his black stallion before dinner. Everyone picks up slices of cake, moves outside again and shots of firewater are topped up. Knútur is sitting next to Pétur, smiling into the candles' flickering flames. Pétur begins to sing and the others join in. We clap and cheer as the song comes to an end.

Pétur puts down the guitar, and everyone turns to refill their glasses and hand around more of the cakes and biscuits.

'Oh, presents!' says Joanna, clapping her hands.

'I haven't got any,' I say.

'I know, I know.' She flaps a hand. 'But we made these with Anna's help! Actually, lots of help. She spins the wool from the sheep into yarn and makes jumpers. We didn't have time to do that, so some of you have scarves and some of us got mittens! And you, Frankie!' She hands round a woollen gift to each of us, tied with string and a tiny piece of birch branch. 'You've all been so kind to me, and what with me not having the money to buy you presents, I wanted to make something. Meg had the real skills, though.'

I pull at the string, and release the piece of birch, hold it to my nose and breathe it in. It's a smell I will never forget and will always associate with this place, here, tonight. The happiness I'm feeling. I unravel the thick, chunky-knit scarf as Frankie and Meg do the same. Joanna, I see, is already wearing one.

'It's perfect,' I say, wrapping it around my neck for extra warmth. 'Thank you.' I beam, as does Frankie.

'Happy Christmas,' says Joanna.

'Do you know?' I say. 'It's been one of the happiest I've had in a long time!'

And the others all agree.

'It may not have been planned. It may have been a rollercoaster of a ride, but it's been amazing.' We all raise our glasses.

'To friendship!'

Anna is now in her rocking chair, which Kristen has moved outside for her. I'm not sure if he did it with her in it or not. She rocks and I go to thank her for the gift.

'Freya,' says Pétur, and comes to me. My heart is pounding, as it always is when I'm near him. 'Thank you for all of this.' He holds out a hand towards the plates of food in people's hands.

'It was . . .' I was going to say it was nothing. But it wasn't. It was everything.

He takes my fingers and my insides burn with yearning to be back in his arms.

'Here, happy Christmas.' He turns over my hand, pulls out a little fabric parcel from his pocket and places it in my palm.

'What? But you gave me the book.'

'That was your Christmas Eve gift. This is your Christmas gift,' he says, and I slowly open the pouch to find two silver earrings in the shape of stars. 'To remind you of your time here,' he says, 'and the stars.' He looks up at the night sky.

'May I?'

I nod, barely able to speak as he puts the earrings into my ears gently. 'Thank you so much.' Then, plucking up all the courage I have, I say, 'I . . .'

'We could . . .'

We speak at the same time, then laugh and fall silent, just our fingertips touching and the sound of the fire crackling.

'I think it's time I . . .'

And just as I'm about to tell him everything I've felt

since I arrived at this place, that I have finally come to feel I can trust and care for someone again, that maybe there's a chance we could stay in touch, there's a low rumble. But it's not an avalanche this time. It's an engine.

36

'Hey!' shouts Kristen. We stop looking into the beautiful night sky and turn to where he's pointing down the road. There's a light . . .

A snowplough!

'They came! On Christmas Day!' I say, shocked.

And behind it another vehicle, honking its horn and flashing its lights.

We have what we've all been waiting for: a way out.

'It's a car!' Meg shouts, her hands over her mouth and nose with her new mittens on.

A huge four-wheel-drive vehicle to be precise. And another behind it. There's the toot of a car horn. Lots of toots.

'Hey!' Kristen and others wave at the procession behind the snowplough, pushing a path through the snow for the other cars to follow. The snowplough driver waves and smiles, clearly pleased to be helping bring families back together on Christmas Day and lead this procession.

We watch the vehicles drive slowly towards us. It feels overwhelming. The bubble we've been in for the last week has burst, an explosion of noise and excitement. The waiting and anticipation are over. In the driver's seat of the first four-by-four is the Light-seeker from the hotel. He smiles widely.

Suddenly a passenger door swings open on one of the other cars.

'Meg!' A familiar figure throws himself out into the snow.

'Tom!' He looks so clean and shiny, in new, presumably quickly bought cold-weather gear, as we sit in the clothes we've been in for a week or more, borrowed and homemade. I put my scarf to my lips and watch as Meg upends her drink and throws herself through the snow, wading towards him. They're like young lovers trying to reach each other over a raging river, until finally they fall into each other's arms, two halves fitting back together.

'You came!' she cries, and there can't be a dry eye anywhere. Mine are streaming.

'Of course I did. I love you! I was so worried! I missed you!'

'And I love you, Tom, with all my heart!'

They kiss again, then hold each other tightly, as if

they thought they'd lost each other for good and will never let go.

'I really do love you! I'm sorry, all the wedding stuff.'

'That doesn't matter. What matters is that you're here! Alive!'

'And so are you!' she says. 'And I promise with all my heart I'll always be there for you. Through the good times and the bad.'

'For better or worse,' he says. 'I love you and I want to be with you always. I don't need or want a big wedding. I just want to be with you.'

'Me too! You're all I need!'

Finally they kiss again, and we all spontaneously clap. If ever there was the joining of two people, making their vows to each other, that was it. Genuine, heartfelt.

I find myself turning instinctively to look for Pétur.

He's beaming at me and I feel my heart sweep, as if it's dancing with the Lights. Maybe I should follow my heart too.

I smile back. Perhaps I shouldn't miss my moment again. Perhaps I should stand up for what I want and not be scared. I bite my bottom lip. Isn't that what this has been about, learning to seize the day? He looks at me and I know what I want, where I want to be . . . who I want to be with. I'm going to tell him.

'Pappa! Pappa!' A shout breaks through my thoughts as the driver's door of the second car opens.

Pétur holds my gaze, then turns away from me in the direction of the shout. I'm stopped in my tracks. A tall blonde young woman, with long legs, like a colt's, in a thick woollen scarf like mine and well-worn warm clothing to match is striding through the snow towards him.

'Hey!' He opens his arms and hugs her tightly. Although she's the same height as him, he lifts her from the ground and swings her round. He puts her back down, smiling. Bright blue eyes, blonde hair, she looks just like him.

'That was a long one!' she says. 'You okay?'

'Of course. As always!'

'Merry Christmas!' she says.

'And you! Freya, this is my daughter,' he says proudly.

'It's lovely to meet you. The work you've done with the safe house is amazing!' I feel as if I've fallen back through the wardrobe from Narnia and landed in the real world with an almighty bump.

His daughter, of course. This is his life out here, not the bubble we've been living in for these past days.

37

'Okay, let's get you guys back to the hotel,' says Tom, clapping his big gloved hands together and smiling.

I can't speak: I haven't the words to say what I'm feeling, now that our time together is over.

Tom helps Meg up into the four-by-four and they cuddle up closely for warmth. Pétur is looking at me and I'm trying not to catch his eye. It's time to go and get on with our lives. He has an exhibition in London to get ready for. I have a restaurant to get back to, hopefully.

I hug Anna in her chair, then Hildur, Margrét, María and Knútur, thanking him and telling him to stay safe.

I stand back to let Joanna step into the truck, while I try to eke out every last breath in the freezing, crisp, clean Icelandic air. Almost without realizing it, I put my hand to my left earring. The little star seems to connect me to this place.

I look at Pétur, just him, to say goodbye. I'm still trying to find the words.

Joanna doesn't move.

'After you,' I say, holding the door open.

'Um, actually, I . . .' Joanna says, unusually hesitant.

'You okay?' I ask.

'Yes. In fact . . . never better.'

'Good.' I wish I could feel the same. 'Let's go.' I sweep my arm towards the open car door, my cold breath forming plumes of steam around me.

'I've decided to stay for a bit,' Joanna says quickly.

'A bit?' I'm taken aback.

Meg frees herself from Tom's embrace in the back of the car and leans towards the open door. 'What's going on?' she says. 'It's freezing!'

'I'm going to stay,' Joanna says. 'Help out with lambing, come the spring.'

'Lambing!' I say.

Meg and I look at each other. 'You!' we say.

She throws back her head and laughs. 'Let's just say I've realized I need to follow my heart.' I have never seen her look so beautiful.

We turn towards Kristen, who is also beaming.

'Well, this is a turn-up for the books,' says Meg.

I turn back to Joanna. 'Do you want me to get in touch with Tony?' I ask.

'I doubt they'll even notice I'm not there. As long as Christmas is planned and delivered to them. He was going to tell his children after Christmas dinner that we were separated and getting a divorce, then take a cruise with his new partner, Julie, in the new year. It really won't make any difference that I'm not there. In fact, I think it will be better for everyone.'

'Good for you. Do it. Follow your heart!' I say, and hug her tightly. Finally, we release each other.

Joanna sniffs, straightens and walks away from us. As she does Kristen steps forward and slides his arms around her, as they slip into a slow, passionate kiss. We cheer and clap.

'Go, Joanna!'

She pulls away, turns and waves, one arm around her lover and the other waving madly at us, grinning from ear to ear. Joanna, an Icelandic sheep farmer! Who'd have thought it? My heart swoops and soars for her, then squeezes as I think of what I'm leaving behind, who I'm leaving behind. And suddenly I'm standing in front of him, holding the book he gave me, mottled and worn.

'I don't feel I should take this. It's yours,' I say.

'I want you to have it. A reminder of this place,' he says, wrapping my fingers around it.

I wish . . . I wish I had the bravery of Joanna. But I haven't. I've only just started out on this journey, finding out about the new me. I'm not there yet.

'Thank you. For everything,' I say, my voice quiet, with a rasp in it. 'I – I won't forget my time here. I've learnt so much.'

'Me too,' he says, his cheek next to mine, so I can smell him, breathing it in like I'm bottling it, like fresh Icelandic air. A smell I never want to forget. Then, quickly, I get into the car barely looking back. I can't.

The drive to the hotel is silent and hot, the car heaters on full blast. I pull off my coat, hat and scarf. I stare out of the window at the snowy landscape I've come to know and love. And once again the tears begin to roll.

38

New year passed in a flash, along with the months that have followed leading up to opening the new restaurant.

I smooth my chef's whites with the new restaurant name embroidered in gold just under the collar.

Getting it up and running has been exhausting and demanding. But it happened. Wilfrid gave me the executive-chef job and I've been here making it happen, with builders and decorators, the best I can, trying to put Christmas as far to the back of my mind as I can.

Now, in the kitchen, opening night is finally here, everything we've been building up to for months. I don't understand why I'm not more excited. It's everything I've wanted . . . wanted, a voice repeats in my head, and I have to push out the image of Pétur on his horse in Iceland six months ago.

I stare at the salmon in front of me, just arrived from the fishmonger, early this morning. I stare down at the plate presented to me to try.

I lift it to my nose and breathe in. Nothing. I try again. A faint hint of the mix of herbs and spices Wilfrid has insisted on. Nothing distinct. I pick up the fork that's been placed there for me. This is everything we've discussed in the dish and yet I'm not feeling anything for it. I cut off a piece of the smoked salmon. It's soft and pliable, bright in colour. I raise it to my mouth and let it sit on my tongue, hoping to feel transported back to Christmas and the salmon we had there. But I'm not. My heart plummets. It's a mix of flavours, unique, complicated, but it doesn't take me anywhere. Just leaves me disappointed. I stare at it and turn to the sous-chef.

'This salmon has no flavour!' I tell him.

'It's the best around!' he says, ready to get back to prepping the rest for this evening's taster menu.

'Wait!' I go to the bar, grab a bottle of vodka. I pull off the lid and take a swig. It's not firewater, but close, then add some to the dish, much to the sous-chef's horror.

'Have we got any berries – bilberries maybe? And it could do with some smokiness. A real taste of where it's come from.'

The staff stare at me as if I've gone mad.

'But . . . that's not how it is on the menu,' says my

sous-chef, concerned. 'Here, I can take over if you like.' He tries to take the dish from me. I put a hand on it and tug it back, firmly.

'You've wanted my job in here since day one,' I say. 'I know you hoped I wasn't going to get it, after missing Christmas, but right now I'm in charge. And while I am, we'll do things my way.'

'Shouldn't it be Wilfrid's way?' His eyes narrow.

I hear a sharp intake of breath from the rest of the kitchen.

I breathe in, deeply. Better, I think.

The staff are watching me anxiously.

'Shouldn't we be getting on with the meat course?' says my sous-chef.

'Soon. It's okay. We have time,' I say. I take a piece of the salmon from the packaging it arrived in. I trace my finger around its outline and wonder where it's come from. Then I add more of the vodka and strip away all the other unnecessary flavours.

I sniff it again, then let it sit on my tongue. It's better. I can feel myself right back there, in the snow, in the hot spring, watching the whales, riding out, in the lava cave, under the waterfall.

Now all I need is bread, baked in the ground, to go with it.

'Chef? We really should get ready for service.'

I look at the kitchen team, staring at me.

'Okay, serve the salmon like this,' I say. But no one

moves. 'Serve this salmon, instead of what's on the menu,' I repeat.

'Yes, Chef,' they say nervously, and start to busy themselves around the kitchen. I can't move. The taste of Iceland, of everything I fell in love with there, is still on my lips, reminding me why I want to do this. I'm nervous, but something in me tells me I have to do it. And as the doors open and the diners arrive, I finally feel I'm stepping out onto the brightly lit stage, the Northern Lights dancing overhead, and it's time to seize the day.

'What is the meaning of this?' Wilfrid roars.

I was expecting it, of course. It's halfway through service. The kitchen is hot, busy and adrenalin-fuelled. The salmon has been served and we're plating the next course to go out.

I mop my brow, doubled over the work bench, concentrating.

'Can we talk about this later, Wilfrid?' I say, resigning myself to the strip that will be torn off me.

'No! We can't! I didn't create this!' he bellows.

I straighten. 'No, I did. I took what was there and made it better. It was down to me, no one else.' The kitchen crew breathe a sigh of relief.

'Made it your own! It's my name above the door!' He points a fat finger towards the front of house.

'And people are loving the food. It's still your food.

The critics are out there and the plates are coming back empty.' I point to the washing-up area.

'You changed the menu without consulting me!' he rages.

I sigh. 'Just stripped it back and elevated what was there already. It's still your menu!' I stop. Why am I giving someone else credit for my work yet again?

'Food magazine critic reckons the palate cleanser was fantastic,' says the waitress, bringing back the empty plates. 'And the *Daily News* wants to know what you did to the smoked salmon. Everyone's raving about the flavours.'

'The bookings site has crashed and Instagram's gone nuts. Everyone's talking about Wilfrid's new Taste restaurant,' says the receptionist, bursting into the kitchen.

Wilfrid looks at me. I stare back at him. Slowly he nods, then smiles. 'Seems my menu's hit the mark again,' he says, and raises to me the glass of champagne he's holding. 'Thank you for executing it so well, Chef. You'll join me in the restaurant when you've finished plating up. I'd like the press to meet my team.'

'There's a TikTok of the smoking molten chocolate cake, like a smouldering volcano, someone's leaked online,' says the waitress, reporting back from the restaurant.

I see the young washer-upper shove his phone into his trouser pocket with a small smile.

'Another of your tweaks?' Wilfrid raises an eyebrow. I dip my head.

'I'll have to make sure other restaurants don't try to poach you!' He sips his drink. 'Now, join me, please.'

I begin to pull off my apron.

He turns towards the kitchen door.

'Monsieur Jean Paul Saison has asked to speak to you, Chef,' says the receptionist. 'He's asked if you would join him at his table. He says he would like to discuss your career with you.'

The kitchen staff are whispering.

'*The* Jean Paul Saison!' they say, clearly impressed.

'That would be my dream!' I hear the whispers.

'Oh, wow!'

'Perhaps,' says Wilfrid, turning back to me, 'a pay rise would be in order. We'll speak about it in my office tomorrow.'

'And that hot chef, Mark Martin, from the Epitome restaurant group, asked if you'd be free for a drink after service. He says your food was amazing, as it always was. He'd love to talk to you about a collaboration.'

Mark! He was here tonight.

'It would be great publicity for us,' says Wilfrid, and I stare at him as if he's just asked me to swim with sharks.

'Over my dead body!' I say. The kitchen staff take another sharp breath of shock.

'Oh, and someone is at the front desk. Says it's really important he speaks to you.'

'Who is it?' I turn to her.

'Someone called Pétur Snorrison?'

I don't need telling twice. I rip off my whites, toss them onto the counter and head for the double doors. What if something's happened? What if Frankie's company are still trying to move in where Knútur's hut is? What if it's news about Knútur? And my heart leaps into my mouth.

'You're all good with the chocolate volcanoes, yes?' I tell the sous-chef.

He nods, like a rabbit caught in headlights not knowing which way to run.

I push open the double doors and the noise from the hot, busy restaurant hits me, like a firewall.

'Chef! Chef! I would like you to join me in the restaurant!' Wilfrid stops me and insists.

'I'm sorry, Wilfrid. There's someone I need to speak to.'

'Look, I've said I'm prepared to overlook your creative touches, even discuss a pay rise. Let's get it all sorted in the morning. But now let's go and tell the press about the menu. The concept.'

'There isn't one, Chef. It's just a bunch of chemistry. What goes with what flavours. There's no story to your food. There's no journey. There's no expression of who you are, what this food means to you. The creative touches, as you call them, are elevating these dishes because they mean something. They're a reflection of the landscape where the food I love comes from.

335

Where it's inspired, grown and nurtured by the community who grow it. A community where if you don't work together you die. A community I care about . . . very much.'

He's flabbergasted. As are the kitchen staff. Some are muttering, others clasping their hands together as if in applause.

'Tomorrow we'll meet. We'll talk. Bring some ideas.'

'I'm sorry, Chef. I need to find a way to tell the world about my food. Who I am and why I cook. I don't know how yet. But it's not hiding away in someone else's kitchen. Here.' I toss my hat to the sous-chef. 'I know you'll follow his recipes to the letter. You'll be fine. Good luck.' Grabbing my coat and bag, I leave through the restaurant to calls of 'Chef!'

'Congratulations!'

'Chef!'

Through the round of applause and the calls to join them at their table, I see him. Mark. Familiar, smooth Mark, holding out a hand to a spare seat to join him. He stands and smiles at me. 'Our chef, ladies and gentlemen,' he says. They clap and he pulls out the seat.

I shake my head. 'Never,' I say, and head for Reception with my heart in my mouth. Pétur, just as I remember him, if without the hat and the big coat, is waiting for me.

'Sorry, I didn't mean to interrupt you. I meant to meet afterwards,' he says. 'It's just I couldn't be here for the exhibition without seeing your new place for myself.'

'Come on! Let's get out of here, quick! It's not my place, not any more!'

'Sorry?'

'You were just the kick I needed to remember everything I learnt,' I say, grabbing his elbow and heading out of the front door before anyone can come after me. We'll go to a small bar around the corner where I can hear what he has to say and where I can grasp what I've just done.

39

'Hey! You're back!' says the young woman on Reception. I recognize her. She's the girl from the kitchen when I arrived here on that first day, having been bawled out by the chef. It's about the only thing I do recognize about the place. It's so different without all the snow and candles. Now everything is light and bright. The snow-covered expanses are moss and grass, with glistening rivulets cutting across them, like crystals tumbling from a jeweller's palm.

I look at the young woman.

'Didn't you work in the kitchen here?'

She nods, seemingly pleased I've recognized her. 'And you're that chef. The one who works for Wilfrid Gallerhan! I googled you after I'd met you. Asked Reception for your name.'

'I *was* the chef,' I say. 'I left!'

'You left? Why?' She's clearly shocked that I would leave such a well-known chef and restaurant. 'Sorry, that was rude.'

'No.' I laugh it away. 'It's fine. I just . . .' In her I see a younger version of myself. I wish I'd realized what I wanted to do and hadn't left it so long. That I'd come to this point sooner. But life had other plans. 'I just realized it was time to believe in myself, my own food and why I like to make it.' She cocks her head, interested, almost hanging on every word. 'I like to create memories on a plate. Take people to a place they want to remember, a place, a time, the people they were with. I want it to be—'

'Like Instagram! Your happy memories in the making!' Her face drops. 'Sorry again.' She's clearly thinking she's overstepping the mark, and that may be because she's worked in the kitchen here for too long, where an opinion on the food was not welcomed.

'Don't be sorry! That's exactly what I mean! Happy memories in the making. A place you want to return to, to remember, to revisit.'

'That is so cool!'

'So, how come you're not in the kitchen?' I say, signing my check-in paperwork.

She shrugs. 'I guess Chef didn't think I had what it took. I'm on housekeeping now, covering Reception for lunch shifts.' She looks like the wind has been taken out of her sails. I put the pen down on the desk.

'You mean he didn't like someone who stood up for themselves and had their own ideas. More than he did, judging by the food I ate here.'

She smiles again. 'Well, your room is all ready for you. Enjoy your time here. I hope it makes memories for you that you want to revisit.'

'Thank you, I do too! And . . . don't worry. Sometimes when you think it's the end of the journey, it's not. It's just a bump in the road . . . or maybe an avalanche!' I take my key card.

She looks at me quizzically. 'Good luck, with whatever you do next,' she says.

'Thank you,' I say. '*Þakka þér kærlega fyrir.* But it's not luck I need, it's belief in myself.' I take the keycard to my room and the keys to the four-by-four waiting outside for me and head outside with butterflies in my stomach.

40

The landscape is so very different – I hardly know it without its white winter coat. But it's just as beautiful in its summer dress.

But I recognize where I am, even without a snow-covered roof. It still pulls at my heartstrings, and the memories tucked away in there. I stop the car and put on the handbrake. I stare at the red-roofed farmhouse and try to push away the memory of the nights I spent here.

But I don't get out. Instead I release the handbrake and drive on over the uneven track. The last time I did this route I was on horseback, following a pile of stones, over a blanket of snow, but I seem to know my way. I can feel it. I have to look up Joanna. I know she's doing great, from the WhatsApp messages she sends us when she has signal and her Instagram account, as an Icelandic sheep farmer. And it's wonderful having her updates on Knútur too, letting me know he's well and enjoying life in his hut by the sea in the spring. He's even letting the locals do some work on the hut to insulate it and make it sturdier. I'm dying to see it. But right now, I have business I need to sort. Nothing else can happen until I do.

I stop the four-by-four and turn off the engine. The waterfall is spilling, tumbling and gushing over the mountainside, and there, just along from it, a lone figure is standing by the river as it tumbles and gushes over the rocks out towards the sea, the harbour and Knútur's home. My heart lurches and squeezes.

Slowly I push open the door and step out, shutting it quietly behind me. It feels so good to be back. I take big deep breaths of the clear riverside air, under the blue sky, full of white fluffy clouds, where the mountain tops meet it. But as good as it feels, I'm as nervous as anything. My hands are shaking. I run them down my thighs and take a deep breath. I take a step forward, feeling that it could be the start of a whole new journey. I see Jón spot me and sit up next to his owner. I know I'll be outed at any moment, if I haven't been already.

I walk towards him and his owner, in the warm sun, his broad shoulders underneath a T-shirt, making me feel everything that, once, I didn't want to feel. Everything I was trying to fight feeling. He doesn't turn around. And then I see it, and catch my breath.

A splash!

There in the water.

I stand and stare and as I do there are more splashes, here, there, and everywhere. And not just splashes. I see them, the huge, majestic fish as they leap from the water, curling, bending, reaching, like Olympic pole-vaulters, throwing themselves with considered style and grace out of the water, heading upstream. Trying, again and again, never giving up. Until finally, exhausted, they make it. And those that don't die trying.

Slowly, he turns to me, a wide smile growing on his face as he sees me. My heart explodes, like one of the geysers, bursting skywards.

'They came back!' I say, with a crack in my voice. I feel the prickle of tears in my eyes, watching as they leap and land.

He nods, still beaming.

'So did you.' His lazy smile curls his lips. And I don't know what to say. 'They came home,' he says, turning back to the fish. And that is exactly how I feel.

'So, you gave my idea some thought?' he says, look-ing out over the river, to the mossy rocks beyond and the tall craggy cliff face, where I can see pairs of puffins cuddling up together on the ledges.

'I have,' I say. I was hoping I'd still feel the same when I got here.

I look at the river and the fish. 'This is right.' I watch the wild salmon. 'Not the farmed ones, killing them off.'

We fall into silence.

'They've gone, you said when I saw you, the salmon-farm company,' I say.

He pushes his hands into his pockets. 'Yes, and they gave us a statement of promise that they would never look at this area again.'

'I know. I had another visitor come and see me back in London.'

'Oh, yes? Your ex?' His face tightens.

'I told him where to go on the night of the opening. No, after that. Frankie got in touch and came to see me.'

He raises an eyebrow.

'She sold her share in the business to the other shareholders, her partner's family, on the condition they never again considered here as a site for a farm. She got them to send the statement of promise.'

He nods slowly. 'She sold out her share? And she came to see you?'

'She really is sorry about the trouble she caused for Knútur. And she understands how wrong the salmon farm would have been there. She wants to make amends,' I say. 'She's moving on.'

He's standing right in front of me now. My heart is beating hard.

'Looks like we all realized things about our lives while we were here.'

He's interested.

'I know now that Laura didn't leave me. She's always

been here. I just needed to look up to realize it. I felt so angry. I just hid my head in the sand.'

'Or in the kitchen.' He takes my hand lightly by the fingers, just touching the tips.

'Frankie wants to be my business partner, invest in me and a restaurant.'

He stares at me, then drops my hand. 'So you're moving on too?'

I'm stunned. 'No! I'm taking over the restaurant here, at the hotel in town, in my own name, with my own recipes, from the memories I made here. Why don't you come and see it?'

41

'This is me opening here,' I point to the papered-over windows, waiting for new life to be breathed into it. 'Frankie's my business partner.'

'So you really are here to stay? It's not just a dream.'

I smile, letting the reality settle in for me too. 'We plan to put this place on the map. She's invested her money, from selling her share in the family business, in this place and me to become a celebration of Icelandic food. Hildur from the safe house is going to join us. We'll train more people who come through it, if they want. To give them new skills. But . . .'

'But?' He cocks his head.

'I can't do it without you. Without the salmon. I need you! I want wild salmon to be at the heart of the menu. I want the smokehouse to be part of this. We'll need more staff, of course, but I want to put all the

flavours of this place on the plate. No imported products. Everything that tastes of the fire, the ice, the hot
springs and waterfalls. I want them to taste where the
food comes from.'

'I think your idea is . . .' He's standing in front of me.
I can smell him. I want to touch him. I want him to
touch me.

'. . . incredible,' he finally says, and then, slowly, he
takes my face in his hands and kisses me, like I've
dreamt of being kissed ever since I left here.

He reaches into his pocket and pulls out a small
square box.

'You made it! The centrepiece for your exhibition?'

He opens it and holds it out to me. 'I was offered the
chance to stay in London, base myself there, build the
business,' he says. 'This was the centrepiece. I made it
for you. For when you came home. Because I hoped
you would, one day.'

I catch my breath.

It's a silver ring. The king of fish in shining silver,
lots of them, tiny but all swimming upriver, leaping,
intertwined, glistening, shimmering scales in their bright
silver setting.

'I know it's time I took a risk too.'

'So you're going to London?'

I hold my breath. I've come all this way, and now
he's leaving. He looks down and it seems like for ever
before he looks up at me. And shakes his head.

'I'm exactly where I want to be, if you want to be here too. I don't want any of this, if you're not by my side.'

'But London?'

'Why would I move somewhere else, when all of my inspiration is right here?' he says.

'Home,' I say, with a widening smile as what he says slowly sinks in.

'*Heim*,' he repeats in Icelandic, sliding the ring onto my finger. I look at it, and it feels exactly where it should be.

'*Heim*.' I beam. 'Sounds like a good name for the restaurant.' I turn to see Frankie smiling, next to the receptionist, to whom I'm about to offer a set of chef's whites and invite her back into the kitchen, where she should be.

'Now, this is living my best life . . .' I say. 'Sometimes you have to take time to stand and stare to realize what's been and where you want to go.'

Pétur takes my face in his hands and kisses me again, and I know, like the salmon, I've come home, and that it was well worth the journey to get here.

The breeze on my face is making me feel alive, and I know Laura's all around me. She never went anywhere and she's cheering me all the way.

ACKNOWLEDGEMENTS

My love for Iceland started many years ago. And it's all down to my friend Anna Sigurdadottir. We met at university in London where we read Media Studies, specialising in radio. Anna brought her family, her husband and children from Reykjavik to experience life in the UK, whilst she studied at the Polytechnic of Central London. I thought she was so brave. Especially in the final year when the family returned home ahead of her.

After university, we stayed in touch, and I was determined to visit Iceland and meet up with Anna again. I loved it there. And we were made so welcome by Anna and her family. We returned and returned again with our children. I love returning there, and meeting with Anna, and falling into that comfortable friendship, as if no time has passed since we last saw each other. That's real friendship.

Acknowledgements

When I wanted to write this book, it was Anna I turned to first, and I really hope I've done the country and the subject justice. Any mistakes are entirely mine! But I hope you feel the love I felt for the place when I first visited and what a special place it holds in my heart.

This book is also about friendship. Anna and I have been friends for over thirty years. And we may not speak often or see each other, but I know that we will always be friends, as I say, as if no time has passed.

The other reason I wrote this book is because it seemed to be a dreadful year of losing people, women, mostly my age who I knew; losing friends. This book is dedicated to those and the families and friends they've left behind and the empty seat at the table where they should be.

As Dame Deborah James podcaster and cancer campaigner said just before her death at such a young age, 'Find a life worth enjoying; take risks; love deeply; have no regrets; and always, always have rebellious hope.' I can't put it any better than that.

My thanks as always to my wonderful team at Transworld for all your support and to my agent David Headley.

Read on for some delicious Icelandic Christmas recipes and more information about Jo's uplifting and heart-warming books . . .

Roast lamb with potatoes and stewed rhubarb

This is my Icelandic twist on a classic festive roast dinner, the perfect centrepiece for a Christmas feast!

Ingredients

500g rhubarb, cut into 3cm chunks
500g caster sugar
1 lemon, juiced
2kg leg of lamb
Bunch of rosemary
6 bay leaves
2 tbsp olive oil
2 large onions, thickly sliced
1.5kg potatoes
100g brown sugar
20g butter

Method

1. Firstly, make the stewed rhubarb. Add the rhubarb and sugar to a pan over a low-medium heat and cook for around 20 minutes or until the fruit is soft. Add the juice of a lemon and set aside for later.
2. Preheat the oven to 220°C/200°C fan/gas 7.
3. Make incisions into the lamb using a small sharp knife, at an angle, about 5cm into the meat. Insert a short sprig of rosemary and a bay leaf into each incision. Season the meat all over with salt and pepper, then rub the lamb all over with the olive oil.
4. Chop the onions into thick slices and place in a large roasting tin. Transfer the prepared lamb on top of the onions. Roast for 20 minutes.
5. Lower the oven to 190°C/170°C fan/gas 5 and cook for another 15–20 minutes per 500g (1 hour–1 hour 20 minutes for a 2kg leg).

6. With 30 minutes to go, add the peeled potatoes to salted room-temperature water and bring to the boil.
7. To check that the lamb is done, you can also check the internal temperature of the lamb. It will be 55°C for medium (pink) and 70°C for well done.
8. Cover with foil and rest for 15 minutes before carving. Save the tray juices as a sauce.
9. Remove the potatoes once they are fork-tender. Allow them to cool slightly before peeling and slicing into 1cm slices.
10. Add some butter to a pan and place over a medium heat. Once melted, add the potatoes and cook for 3 minutes or until they are golden brown on one side. Turn them over and repeat.
11. Once the potatoes have an even golden crust, remove them from the pan. Then add the brown sugar to the pan until melted. Place the potatoes back in the pan and coat them until caramelized.
12. Reheat the stewed rhubarb over a medium heat.
13. Then carve the lamb and serve with potatoes and rhubarb jam. Lamb goes particularly well with a glass of full-bodied red wine.

Kjötsúpa (lamb stew)

This traditional Icelandic stew is heart-warming and comforting, made with the most simple but flavourful ingredients – this is my perfect meal for a cold winter's day.

Ingredients

1kg lamb, either shoulder or neck works best
4 large carrots, roughly chopped
4 parsnips, roughly chopped
1 medium swede, chopped
5 waxy potatoes, chopped. King Edwards would work well
1 large onion, chopped
Salt
Pepper

Method

1. Place meat in a large soup pot and cover with water.
2. Slowly bring to the boil and then reduce the heat to low.
3. Simmer the meat for about an hour, until it's very tender and falling off the bone. During the cooking process, skim away any surface scum.
4. Add the chopped vegetables and simmer until they're tender, about 30 more minutes.
5. Serve *Kjötsúpa* hot with crusty bread lathered in butter. It might not be geyser bread, but it will be delicious!

Fish stew

As Eliza and Pétur show in the book, this is a delicious meal to share with your partner. This classic fish dish is fresh, tasty and sure to impress!

Ingredients

50g butter
1 onion, chopped
300ml whole milk
750g cooked fish, a white fish such as haddock or cod would work best
750g cooked potatoes, boiled and peeled
2 tbsp flour (if necessary for thickening)
Bunch of fresh chives for serving

Method

1. In a large saucepan, melt the butter on a low heat and add the onion. Cook until the onions are soft and translucent.
2. Gradually add in the milk and simmer for 5 minutes. Stir regularly to ensure that it doesn't stick.
3. Flake the pre-cooked fish using a fork and season with salt and pepper (Freya's top tip!). Add to the milk mixture.
4. Cut the cooked and peeling potatoes into chunks and add to the pan.
5. Keep a low heat under the saucepan until everything has heated through, this should take a few minutes.
6. Place into bowls to serve and add chives as a garnish.

Rhubarb and *skyr* no-bake cheesecake

This was the cheesecake that Eliza taught the women in the safe house how to make. It's a really great option for a Christmas dessert as it requires no baking and is absolutely delicious – a real crowd-pleaser with an Icelandic twist!

Ingredients

Cheesecake

350g digestive biscuits, crushed
150g unsalted butter, melted
2 tbsp honey
750g *skyr* yoghurt
100g caster sugar
1 tsp vanilla extract
260ml double cream

Rhubarb jam

500g rhubarb, cut into 3cm chunks
500g caster sugar
8g sachet of pectin
1 lemon, juiced

Method

1. Crush up the digestive biscuits using a food processor or rolling pin.
2. Melt the butter and honey and pour over the biscuits. Mix to combine.
3. Put the biscuit mixture into a lined 9-inch springform cake tin and press it into an even layer.
4. Place in the fridge while you prepare the *skyr* mixture.
5. Add the *skyr* and sugar to a mixing bowl and beat to combine.
6. In a separate bowl, whisk the double cream and vanilla extract until soft peaks form. Then fold this into the *skyr* mixture.

7. Pour the mixture on top of the chilled base and place back in the fridge and chill for at least 4 hours, ideally overnight.

8. In the meantime, make your rhubarb jam topping. Place the rhubarb, sugar and pectin in a large saucepan. Heat gently until the sugar dissolves, stirring continuously.

9. Once the sugar has dissolved, add the juice of one lemon and turn the heat to high.

10. Boil the mixture for 10 minutes until the fruit is soft.

11. To check that the jam is set, spoon some out on to a plate. After 2 minutes, push your finger through the jam and if it wrinkles, it's ready.

12. Leave the jam to cool.

13. Once the cheesecake has set, top it with rhubarb jam and place in the fridge for an hour.

14. Slice, serve and enjoy!

If you enjoyed *Keeping a Christmas Promise*, Jo Thomas' brand-new feel-good novel *Summer at the Ice Cream Café* is available to pre-order now!

Beca has decided it's time for a fresh start in the seaside village where she grew up. After a decade in the city building her business, she's ready to escape the humdrum. And when she sees her dream home for sale it starts to seem like fate.

But when she arrives and visits her grandparents' ice cream parlour, she discovers that the new owner, her ex-boyfriend Ed, has stripped the heart out of it. She vows to honour their legacy. With the help of a long-forgotten recipe book and a boat house on the coast, Beca decides to follow in her family's footsteps making delicious ice cream.

As a fierce rivalry develops, Beca must rely on her oldest friend, Griff, to help her make the parlour a success. But when disaster strikes, is Beca about to discover that true happiness has been right in front of her the whole time?

For more food, love, family and fun be sure to read Jo's other escapist and uplifting novels which are available now

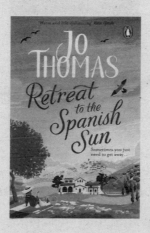

Sometimes you just need to get away . . .

Eliza has a full house! After her grown-up children moved out, she downsized to a smaller property . . . but now they're all back. Every room in the house is occupied and Eliza just needs some peace and quiet to work.

When an ad pops up saying 'house-sitters wanted', Eliza can't resist the chance to escape to a stunning finca in southern Spain for a few weeks to help her focus on achieving her dreams. But it isn't long before Eliza gets caught up in the charming local way of life.

The warmth of the late summer sunshine, delicious local food and friendly village café show Eliza that the life she's always wanted is within reach. And with the return of handsome house-owner Josep, could there be another reason for her to stay in Spain a little longer?

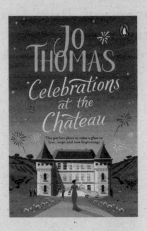

The perfect place to raise a glass to love, hope and new beginnings . . .

When their grandfather·dies, Fliss and her sisters are astonished to inherit a French château! Travelling to Normandy to visit the beautiful if faded house, they excitedly make plans over delicious crêpes and local cider in the town nearby.

They soon discover the château needs major work and a huge tax bill is due . . . Unable to sell but strapped for cash, Fliss determines to spruce up the elegant old rooms and open a B&B.

But Jacques, the handsome town mayor, is opposed to her plan. When it becomes clear that the only way to save the magnificent castle is to work together, Jacques and Fliss discover that they have more in common than they think . . .

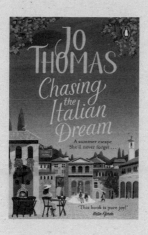

A summer escape she'll never forget . . .

Lucia has worked hard as a lawyer in Wales, aiming for a big promotion she hopes will shortly come her way. Finally taking a well-earned break at her grandparents' house in southern Italy, the sunshine, lemon trees and her nonna's mouth-watering cooking make her instantly feel at home.

But she's shocked to learn that her grandfather is retiring from the beloved family pizzeria and will need to sell. Lucia can't bear the thought of the place changing hands – especially when she discovers her not-quite-ex-husband Giacomo wants to take it over!

Then bad news from home forces Lucia to re-evaluate what she wants from life. Is this her chance to carry on the family tradition and finally follow her dreams?

Will she fall in love under the Christmas lights?

Residential-home caterer Connie has had one online-dating disaster too many. Hurt in the past and with her son to consider, now she's feeling hesitant. Then one of Connie's residents sets her up on a date at a beautiful German Christmas market – with the promise she'll take a mini-bus full of pensioners along with her . . .

Amongst the twinkling lights and smell of warm gingerbread in the old market square, Connie heads off on her date with a checklist of potential partner must-haves. Baker Henrich ticks all the boxes, but when Connie meets Henrich's rival William, she starts to wonder if ticking boxes is the answer.

Will Connie's wish for love this Christmas come true, and if so – with who?